Embers

Stephanie McDonald

RINGWOOD PUBLISHING
GLASGOW

First published in Great Britain in 2021
by
Ringwood Publishing, Glasgow.
www.ringwoodpublishing.com
mail@ringwoodpublishing.com

ISBN 978-1-901514-99-5

British Library Cataloguing-in-Publication Data
A catalogue record for this book is available from the British Library

Printed and bound in the UK
by
Lonsdale Direct Solutions

Embers

Prologue

The rain lashed at her face, its ferociousness taking her a little by surprise. She recovered quickly, launching the full weight of her body against the force of the wind that was striving to pin her back against the house. Not even the harshest of elements would stop her now, nor slow her down. She was prepared for this. At this critical juncture in her life, she felt prepared for anything; ready to take on any opponent, be it in human form or one sent by Mother Nature herself. Nonetheless, her hushed prayer was for an easy, obstacle-free getaway.

She had no time to waste in checking, but she assured herself that she had brought with her everything that she was going to need. Anything that she may have forgotten could be easily replaced anyway, if needed. The contents of her backpack were merely bonus items, possessions whose sheer presence would make her life a little more straight-forward, but she wouldn't find herself in dire straits if she had happened to leave some behind.

The only item she truly needed was stored safely in the zip-fastened inside breast pocket of her waterproof jacket. She rested her fingers against it as she walked hurriedly, the sounds of her movement through the trees masked by the harsh howling of the wind and the whipping sound made by the driving rain that had chosen the perfect night, from her point of view, to drift in from the south. The photo was in there, for certain. She breathed a sigh of relief, safe in the knowledge that there could be no going back now.

Without glancing back at the house, she started to break into a jog, drawing energy and impetus from the sweet sensation of victory that was born of having made it this far. She had been confident that she would, of course – she would not have attempted it had she not been ninety-nine per cent sure it would work – but still, her heart pounded with equal parts excitement and fear, loud enough that she could hear its urgent rhythm in her ears.

He hadn't stirred, she was sure of it. He wasn't behind her, running after her, intent on dragging her back. She was free.

She felt raindrops mingle with the tears on her face, and a smile take over her lips, as she powered on.

Part One

Chapter One

Graham
Now

'Pikey, it's your turn, mate,' Colin yelled, struggling to make himself heard above the music blasting from the speaker above his head.

'Two secs, mate,' Graham Pike replied, from where he was stationed at the bar. He had managed to get served in surprisingly super-quick time, quicker than anyone else in his party had all evening, and the bartender was pouring the heads on the fourth round of pints he had ordered for himself and his friends.

'There we go, lads,' he announced, placing a tray containing four pints of Carling on the table he and his mates had been occupying for the last two hours. 'My turn, is it?' He took an inaugural sip of his drink before assuming his place at the pool table. He potted the last of the striped balls and re-located to the opposite end of the table to take a stab at the black, aiming to clinch the game.

'Here, Pikey, your phone's going again,' he heard Irish Eoin call from behind him.

Owing to the unfortunate circumstance the group of friends had found themselves in, namely two of them sharing a first name (to the naked ear, at least), Eoin had become known as 'Irish Eoin', while English Owen was allowed to remain simply 'Owen'. The difficult decision had been made after due discussion. It was deemed only fair that, with

Owen having known Graham and Colin since their student days, hence being a 'founding member' of the group, as they had collectively agreed, he had been afforded the right to be known by his Christian name alone. Irish Eoin had protested a little, but nonetheless accepted the moniker forevermore.

'It's been going mental since you've been at the bar,' Irish Eoin added.

Graham sighed, deliberating over the order in which he should enact the steps he was imminently required to take: check who it was that had been bombarding his phone and then take his shot at glory, or vice versa. He played the shot quickly, under pressure, and fluffed it. He needn't rely on a sixth sense to suss out the identity of his harasser, and the prospect of having to follow up on the unsolicited contact had knocked him off his stride.

'Better luck next time, mate,' Colin teased him, slapping him on the shoulder. 'Spilled your pint on your hands, did you? Messes with your grip, it does. Shame.'

Graham smiled back weakly.

'Jesus, mate, seventeen missed calls,' Irish Eoin exclaimed, holding up Graham's illuminated phone just as another missed called registered, supporting his earlier assertion.

'Yeah alright, Foghorn Leghorn,' chided Graham, swiping the phone from his bemused friend's hand. 'Why don't you yell a bit louder? I don't think that guy all the way on the other side of the room heard you.'

'Something up?' Colin asked, wearing a typically suspicious expression. He had taken his own shot and had also failed to pot the black, leaving Irish Eoin to cue up with a view to winning the game and putting himself and Graham in the overall lead by four games to three.

Graham checked the call history, saddened but not surprised to have his suspicions confirmed. He blinked for a long second, letting out a frustrated sigh.

'I'm not sure,' he answered honestly, having to raise his voice above the music, as the familiar refrain of 'Mr Brightside' rang out and the majority of the pub patrons engaged in an impromptu singalong. 'Let me just nip out and see what it's all about.'

Before Colin could make his objections heard, as Graham instinctively knew he would, Graham began weaving his way through the tightly-packed group of people who stood between him and the exit, most of whom were now bouncing up and down and singing, '*I ne-ver*,' in unison at the top of their voices.

He made it outside and a shiver took hold of him as his body adjusted to the sharp contrast in temperature. It was a crisp October night, and he had come out in only his shirtsleeves. He felt the chill now, even though he had sweated from every pore only a few seconds ago inside the crowded pub.

'Shit!' he yelled, taking a couple of young women by surprise as they neared the doors, heading inside. 'Sorry,' he said, holding up his hand in an apologetic gesture. His swearing was justified, however, as he would have explained to them had they not scurried away from him as though he were a threat.

Along with the seventeen calls he had missed in the short space of time since he'd stepped away from the game to go and deliver his round, he had received a voicemail as well, and the expletive had escaped from his mouth like a reflex as he listened to the contents of the message. It was tame, too, in the circumstances.

'Please call me, Gray,' Angie begged, sounding upset and desperate – nothing new there, then. And as was always the case, Graham's first instinct was to go to her aid. He'd had several years to work on managing this urge somewhat, and had succeeded in programming his sensible self to kick-in and swat away the notion of him being at her beck and call.

He called on the part of him that felt very strongly that he was entitled to a life of his own, a life which did not involve being on hand to play the hero when someone was in need of a white knight – someone he had long since relinquished any commitment to.

But inevitably, infuriatingly, his conscience would strike back with a vengeance. He could never suspend his grip on reality sufficiently to consider that it could be positive news when Angie got in touch. Conversely, his mind went straight to the worst-case scenarios which might apply to his tragic ex-wife, and sent memories of previous calamities flooding into his mind.

His right mind and his conscience would come to blows, and the vicious circle would continue on and on, driving him to distraction. The chance of him passing a carefree night with his friends had come and gone.

He made his way back to the pool table with a stoop to his shoulders and a heaviness in the soles of his feet. Colin, as always, was the first to diagnose the visible symptoms.

'Whatever it is, Gray,' he said gravely, 'you know it'll just be the same old bullshit.' Colin spoke from experience. He had been drafted in to assist with the fallout plenty of times in the past, enough to know that Angie was the woman who liked to cry wolf. No one knew better than him that Graham had been bitten many, many times by her deceit, and no one resented her more for the way she had monopolised his friend's life. Except that now, she was no longer his wife, and she no longer had a right to his time, or his attention.

'She sounds like she's in a bad way,' Graham informed the men collectively, feeling uncomfortable at having to air his private affairs at such a volume, in such a busy venue.

'No fuckin' way, Gray,' Irish Eoin objected in typical fashion, dropping his cue down on the pool table in frustration. 'You can't leave, mate.' He draped his arm over Graham's shoulder, towering over him by four or five inches. 'That lass over there's been giving you the eye all night. Look, she's looking over now, look!'

Graham glanced over at the woman, who gave him a bashful smile and appeared to blush at the recognition. He responded with a polite, apologetic smile, then looked away, embarrassed. His mind was already, irreparably, tuned into other things, leaving him at a loss to respond in any other way.

'Well, one of you will have to give her my number and if she's interested, she'll call,' he said wistfully, retrieving his jacket from the back of the booth that the men had reserved earlier, and putting it on.

'You're really going?' Colin asked, his tone and facial expression like those of a child whose best friend had announced they were about to leave their birthday party. It was neither Colin's birthday nor a party, but it was a night out that had been some considerable time in the planning, owing to Colin and Owen's relatively recent additions to their respective families and, as a result, their availability on Friday nights (or any night, for that matter) having dwindled somewhat since. Irish Eoin was not a father, nor did he have any responsibilities of note, but he was rugby-daft, and his team's games annoyingly tended to fall on Friday nights. In summary, this night out was important to everyone, for various reasons. Not least for Graham, who valued his friendships dearly.

'I'm really sorry, man,' he told Colin, giving him a one-armed hug and waving to the others before battling through the crowd again. He didn't wait around to witness Colin's disappointed, annoyed expression, or the 'Fuck's sake!' that all three men whispered under their breaths. No one could hear anyway, above the incessant thud of the music.

Chapter Two

Graham
Now

'Angie!' he bellowed, nearing the end of his tether at her refusal to open the door. Or worse, he considered, her inability to open it. What the hell had she gotten herself into this time? He banged even harder on the solid wooden door, registering the pain in the butt of his hand but carrying on regardless, fuelled by the fear of what he might come across if he was forced to knock it down. Under normal circumstances, kicking a front door in wasn't high on his list of fun things to do on a Friday night. When said door was already bearing the marks of an attempted kicking-in, owing to the undesirable location of Angie's flat, Graham would rather have been anywhere else.

Finally, he heard the rattle of a chain on the other side, and Angie tentatively teased open the door.

'Oh, Gray, it's you,' she said gratefully, throwing her arms clumsily around him. 'You came, I knew you would.'

She was oddly dressed for a Friday night, in multi-coloured yoga pants and an oversized sweater, and her eyes bore the signs of drug use. Legal or illegal drugs, Graham couldn't say for sure. He gently removed her arms from around his neck and bit down gently on his lip to keep his composure.

'Why did you call me here, Angie?' he asked, making no attempt to disguise the anger in his voice.

'Oh, Gray,' Angie repeated, and slunk inside, into the hallway, confident that Graham would follow her. 'It was awful,' she told him, tears suddenly appearing out of nowhere. 'Look what they did.'

Graham came into the living room behind her, as she had known he would, and his mouth gaped open as he observed the scene before him. The room looked as though a hurricane had swept through it, scattering possessions all over the floor. Bundles of stuffing from inside the couch were dotted all around, glass from photo frames littered the carpet and there was a conspicuous void where the television had once stood.

'What the fuck happened?' Graham asked, his temper barely in check. 'And what do you mean, look what *they* did? Who the fuck are *they*?'

'Oh, don't yell at me, Gray, please! You know I can't take it when you yell at me!' Her voice shook and she stamped her foot like a toddler throwing a tantrum, staring at the floor. She couldn't look him in the eye. Graham knew that what had occurred earlier in the evening had been of her own doing; she had invited this chaos to her door.

He nodded sarcastically, his lips locked in a tight grimace. 'You're right,' he said contrarily, surveying the damage to the room in more detail. 'Seventeen missed calls, a voicemail, twelve quid in a taxi, five minutes waiting for you to open the door and storm El-fucking-Diablo having ripped through your living room, but I shouldn't yell at you.' He'd lowered his voice to speaking level, but anger was fizzing around inside him like a soluble antacid making contact with water. He wearily sat himself down on one of the least affected sections of the couch and crossed one leg over the other, placing one arm across the back of the couch and the other on his shin.

'So, why don't you tell me what went on then?' he suggested, surprising himself by managing to keep his rage under control. His voice was laced with disgust and disapproval, but at least he wasn't raising his blood pressure by going on an all-out rant. Yet.

Angie came and sat on the couch with him, having the good sense not to get too close. In all the time that she had been testing his patience he had never lashed out at her physically – and he never would. Besides, by now she knew that any attempt to touch him would be met with strong resistance, and he would simply edge further away, or even leave, if she tried.

'It was so awful,' she said, the crocodile tears making a comeback. Graham rolled his eyes but resisted the urge to tell her she'd already said that. 'There were three of them, and they just trashed the place. Look.' Her eyes swept around the room, widening as though she was taking in the scene for the first time.

'Yeah, I can see that,' Graham answered, the longing that he felt to be away from this cursed place and back in the pub with his friends overwhelming him. 'How did they get in?' he asked, knowing that there was a good chance he wasn't going to like the answer. The front door – the only entrance to the flat – wasn't in the best shape, but it definitely didn't appear to have been breached, and unless Spiderman had paid her a visit, he was quite sure whoever had made the mess hadn't come in through a window on the seventh floor.

Angie let out a deep breath. 'It was a date,' she admitted, ignoring the wry laugh that her confession evoked in Graham. 'Tony – he was the one I was supposed to be seeing – he seemed like a really nice guy, initially.' She sniffed and wiped away a tear. 'But when he showed up, he had brought his two mates with him, and they just barged in, and I didn't know what to do …' She buried her face in a tissue as her words trailed off.

'Wait,' Graham said, sitting forward, holding up his hand in a halting gesture. He swallowed, delaying asking

11

his question, feeling sick as he imagined what might have gone on. 'Did they hurt you?' he asked, screwing his eyes closed as though it might reduce the impact of the answer he was anticipating.

'What? No!' Angie appeared horrified at the notion. 'No, it wasn't like that,' she explained, a little too flippantly, Graham thought. 'They didn't touch me, they just went around making all this mess.' She pointed to the debris. 'Laughing like kids, they were, like it was just a big prank. They were on something, definitely. But Tony wouldn't have let them hurt me.'

Graham wasn't sure whether he believed what she had told him or not. He had lost the knack for reading her long ago, if in fact he had ever possessed it.

'You know him well, do you?' he asked cynically.

'Well, no, not really, I suppose,' Angie conceded. 'We were only meeting for the first time, tonight, but we've been chatting online for a while, and he seemed really nice.'

Graham covered his face with his hand, letting out a deep sigh. 'Yeah, pops round for sex; brings his mates; robs you blind; wrecks your place. Sounds like a real gent. Did I miss anything?'

Angie stayed silent for a moment, and Graham noticed that she seemed to be swaying a little. He could smell the alcohol seeping from her pores from where he sat a few feet away, and he only hoped that she hadn't been stupid enough to take anything else along with it. 'Don't have a go at me, Gray,' she pleaded again, struggling to keep her eyes open. 'I'm sorry. You know I'm sorry.'

She leant over and tried to rest her head on his shoulder, but he rose from the couch and let her slide onto the cushion, her fall almost comical.

'Yeah, Ange, you're always sorry, aren't you?' He could feel a rant building, but he looked at her and, not for the first time, he found himself gobsmacked at just what a sorry, pitiful creature she had become. She hadn't bothered to lift herself back up to a sitting position, and was staring listlessly, possibly at Graham, possibly at a blank space on the wall, he couldn't tell. She weighed less than she ever had in all the years that he'd known her, and even though the yoga pants she wore were supposed to be loose, they hung baggy and gaping on her tiny legs. Her eyes were heavily smudged, with streaks of mascara having formed on her cheeks, and her eyes were vacant, dark pools. He couldn't prevent a gasp escaping from his mouth, and he couldn't keep track of all the emotions he was experiencing at once: anger, resentment, pity, sadness, fear.

He leant back against the wall closest to the door and folded his arms. 'So, have you called the police?'

'No,' Angie replied, coming back to life again and sitting up, 'and I'm not going to either.'

'What do you mean?' Graham was incredulous. 'They robbed you, Ange. They ransacked your place. Left you with next to nothing. Why would you let them get away with that?'

'Because you know what'll happen, Gray,' she hit back, irritated. 'They'll come in here with all their questions, poking their noses into my life. "How do you know Tony? Why did you give him your address? So, you let him into the flat?" Blah, blah.'

'Valid questions,' Graham muttered, not sure if she heard him. There was no point in asking why she had called him, begging him to come around. He knew the answer.

'I can't be doing with it, Gray,' she explained, as though the pursuit of justice were nothing but an inconvenient obstacle to her contentment. 'I'll clean the place up myself; get a new telly when I've scraped a bit of cash together.'

She stuffed a stray strand of unwashed hair behind her ear, and Graham's stomach lurched with sorrow at the plight of the woman he'd once loved so desperately, so obsessively.

There had been a time in his life when he had felt like he lived only to be with her, to make her happy. When she had first entered his life, he couldn't imagine her ever not being in it. He didn't want to. Now, even though he still couldn't find the resolve to turn his back on her, she had become the bane of his life. It stabbed at his conscience to think it, but a huge part of him wished that he could be rid of her once and for all, and his perceived responsibility towards her.

'I'll help you clean up,' he said quietly, knowing that no amount of explaining to her where she had gone wrong – again – would change anything. She had been damaged beyond repair a long, long time ago, and Graham's role now was just to be there, and to apply a sticking plaster to her perilous circumstances every now and again. Far more often than he cared to acknowledge, or admit.

They worked in silence, Angie following him around the room with an open refuse bag as he tossed the tufts of foam from the couch into it, then took time and care wrapping the larger shards of glass in newspaper and the smaller ones in three layers of plastic carrier bag. 'I'll take this out on my way out,' he offered, and Angie nodded silently.

After fifteen minutes the room looked less like a bomb had hit it and more like a band of teenagers had held a house party and hastily tried to tidy up afterwards.

'Right,' Graham said, stretching out his upper back to release the muscles which had suffered from all the bending he had been doing. 'I'd better go then,' he told her, reaching for his jacket. 'You're sure about not going to the police?'

Angie nodded again. She looked ever so slightly more sober than she had when he had arrived thirty minutes earlier, but it would take a few hours of sleep for whatever had intoxicated her to leave her system.

'Will you see me into bed, Gray?' she asked quietly.

Graham tutted and turned his head in annoyance, but she reached forward and latched onto his elbows. 'Please, Gray,

I got a real scare tonight. You know how hard it is for me to get to sleep at the best of times. Please, just until I drift off, then you can go. It's not like I'm going to try anything, come on.'

He looked down at her, a full foot shorter than him (he wondered whether she'd always been that short, or whether years of abusing her body had caused her to shrink in height as well as stature), and for a fleeting moment he felt compelled to grab hold of her and hug her tight, and never let her go. The moment and the urge came and went, notions of reclaiming the feelings of love that he once harboured for her disappearing like puffs of smoke into the air, and he simply huffed, extracting himself from her grasp and laying his jacket back down on the arm of the couch.

'I'll stay until you're asleep, and then I'm off, Ange,' he told her forcibly, making for the bedroom without waiting around to gauge the reaction on her face. He couldn't stand to witness the pitiful gratitude that he knew would be written all over it.

Her bedroom was, to Graham's great surprise, immaculate. A small table lamp lit the room, and although sparse on furniture, it was a pleasant-looking space. A plain, wine-coloured duvet set covered the double bed, and there were three small cushions resting up against the pillows. A chest of drawers stood under the window which faced onto the rear of the property, and although the curtains were drawn, the glow of the street lamps seeped in. A sturdy wooden wardrobe that hadn't been there the last time he had a reason to 'visit' took up the length of the wall on the right side of the room. There was no mess, no clutter, no trace of the chaos that seemed to follow Angie around wherever she went. But that was Angie all over, he reminded himself. She was the ultimate enigma.

Angie appeared from the bathroom, having brushed her teeth. If he didn't know any better, based on the previous sixty seconds, he would have sworn that she was a normal person, living a normal life. But he did know better. Infinitely so.

'Thank you, Gray,' she told him, climbing into bed still clad in her yoga pants. She had removed the huge sweater and was wearing a plain white t-shirt, and Graham noted just how emaciated she had become.

'Do you want this off?' he asked, his hand hovering over the lamp switch.

'Please,' she answered, her eyes already closed.

Graham switched off the light and took a seat on the edge of the bed, hoping that it would take only a matter of minutes for Angie to nod off. It was already gone one o'clock in the morning, and he was shattered. He had been looking forward to a chilled, enjoyable evening with the boys. Instead, he felt an uneasy suspicion that the night still had scope to deteriorate further.

'Why didn't you save me?' he heard Angie ask from behind his back.

He sighed and rubbed his temples with his hand, far too tired to embark on the kind of conversation that he knew was coming, rueing the fact that his sixth sense for unpleasantness seemed to be on point once more.

'Let's not do this, eh Ange?' he pleaded, like a father trying to coax his child to settle down.

'You said we'd always be together, Gray,' Angie continued sadly. 'You promised. You were supposed to save me. From myself.'

'I tried,' Graham whispered, meaning it. 'You know I tried.'

'But you left me!' Angie cried, her voice thick with tears.

She had sat up now, and Graham could feel the warmth of her breath on the back of his neck. This was an exchange that had taken place many times in the past, always when Angie was drunk, or off her face on something, and he had long since given up rising to the bait.

'Let's not rewrite history, Ange, okay?' he suggested, standing up and gently lowering her down to a horizontal position as though she really were a small child. 'Just try and get to sleep,' he urged her. 'You'll feel better in the morning.'

'Don't leave me, Gray,' she said, gripping his arm.

'I'm not leaving!' Graham snapped, then lowered his voice again. 'I'm not leaving right now, alright? I'm going to wait right here until you fall asleep, and then I'll go. Don't worry.'

She stared at him for a few seconds as though she were about to protest, but eventually she seemed to be placated, and rested her head on the pillow again, defeated.

Graham tiptoed around to the other side of the bed once he was certain that she had closed her eyes and laid himself down, waiting for the tell-tale sounds of her breathing to confirm that she was out cold, and that he could escape.

He checked his phone, taking care to dim the screen so that its brightness didn't disturb Angie, and saw that he had a missed call and a text message from Colin.

Mate, just want to check you're OK. Call me tomorrow.

Graham put his phone back in his pocket and stared out of the window at the foreboding darkness. Was he okay? In the small room, the word 'No' echoed off every wall.

Chapter Three

Graham

Then

It was her accent that first caught his attention. His ears were not well attuned to other dialects – he had never lived anywhere other than home; had never even left the county. At the age of eighteen, mingling with other students from far and wide, it had struck him that it might not be 'cool' to admit this; that his uninspiring past may paint him in something of a pathetic light, especially when (or if) he got around to chatting with the opposite sex. But while he was growing up, being a home-bird hadn't seemed out of the ordinary at all. On the contrary, it had seemed wonderful.

Pike family holidays, when they could afford them (not too often, regrettably), were usually enjoyed at a caravan park a mere forty-five minutes from home. When his peers at school had spoken of their annual jaunts to water parks in Spain, or fancy campsites in France, he had sometimes felt the tiniest twinge of jealousy, but he had nonetheless cherished his family's little adventures down the M25, not least because his mum and dad always did everything they could to make the experience a hundred times more exciting than it technically should have been.

Sandwiches, soft drinks and yogurts were packed into a cool box for the journey, even though they were only ever likely to be on the road for under an hour, door to door. His dad would be in charge of the cassette player, and with a little help from Graham, would devise a playlist that would whip up the appropriate enthusiasm for the trip, with 'emergency' songs in reserve just in case they happened to run into a bad traffic jam and find themselves in need of some especially cheery music to keep their spirits up. Queen, Spandau Ballet, and some of the earliest incarnations of the *Now!* series were firm favourites.

Graham had never once regretted or resented the fact that he hadn't travelled beyond the boundary of Kent in his younger years. And now, aged eighteen, he was oddly thankful for it. Had he already lived the adventures, and done the gallivanting that the other kids had done when he was a child, he would have no doubt remembered all the things that a child was programmed to remember: the swimming pools with their amazing flumes; the sea-swimming; the ice cream. Insignificant things that could have been dragged and dropped from any holiday resort in Western Europe. Now though, he was an adult; he had a whole world to discover, and could make note of all the details that an adult would appreciate. Landmarks. History. Culture. A world that was as brand new to him as the day he was born. And that, actually, was a wonderful feeling, Graham thought.

Her voice seemed to transcend all the others as she chatted with her friend a few yards away, even though in reality she wasn't speaking all that loudly. He glanced over out of curiosity, and his eyes lingered for a long moment when he saw her face. The sun was in her eyes, and she held her hand across her brow to shield them, but Graham got his first taste of their power even from ten feet away. Her hair was swept away from her head by a plain white headband, and in the light of the sun it looked like the golden flax he had read of in fairy tales as a child. She was tanned, he noticed, and he wondered whether that was a result of the unusually hot summer that they were gradually waving goodbye to in the south east, or whether she had recently been abroad. Perhaps she and her friends ate out here in the courtyard every day, soaking up the sun in between classes. 'Probably abroad,' he muttered to himself, accidentally saying the words out loud. For a second he thought her eyes had locked on his, and he averted his gaze so swiftly that he heard a crick in his neck at the suddenness of the movement. Feeling a flush of embarrassment, he was tempted to gather his books and hurry away from the outdoor seating area, but he still had twenty minutes before his next class was due to start, and half a cup of coffee to finish off. And besides, what was he running from? So, a beautiful girl had looked at him. Was he really such a loser that he had to retreat at the first sign – or not – of interest from the opposite sex? Whoa, he thought, acknowledging that he was jumping the gun. He couldn't even be sure that the fair-haired beauty seated at his eleven o'clock had noticed him, let alone experienced anything like the new, nervously-excited sensation that had struck him like an electric shock. He buried his face in his coffee cup, lamenting his decision to opt for it in place of a soft drink when the still-hot liquid sent his temperature spiking even further.

'Have you moved onto module two already?' The voice was now familiar, the accent even more pronounced now that she was much closer than before.

'Er, yeah,' he muttered, quickly scanning around him to check that she was actually talking to him. She was.

'Bloody hell, I'm barely halfway through the first one,' she told him, slinging a canvas bag over her shoulder. 'I'm finding it pretty tough.' There was a pause while Graham tried to formulate a response. 'I haven't noticed you in the class before,' she added.

She wore shades now, and for a second Graham wondered why only a few moments ago she had been relying on her hand to keep the sun at bay. Her friend seemed to have vanished into thin air, and she was inches away from him, her floral-scented perfume filling his nose.

'Er, me neither,' Graham replied, addressing her last point first. His blushing threatened to spiral out of control. 'We're still only supposed to be on module one,' he added, going back to the remark she had made earlier. 'I just like to get a head start.'

'O-kay,' she replied, drawing out the word.

This was why he had been about to run. This was exactly the kind of embarrassing, excruciating encounter he had been fearful of. And now it was happening. With a girl he had fancied at first sight.

She lifted her head and took a deep breath in, and behind the shades Graham could see that she had closed her eyes. 'I love this weather,' she said, basking in the glow of the sun. 'I wish it could go on forever.'

'Me too,' Graham concurred, desperately seeking some conversational inspiration from somewhere. 'It makes me think I might like to go and live somewhere hot. Somewhere where it's like this all the time. Or at least most of the time.'

She shifted her head back round to face him, a guarded smile playing at her lips. 'Hmm. I've been thinking that all my life,' she said, with a hint of sadness in her voice. 'Anyway, we should head to class, don't you think?'

It took Graham a few seconds to register what the 'we' in her sentence alluded to, leaving him scrambling to gather his books and load them into his rucksack, loath to give her time to change her mind.

'I'm Angie,' she announced when he was ready, holding out her hand.

'Graham,' he reciprocated, marvelling at the softness of her skin as they shook hands.

'Good to meet you, Gray,' she said, leading the way to the Hunter Building where their class was held. 'You don't mind if I call you Gray, do you?'

'Not at all,' Graham confirmed, enjoying the way his

name sounded in her voice, her accent. In that moment, she could have called him anything she wanted, and he wouldn't have cared.

Chapter Four

Graham
Now

The beers Graham had drunk earlier had caught up with him, and he had dozed off without meaning to. His body was deliberately curled away from Angie, facing the window. He had listened out for signs that she had fallen asleep for a few minutes, occupying himself by trawling through the evening's football results on his phone, but his eyes had been too damn heavy, and he'd ended up out for the count in no time.

He couldn't be sure what he'd dreamt of, if he'd even dreamt at all, but the animosity and anger that he had felt earlier had dissipated. Now, he was simply tired.

He was roused back to consciousness with a start by the sound of high-pitched screaming piercing his ears.

'No!' he heard Angie cry. 'No, please, please!'

Graham jumped up, the glow of the streetlights outside offering sufficient illumination of the room so that he could see Angie tossing and turning, her eyes still closed, her face screwed up in fear.

'Ange. Angie!' He raised his voice and touched her shoulder to rouse her. He knew from experience that the kindest thing to do was to wake her from her nightmare as opposed to letting it carry on. Her eyes flew open and he saw the terror in them.

'No!' she screamed again, pulling away.

'It's me, Ange, it's Gray.'

It took a few seconds for her to reach full consciousness and realise that she was in no danger, that it was Graham in the bed with her; that he was the one with his hands on her. She looked at him and burst into tears, sitting up and burying her face in her bony hands.

Graham hesitated for a moment, still bleary-eyed from sleep, but he couldn't not comfort her. He shuffled forward, putting an arm around her shoulders which were shaking in time with her sobs. At his touch, she turned to look at him, and there was no doubt that, unlike the ones he'd seen her turn on like a tap earlier, these tears were one hundred per cent real. And he knew the dark place they had come from.

'Gray,' she said, her voice small.

'Shh, it's okay,' he murmured, an empty reassurance. He drew her closer, and her head rested on his chest. She continued to cry, but as the moments passed Graham could feel her heart rate gradually returning to normal; her sobs becoming softer and further apart. He gently rocked her like a child, stroking her hair and reminding her that he was there; that no one could hurt her now.

Several minutes passed like that, until Angie's sniffs were the only sounds that shattered the silence in the room.

'I didn't know you still got them,' Graham whispered softly.

Angie straightened up and faced him. 'Always,' she conceded. 'They'll never stop, Gray,' she told him, the bad dream apparently having sobered her up considerably. She looked exhausted, and Graham wondered how much of that could be attributed to the fact that sleep, for her, brought with it a world of pain. As it had done for much of her adult life, since she had re-opened the door to the memories that were responsible for her anguish.

'What about the pills?' he asked. 'They used to work, didn't they?'

She wriggled away from him, waving away his question. 'They don't work, Gray, nothing works. God knows I've tried enough options.' She gave a wry laugh as she took a sip from the glass of water that sat on her bedside table. At least, Graham hoped it was water. 'Nothing works,' she repeated, staring at the ground in resignation.

Graham sat still in the darkness, unable to think of anything comforting or helpful to say. She wasn't his responsibility, hadn't been for a long time, but still he felt a compulsion to care for her. She was a person in pain. It didn't matter what she had done, in moments like these. In these moments, he longed for her to find a way to put the demons of her past to rest and move on; to find happiness. Or if happiness was too far out of reach, then perhaps peace was a decent compromise.

'We can talk, if you want,' he suggested after a long silence. 'My chat was always pretty effective at sending you to sleep, remember?'

She laughed softly, appreciating his change of tack, and gave a little nod. 'I do remember,' she said with fondness. 'Or those rotten films you used to make me watch. God, you had shitty taste in movies.'

He laughed too, glad too of the shift in tone. 'Yeah, I guess I did,' he conceded. 'I like to think my tastes are a bit more refined than that now.'

Angie let her eyes close for a second, as though testing the water to see what would happen if she did. 'Go on then,' she urged, her smile at odds with the tear tracks that she hadn't yet swept away from her cheeks. 'Bore me to sleep.'

'No problem,' Graham replied, shifting his weight back so that he sat upright against the headboard, while Angie lay down and closed her eyes again.

Chapter Five

Graham
Then

Neither of them had felt the need or the desire to have a big, extravagant wedding.

Graham's parents had insisted on doing what they could to help out with the costs, despite his firm protestations, and their persistence only motivated Graham to keep the overall budget down as low as he could.

Angie had assured him repeatedly that she had no preconceptions or demands for the day. She wasn't one of those women who had been planning her wedding since she was seven, dreaming of puffy dresses and massive cakes with tiers the size of car tyres, as she had explained when the subject had first arisen. In fact, she told him that the thought of all the pink, pomp and ceremony made her feel quite nauseous.

Like Graham, the only thing that really mattered to her was that they were to be married. That they had found each other. Where and when they would say their vows, and how much the event was going to cost, were inconsequential matters.

The term 'other half' could have been conceived with the two of them in mind, she had commented once, and he had no inclination to contradict her. From the first time they had kissed, he had known. If he was honest, from the very first time they met, he had dared to hope, but that kiss had sealed their fate.

She was the yin to his yang. The Juliet to his Romeo, although their love wasn't going to be ill-fated like the young, star-crossed lovers in Shakespeare's tragedy. He and Angie were young, and so in love with each other that sometimes it seemed to physically hurt, but that was where the similarities between them and the tragic sweethearts from Verona ended.

They were going to be one of love's great success stories. They were going to be the poster couple for marriage. They were going to travel – they had already begun making plans, and promises – they were going to live life to the full, and they were going to do it together, hand in hand, smiling. Graham could already picture the photo albums filled with their adventures, propped up beside the albums filled with mementoes of their big day.

They shared the task of organising the ceremony and the reception, opting for a registry office in accordance with their mutual lack of faith of any description. Angie had revealed, shortly after she and Graham had begun 'going steady', that she was, in effect, an orphan. Both her parents had been killed in a car accident when she was only seven, she told him, leaving her to be raised by her surviving grandparents, both of whom had also sadly passed on by the time she had embarked on her studies at the University of Kent at the age of nineteen.

The absence of siblings was where she and Graham shared a tiny amount of familial common ground, but aside from that, their childhoods could not have been further apart. She was a Northerner, born and raised in the heart of the city of Newcastle. He was a country boy, a true Southerner who had grown up in the garden of England and had never been north of Cambridge. He had known a childhood of limitless love and affection, of comfort and security. She had known a wealth of anguish before her age had even hit double figures, and had not a single relative to call on at the tender age of twenty-two.

Angie had shrugged off his condolences when he had offered them profusely, his heart bleeding for her. 'It is what it is,' she had mused with a smile, but Graham had caught the flicker of sadness behind her eyes when she had said it.

He had offered to warn his own relatives against asking too many questions of her, fearful of how damaging it might be for her to be compelled to recount her haunting past on her wedding day, of all days. But Angie had nonchalantly waved away his concerns.

'Don't worry about it,' she had told him, as they divided up their 'romantic' pre-wedding meal the night before – a Chinese takeaway. 'It's only natural for people to ask. It's not often you come across someone without a whiff of a family unit.' She was matter-of-fact, unemotional. One hundred percent focused on making sure her forkful of chicken chow mein reached her mouth without any of the greasy noodles slipping off and making a mess of her chiffon top.

'I know, but I just can't bear the thought of it upsetting you, having to tell the story,' Graham said apologetically. 'And multiple times, potentially. They won't mean any harm, of course, I just think it would make things easier if I were to forewarn them. They won't mind.'

'You do what you have to do, my darling,' she had urged him, laying her hands on both his cheeks and kissing him, transferring the saltiness of the soy sauce onto his lips. 'My sweet, darling man.'

He had tried to ignore the nagging doubt, to play it down in his head, but there was no denying her reaction had been odd. He couldn't shake the thought, and it vexed him, that Angie seemed to be less perturbed by her unfortunate, some would say tragic past, than he was. He told himself to get over it, that grief did strange things to people, and he couldn't claim to have a wealth of experience on the subject. Far from it. Angie had once explained to him that the best way to get over a tragedy such as the one that had befallen her as a child was to make peace with it, and move on. Perhaps that was simply what she had managed to do, because she'd had no choice but to do it. What doesn't kill you, makes you stronger – wasn't that the saying?

It still niggled at him though, every now and then.

They had shunned conventionality and spent the night before their big day together. They were about to commit to spending forever together, so why should they kick off the most special day of their lives in separate beds, in separate rooms?

Angie's dress was necessarily inexpensive, but her choice had been a master stroke. She had followed tradition by not allowing Graham to set eyes on it beforehand, but not because she believed in superstition.

'That's why,' she breathed in his ear, draping her arms around his neck as he stood open-mouthed, his breath having been whipped from his lungs when she had stepped out of the en-suite hotel bathroom on the morning they were to be wed. She was luminous with joy. The sight of her pierced his heart and froze his mind, and it took him a few seconds to recover.

He wrapped his arms around her waist, savouring the feel of the satin under his hands, the scent of her perfume, the weight of her head on his shoulder.

'You,' he whispered, tears gathering in his eyes for the first time in decades, 'are making me the happiest man alive today.' He touched her chin and gently tipped her head upwards, looking straight into her eyes. 'I love you,' he told her. He planted a kiss on her lips, which were still bare, awaiting the finishing touch of lipstick.

'Well, that's lucky,' she told him, her accent still as strong and delicious as ever, despite her six years spent in the south east. 'Because I love you too, Graham Pike.'

29

She initiated the kiss this time, and Graham had to exercise all his restraint to hold back from tearing the dress off and making love to her there and then.

Tearing wasn't necessary. He gaped in amazement as Angie reached behind her head and started to undo the zip.

'It's fine,' she assured him, noting his surprise, the quick glance to his watch, taking his breath away once more. 'They always expect the bride to be late, anyway.'

Chapter Six

Graham
Now

He didn't need to open his eyes to know that morning had come. Keeping them closed, he tried to get his bearings, tried to work out why his left arm seemed to be draped over something. Something warm. Someone.

It all came flooding back to him as he gently opened one eye, feeling the hangover from the night before strike a preliminary blow to his head. He hadn't had all that much to drink before he had regrettably run out on Colin and the guys, but the events that had followed had landed him with a cracking headache that would most likely last the whole day. Perhaps even longer, if experience had taught him anything.

He tried to retrieve his arm, careful not to disturb Angie, but the slightest change of position was enough for her to be roused. She flinched slightly at first, clearly confused for a split-second as to why there was another person in the bed with her, but laid her head back down with a visible sigh of relief when she realised it was Graham. However bad his hangover felt, he had a suspicion that hers was likely to be far worse.

He extracted himself from the bed, leaving her to doze off again, and cursed himself for not downing a glass of water before he'd gone to bed, like he usually made a point of doing after he had been drinking. Not that anything about the night before had been usual, though. Predictable, perhaps. In many ways, depressingly inevitable, but not usual.

He glanced at himself in the bathroom mirror, noting that he looked as bad as he felt. His eyes were red and told the tale of a restless night. His face was correspondingly haggard, betraying each and every one of his thirty-six years. He would have given anything to brush his teeth, but after searching the cabinets and failing to discover any new, untouched brushes, he resolved to pick up some minty chewing gum before he caught the train home – that would have to do until he got back to his own place and was able to make himself feel human again.

'Do you want a cup of coffee?'

He jumped in surprise as he came out of the bathroom. Angie was on the couch, when he had expected her to be in bed, where he had left her only seconds ago. She rose when he came out, passing him on her way to the kitchen. He followed her and watched while she filled the kettle.

'No thanks,' he told her. 'I'd better get off.'

Angie looked as though she was about to object, but simply said, 'Okay.'

'I'll take out those bags of rubbish for you,' Graham offered again, retreating to the living room to collect his jacket.

'Thanks,' Angie replied. She had pulled on the sweater she had been wearing the night before and was standing at the edge of the kitchen, her arms folded across her chest. A protective gesture, which Graham recognised of old.

Graham hesitated. On one hand, he was desperate to leave, feeling suffocated by the air of disaster that gathered around Angie, and clung to her like dust particles settling on her skin. But on the other hand, he loathed the seediness he was feeling, as though he was bailing on a one-night stand. He wasn't, of course – nothing of that nature had happened between them in years – but he found it hard to shake the feeling, nonetheless. Maybe he should stay and have coffee with her, he thought.

The motion was raised and rejected in under a second. His better judgment intervened, saving him from a journey down a very slippery slope. Angie was like a drug: once you got hooked it was almost impossible to break free from her clutches, and doing so involved unimaginable effort and pain. He had only just been sucked in by her desperate pleas to be rescued, then he had compounded his gullibility by agreeing to stay. If he agreed to coffee, who knew what she might suggest next.

'Right, well I'll be going then,' he said, grabbing hold of the bags they'd filled with the debris that had been scattered around when he had got there. 'See you later, Ange.'

'Bye, Gray,' she answered quietly. She let him see himself out, and made no request for him to stay, but even her apparent resolve didn't make it any less heart-wrenching for him to walk away like that. By the time he had disposed of the bags and made it halfway down the street, he was already fighting the temptation to turn back, to knock on the door and agree to have the bloody cup of coffee with her. But he didn't. Nothing good could come of it. It wasn't fair on Angie to give her false hope; to let her think that there was any chance of them having a relationship beyond what it was: Graham apparently being on hand to clear up her mess whenever it got bad enough for her to think of calling him. And it wasn't fair on him, either, to sacrifice yet more of his time, more of his life, offering himself up as her personal saviour. Colin would have a field day with him if he found out that Graham had stayed the night. Colin could never understand why he let himself be manipulated the way he did, and in all honesty Graham couldn't blame him; most of the time, Graham himself didn't fully understand why he fell in line whenever Angie pulled his strings. He didn't always – there had been times in the past when he'd had the courage to say no – but nine times out of ten, guilt got the better of him, and he capitulated.

He thought about replying to Colin's text from last night while he made the short walk to the train station, but decided to wait until he got home. The digital equivalent of an ear-bashing that he was inevitably letting himself in for was best handled once he'd had the chance to brush his teeth, take a shower and force down some toast and coffee.

His mind went to the last time he had been unable to conceal from Colin the fact that he had been lured into the same hackneyed trap. He hated being dishonest to his friend, but whilst Colin had every right to point out the sheer stupidity in Graham's subservience, Graham had decided that he was already suffering enough for it already, without having to manage Colin's frequent rants as well.

About a year earlier, Angie had engineered a reason to interrupt a golfing trip, and Colin's pent-up frustration had come shooting out like steam from a kettle.

'How much longer are you going to put up with this shit?' Colin had said, his face distorted with anger. 'I mean, for fuck's sake, Graham, it's been what, six years already? Six years since you got divorced, and you're still running to her like a fucking lap dog! When are you going to grow a pair, and tell her to fuck off?'

A small group of men who were biding their time, waiting for access to the seventeenth hole, exchanged surprised glances. Eoin and Owen were several hundred yards ahead, on the eighteenth, but Colin's tirade had been so loud that Graham wondered whether they might still have heard.

Wounded by his oldest friend's words, Graham had been too shocked to speak for a moment. Colin's disapproval of Angie had never been a secret, but his obvious disdain for Graham's perceived weakness had been much more subtle before, and the realisation that he no longer had the unconditional respect and support of the one person he had expected it from, stung.

'Tell her to fuck off?' he repeated incredulously, having taken a moment to catch his breath. 'Is that what you think I should do? And what if it was Liz, eh? What if it was your wife who had been through what Angie's been through, are you really the kind of man who could just turn his back on her? Because if you are, Col, then you're not the man I thought you were.'

Graham had stormed off, uttering a half-hearted apology to the witnesses as he left the green, furious with Colin but also furious with himself, because underneath it all he knew that Colin had a very valid point.

The friends had quickly reconciled afterwards, and Colin's admonishments had been far less harsh ever since, but his sentiment continued to be the same. As did Graham's acceptance of it, and his frustration at being helpless to change grew ever stronger.

He didn't have to wait long for a train and was grateful that the early hour meant there were hardly any passengers on board, and hence, plenty of seats available.

He felt emotionally drained. In light of the fitful, uncomfortable sleep he'd had, his body still cried out for a full eight hours' rest. He laid his head against the back of the seat in front of him and closed his eyes, wishing that the cornucopia of thoughts swirling around in his head would follow his lead in trying to relax. There had to be a way to stop this from happening, he told himself – not for the first time. There had to be a new, untested approach to helping Angie, a means to wrench her from the merry-go-round of self-destruction that she just couldn't alight from on her own. But as he ran through the options, he conceded that they had tried them all. Counselling. Psychotherapy. Intervention. Rehab. What else was left when a person was hell-bent on ruining themselves, and everything and everyone around them?

He buried his face in his hands, willing the train to go faster. He wanted to sleep, properly this time, and he wanted to wake up with an inkling of what he should do next.

Chapter Seven

Angie
Now

The shame was nothing new. The exhaustion was par for the course, part and parcel of the life she had fallen into. That was, if the existence that she survived each day could be described as a life.

She forced herself to drink the cheap, bitter black coffee that she had made, her body desperate for its supposed detoxifying powers and more importantly, its caffeine. It wouldn't provide a hit anywhere close to what she needed, but after last night's disaster she had barely any cash left, save for the emergency stash that she kept hidden inside the butter dish that had never been used for its intended purpose. She would have to be frugal and sensible if she had any chance of making it to 'payday' without having to go cold turkey for a day or two in between.

She had never once asked Graham for money, and she never would. There were some things that were sacred, and although her pride had been decimated to almost rock bottom, she fought to cling onto the remnants that she knew were still there; fragments that she could still recognise, even if no one else could.

A few days of rationing would probably be a good thing, anyway, she reassured herself. She had been scoring pretty hard, consistently, in recent weeks, and far from serving as the anaesthetic that she craved, the stuff she had been using seemed to be making the nightmares even worse. Maybe she would try laying off the drugs for a while, and sticking to just the drink. At the very least, she could score booze on her own. She wouldn't have to invite that low-life, no-mark slime-ball Jackson into her home, and swat his sleazy hands away from her. Fuck that.

She opened the packet in front of her and took out a cigarette, content for the moment to let the caffeine and nicotine do their respective things.

Traces of Graham's aftershave lingered in the air, and she breathed in a lungful of the scent before lighting her cigarette, savouring it for a moment before knowingly eradicating it.

Chapter Eight

Graham
Now

'So, that's enough about me. What do you do for a living?'

Graham came undone at the sudden ambush, having believed he had a few more minutes before the questions would spin back around to him.

'Oh, er, give me a second,' he stumbled playfully. 'I just need to think of something really impressive, but also believable.' He stroked his chin with his fingers and tried to look pensive. 'Nope, sorry, no, can't do it.'

Ellen laughed, and alongside his relief that he seemed to have gotten away with a rather lame joke, he felt a little bubble of optimism rise up inside him. This evening was going well. His date was interested in him, if he was reading the signs correctly. She was chatty; so far, she'd answered Graham's questions with full, informative answers, coming across as open and honest. She definitely wasn't self-obsessed, he had concluded. Case in point: she had batted the spotlight back to Graham as soon as she had cottoned onto his tactic of trying to find out as much as he could about her before offering up any kind of resumé of his own life.

She was witty. She was pretty. Hell, who was he kidding? She was stunningly beautiful, and when she smiled it got to him in ways he had almost forgotten about. When she laughed genuinely at his exclusively childish humour, well, that was even better.

'Honesty is the best policy,' she reminded him. 'Go on, just tell me. It can't be that bad.'

'You mean compared to being a vet?' Graham checked. 'Yeah, it's pretty bad.'

'Oh, go on,' she repeated, tapping his arm in mock frustration. It was only the slightest contact, but it settled the question of whether he had done the right thing in agreeing to come on this date. It had only begun fifteen minutes ago, but it was turning out to be the perfect tonic for an otherwise shitty period in his life.

'I'm an underwriter,' he said, screwing up his eyes as though to shield himself from her response.

'What's that?' she asked, with a giggle.

'I've got no idea,' Graham replied jokily. 'I've been working there eleven years and I still don't know what an underwriter actually does.'

She laughed again, then excused herself from the bar. Graham didn't take his eyes off her once during the seconds it took her to walk to the far end of the restaurant and disappear into the ladies' bathroom.

He let out a breath of relief at having made it successfully through the first quarter of an hour without making any major faux pas – at least, he sincerely hoped he hadn't – and felt a twinge of excitement about what the rest of the evening might have in store. It had been a long time since he had been brave enough to go on a proper, official date, and even longer since he had met someone that he genuinely felt a connection with. Assuming Ellen didn't suddenly make an excuse to do a runner on her return from the ladies', or worse still, didn't bother to return (a prospect that suddenly caused Graham to break into a nervous sweat), there was still a meal to be enjoyed, which meant at least another hour or so of her company. And after that, he thought, maybe she could be persuaded to join him for a drink in the classy cocktail bar just around the corner.

40

He would be the perfect gentleman when the time came to bid her goodnight, but the thought of spending another few hours with her was enough to make him feel quite heady. It was a feeling so alien to him that he took a few moments to compose himself and acknowledge what was happening, wiping his forehead with his napkin to brush off the beads of perspiration that had broken out there. He was as nervous as a teenager on their first venture into the world of romance. But it was a good feeling. He liked it. Still, he made a mental note not to get too far ahead of himself.

'Shall we move over to the table?' he asked as soon as she came back, eager to lock down her attendance for the next part of the date.

'Absolutely,' Ellen replied, her smile still reaching her eyes, bolstering Graham's ever-growing confidence.

'After you,' he told her, returning her smile. He could not, and did not, even try to stop his eyes roaming over every detail of her figure, taking it all in as she walked a couple of paces ahead of him.

She was a little younger than him, he guessed, although he hadn't been absent from the dating scene for so long that he would make the mistake of asking or making a stab at working out her age. Twenty-one was the stock answer to give when pushed for a guess, wasn't it? Within the safety of his own mind, he estimated that she was already in her late twenties, although she could genuinely pass for twenty-five, he thought. Another ripple of sweat threatened to break out as he contemplated the consequences if that were true. Did she know he was thirty-six? Would she really be interested in someone perhaps seven or eight years older than she was?

He ran through some logic in his head: the woman he was having dinner with was a well-established vet with her own successful practice, so she would have had to have been nothing short of a child prodigy to have achieved everything she'd achieved so far if she was not, in fact, nearing the milestone of the big three-oh. Whilst it was possible that she had skipped some grades, it was probably more likely that she just looked younger than her years. Less than a decade of a difference between their ages was perfectly palatable, he concluded.

Aesthetically, Graham had already assigned her to a league far higher than his own. Ellen stood about five feet tall, and had a naturally slim, toned figure. Initially he had been blind-sighted; there was something about her stature that was at odds with his vision of a traditional vet, but as he tried to conjure an image of what that was, he realised he only had one frame of reference to base it on. The last vet he'd had dealings with had been on hand to navigate his family's dear old Labrador Loki to his final rest, around five years previously. This particular vet had been a white-haired, perpetually-tanned gentleman of grand stature, with the largest hands Graham had ever seen. Ellen was nothing like him. And for that, Graham was thankful.

She wore a simple, elegant black dress, which was not so fancy that it was out of place in the mid-priced restaurant they were about to eat in, but also fancy enough that he was buoyed by her making such an effort for their meeting. Her eyes were hazel, and she wore subtle make-up around them, which again was appealing to Graham. If there was one thing that he couldn't make his peace with, it was the orange tinge that several women tended to coat their faces and bodies in, whether for special occasions or simply their everyday lives. He had noticed a couple of said women in the restaurant, and had tried his best to stop his face from betraying his opinion.

He felt the beginnings of a smug smile tug at his lips as he assisted Ellen to her seat before their waiter could oblige. There was a sense of pride in being seen out with a smart, attractive woman who was having an unexpected but happily welcome effect on him, and suddenly he was desperate to break out all his charm.

'Here are your menus,' the waiter needlessly pointed out, laying one each in front of Ellen and Graham. 'And can I get any drinks for you?'

They opted for a bottle of reasonably-priced Prosecco to share, and the waiter left them alone to pick up where they had left off.

'I'm starving!' Ellen admitted, perusing the menu with urgency. 'I have an unfortunate habit of forgetting to eat during the day when I'm really busy, so the last thing I had today was an apple, at about half-eleven.'

'I'm pretty hungry myself,' Graham concurred. 'And this will come as a real surprise to you, but I don't really tend to forget to eat at all.' He playfully tapped his stomach, and instantly regretted drawing attention to it. His waistline had been growing at a rate much faster than he cared to admit recently. He made another mental note, this time to combine more exercise with healthier eating and less beer in an attempt to make his abdomen shrink back a little closer to how it had been before he'd begun to be lax about his routine.

'What do you think you will have?' she asked him.

'Hmm ... the steak sounds good,' he said, after a second's deliberation. 'Can't beat a nice steak. What about you?'

Ellen smiled politely. 'Not for me,' she explained. 'It doesn't really gel with my ethos, to eat the animals I'm morally committed to keeping alive.'

'Ah, of course,' Graham conceded, turning red with embarrassment. 'I'm so sorry,' he added. 'I didn't even think.'

'No, don't be silly,' she told him, brushing his arm again with her hand. Her expression was open; there was no hint of anger or offence. 'You order whatever you want,' she assured him. 'It's my choice, doesn't mean you can't eat whatever you would normally eat.'

Graham smiled back. He was heartened by her response, but in spite of her insistence he didn't feel that it would be appropriate to flaunt his omnivorous tastes in front of her.

'Do you know what? I think I'll try something completely different, in that case. What are you having?'

'Honestly, Graham,' she countered, 'you really don't have to do that, not for my benefit.'

'No, no, I want to,' Graham insisted. 'Really, I'm so unadventurous when it comes to food. It's about time I broadened my horizons. What looks good?'

'Well, I think I'll go for the risotto,' she said, pointing to the dish description on her menu. 'Most restaurants tend to do mushrooms to death in their veggie meals, but this one is mushroom-free, and sounds delicious.'

'In that case, I'll go for that as well,' Graham confirmed. 'I don't think I've even tried risotto before. How ridiculous is that?'

'Almost as ridiculous as being an underwriter,' Ellen quipped, and her face lit up again.

I like her, Graham thought to himself again, mirroring her chuckle and allowing himself a rare moment of reckless abandon. I *really* like her.

Chapter Nine

Graham
Now

'So, she's a keeper?' Colin asked. He had been remarkably and unusually well-behaved while Graham had described his fledgling relationship, refraining from butting in with inappropriate comments or searching questions. In fact, other than a raised eyebrow when Graham had divulged that Ellen was vegan, Colin's conduct had been perfect. Exemplary.

'I think so, mate,' Graham replied. 'And I guess I've got you to thank for it.' He gave his friend a pat on the arm to signify his gratitude.

'Yeah, and don't you forget it,' Colin warned him with a laugh. 'That's, oh, shall we say, eleven years of favours you owe me now?'

'Eleven? Where the hell do you get eleven from?'

Colin rolled his eyes at having to explain. 'One for every digit of her mobile number that I took the liberty of acquiring for you when you couldn't be arsed,' he clarified.

Graham dipped his head, remembering the evening when he had run out so unceremoniously, leaving his friends and his new admirer behind in order to go and firefight Angie's latest crisis. Colin had taken matters into his own hands after Graham's departure and asked Ellen outright whether the glances she had been throwing in his mate's direction had any basis in her quite liking the look of him. They had, she had bashfully admitted, and she had agreed to take Graham's number, declining to give her own to Colin for fairly obvious reasons. After three days, she had plucked up the courage to text Graham, and the rest was recent history.

'It wasn't that I couldn't be arsed,' Graham objected, running a finger nervously around the rim of his pint glass as memories from the night spent comforting Angie bled into his mind. 'You know that.'

'What I know is that you should have changed your number a long fucking time ago, mate. Circa the day after you finally came to your senses and walked out on that nutter.'

'Yeah, okay, Col,' Graham said sharply, holding up a hand in warning. A repeat of the war of words on the golf course was not in his plans for the day. 'Let's just agree that you have no time for her and I'm a mug, and move on, shall we?' he suggested. 'No need to get nasty.'

Colin huffed, and looked set to say something in response, but checked out at the last second.

'I don't want to talk about her,' Graham added, hoping to put the topic to bed.

'Good,' Colin retorted, clearly holding himself back from revealing more of what was on his mind. 'Let's talk about Ellen some more. And you can start paying back your eleven years' worth of favours by buying the next round.'

'Deal,' Graham replied. He tried a smile, but it felt harder to come by than it should have. He was rueing the fact that, despite his desire to talk about Ellen and the happiness she had brought him in the space of the four dates they'd been on together so far, Angie's face was now front and centre in his mind. Memories of that night, the last time he'd seen her, were floating around in front of his eyes. He could hear her screams as though they were being played through an earpiece that had been surgically implanted and could not be taken out.

He hadn't heard from her since then. Not a whimper since he had escaped her flat that morning over a month earlier, leaving her to fend for herself in a world that she just wasn't built for. The lack of contact both heartened him and concerned him, and with his extensive knowledge of her history, the concern far outweighed the relief. He had tried telling himself that the unexpected silence was due to a shift in her circumstances; that she had finally managed to sort herself out. It happened, didn't it? All it took was a trigger, a reason to 'wake up and smell the coffee'. People with difficult pasts often clawed their way out of their misery and found the strength and the will to fight for themselves, for their right to be normal and happy. Perhaps that was what Angie had done. Perhaps the debacle with the young robbers had forced her into taking a long, hard look in the mirror, and resulted in the long overdue realisation that she needed to make a huge alteration in her life. Several, in fact.

As desperately as he had wanted to believe it, however, he had failed to convince himself beyond all reasonable doubt. With Angie, or rather, the version of her that she was now, the only constant was doubt. If he were a betting man, Graham wouldn't have risked a penny on Scenario A being the accurate version of events. Not when Scenario B had the propensity to be some kind of fuck-up of Titanic proportions on Angie's part – one that probably involved drugs, alcohol, ill-advised sexual encounters, or a combination of all three.

The fact that Angie hadn't pestered him for weeks should have been the icing on the top of a very sweet cake which was four enjoyable, drama-free dates with Ellen. She had come into his life at exactly the right moment when, without acknowledging it, he had all but given up hope of ever finding anyone who could reach the parts of him that Angie once had many moons ago. It irked him that he could not shake the feeling that everything seemed to be breezing along just a little too well.

Whenever something was too good to be true, it invariably wasn't true. That was the legacy of his marriage, and one that was hard to shirk.

For Graham, when a beautiful, intelligent, low-maintenance woman showed a healthy interest in him, notions of catastrophe waiting in the wings, biding its time before rearing its ugly head and restoring the generally shitty status quo that his life had adopted in recent years, befuddled his brain.

'What are you thinking about over there, you filthy bugger?' Colin joked, breaking Graham from his reverie. 'I thought you told me it hadn't gone that far yet.'

'It hasn't,' Graham answered promptly, truthfully. 'I was just thinking of all the ways I could possibly fuck this up,' he explained. 'You know I've got form in this area.'

Colin sighed, familiar and clearly exasperated with Graham's tendency to assign himself blame where it was unwarranted.

'You want my advice?' he asked, his voice sincere.

'Sure,' Graham replied, making eye contact with the server at the other side of the bar and waving her over.

'Okay, here goes,' Colin started, blowing out a long breath. 'Firstly – and this is not so much advice as a gentle reminder – you were not responsible for what happened with she-who-will-not-be-named. I know it, you know it, and deep down, even she knows it. You've got to let that shit go.'

Graham nodded gravely.

'Secondly, Ellen is Ellen. She's not ... her. Don't ever make the mistake of thinking of her – or treating her – like she is. Trust her until the day she gives you a reason not to. For God's sake, don't let your Angie baggage get in the way of what could be a really good thing.'

Graham went to speak, but Colin held up a halting hand. 'I know, I know, I said I'd never utter her name, but I'm breaking my own rule for a very good reason.' He leant forward. 'You deserve to be happy, mate,' he told Graham sincerely. 'And by the sound of it, Ellen could be the one to make you happy. Don't let anything stand in the way of that.'

It was a warning of sorts, and Graham knew it. Far from his romantic prospects being the only area of his life that Angie had managed to systematically ruin for him in the years since – and if he was honest, in some of the years before – they had divorced, her behaviour and Graham's response to it had caused friction in all of his relationships, not least in his friendship with Colin. His perceived pandering to her had been the trigger for heated arguments that would never have occurred had it not been for Angie, with Colin insisting that Graham was playing the counter-productive role of enabler, and Graham maintaining that turning his back on a woman in need was something his conscience would never sanction. Their relationship had weathered many storms, but Graham was aware that there was a finite number of times they could have the same fight and come out the other side with their mutual affection still intact. If he reverted to type and let Angie come between him and a shot at happiness with Ellen, he had a feeling that Colin may well have a few choice, less-than-pleasant words to say about it, and this time Graham had no defence to offer.

'Message received and understood,' he assured Colin, drawing a smile from his oldest friend.

Colin gave a curt nod and sat back again, signalling the end of the sentimental period of the evening. 'Right,' he said, 'where's this bloody drink you owe me then?'

Chapter Ten

Graham
Now

'Sorry, sorry.' Graham scrambled in his pocket for his phone, trying desperately to shut it up as quickly as possible. Instead, in his haste, he only succeeded in sending it flying out of his hand and underneath the seats in front of him. He winced as he heard it slide along the floor, the sound drawing tuts of disapproval from the other theatregoers. He couldn't blame them, to be fair.

Why hadn't he just put the thing on silent? Or turned it off? Ellen was with him, seated inches to his right. The guys knew he was going to be at the opera – they'd taken turns to tease him for it – and besides, they weren't known for calling him. His parents never called him on his mobile, preferring to contact him via his landline.

He had no reason to make himself contactable. Totally the opposite, in fact – he didn't want anything to spoil this night.

'Shit!' he whispered, although his hushed tone was pointless in light of the fact that his Kings of Leon ringtone was resonating around the stalls and beyond. A disgruntled audience member three rows in front retrieved the offending object and passed it back, via two more unimpressed patrons. 'Sorry,' he offered again, to everyone in the room. He turned to Ellen and noted that she was staring straight ahead, the tightening of her jaw visible in the soft glare from the stage, enough to let him know that she was pissed off.

He didn't bother to check who the call was from. He switched off the device straight away, cursing himself once more for failing to do so earlier, and clenched his fists in his lap. Anger got in the way of his attempts to concentrate on the spectacle that was playing out on the stage, yards away from the Band A seats that he had been able to procure at a premium. He had been so looking forward to this evening, excited at the prospect of attending his very first opera, not only because he had spent some time watching clips from various productions on YouTube and had fallen a little in love with the arias, but also because Ellen had told him that Madama Butterfly was her all-time favourite opera, and he wanted to revel a little in his own thoughtfulness. He had surprised her with the tickets a few weeks ago, finding pleasure in her thrilled reaction and harbouring thoughts of turning the evening into a landmark one for reasons other than simply playing host to their first shared operatic experience.

He and Ellen had been together for five months, and he felt it was the right time to ask her something very important. He wasn't ready to propose – he still hadn't decided whether he was willing to ever declare vows for a second time in his life – but a next step of sorts was in order, he thought. He was going to ask her to move in with him.

'Are you sure?' Colin had asked him a week ago, his response to Graham's glad announcement more deflating than enthusiastic. 'It's still early days.'

Graham gave a wry laugh, surprised by Colin's dampening tone. 'Well make up your mind, mate,' he retorted sarcastically. 'One minute you're bending my ear about how I should make a go of it with Ellen, dump all my baggage and move on, and the next you're asking me if I'm sure?'

'I'm only looking out for you,' Colin replied, stony-faced.

'I just don't want to see you get hurt again.'

'Why would I get hurt this time?' Graham prodded defensively. A nerve had been touched. 'You said it yourself, Ellen is not Angie.'

'You're right, I did say that,' Colin answered, in a stern manner usually reserved for when he was conducting his business as a solicitor. 'And I stand by it. To all intents and purposes, she's nothing like her, but after all that you've been through, I'm just asking if you're one hundred per cent sure you want to rush into living together so quickly. I just don't see the need for you to hurry.'

'I don't believe this,' Graham said, loud enough that a few other people in the coffee shop looked over, clearly wondering if a scene might about to unfold between the two men. 'You know, mate, I actually thought you'd be pleased for me. You're the one who's been on my case for years to find myself a decent woman, and now that I have, you're trying to put doubts in my head.'

'Hey, hang on a minute, mate,' Colin countered. 'I'm doing no such thing. If there's any doubt in your mind, it's got nothing to do with me. If you ask me …'

His voice trailed off, and he instantly wished he could take the last few words back.

'If I ask you, what?' Graham asked, in an uncharacteristically aggressive tone.

'Nothing, it doesn't matter,' Colin replied quietly, trying to diffuse the situation which seemed to have escalated at an alarming pace. He drained the last of his coffee and pulled his wallet from his pocket, signifying that their lunchtime catch-up was over.

'No, come on,' Graham goaded, unwilling to let the subject be put to bed. 'If you've got something to say, just say it.' Agitation was evident in his face now, and conversations around the room halted, as the other customers eagerly anticipated some early afternoon entertainment.

Colin sighed, resting his elbow on the table and rubbing his forehead with one hand.

'Okay. If you ask me, you're blowing what I said way out of proportion,' he explained. 'You're going on the defensive, lashing out at me for no reason, and that's not like you. It makes me think you're having doubts about the relationship with Ellen, and you're trying to deflect onto me because you want this to work, but you're scared it won't.'

Graham sat silently for a moment, digesting what he'd heard. Colin waited in expectation of an enraged outburst, as did the rest of the now practically silent coffee shop, but it didn't come.

'I thought you were supposed to be a lawyer, not a fucking psychologist,' Graham finally remarked, but there was no aggression in his delivery this time. His lips gave in to a reluctant smile as he leaned forward to rest his head in his hands. 'I want to be with her, Col,' he admitted softly. Colin nodded. 'She's great. She's everything I could want: smart, attractive, fun to be around, mentally stable …'

He sat back and ran his hands through his hair.

'So, what's the problem?' Colin asked.

'Me,' Graham stated. 'I'm the problem. Because I keep thinking that if I don't move things forward, tie her down as soon as possible, I'll lose her. But what if I am rushing things? What if I ask her and she thinks it's a terrible idea?'

'Well then you'll just carry on the way you are now, I suppose,' Colin offered. 'Is that so bad?'

Graham pondered this for a second. 'No,' he conceded.

Colin clearly wasn't convinced that he was getting the whole story, but Graham sensed that his friend didn't feel there was any value to be had in persisting.

'Do whatever you think is right,' Colin advised, and Graham recognised the tactic – Colin was relieving himself of any culpability by relying on Graham's tendency to go with his own gut regardless of anyone else's input.

And Graham had proved him right. He had gone ahead and done what he had planned to do in the first place, shirking off Colin's caution and telling himself that it was about goddamn time he started taking direct action in his life; going after the things he truly wanted. And Ellen was what he truly wanted. He was sure of it.

Except that, when it came to asking the question that seemed to dwell permanently on the tip of his tongue, he hadn't been able to bring himself to take the plunge yet. Even though there had been several perfect opportunities.

He had been ready to pull the trigger one idyllic night just after the pair had made boozy love, following an evening of watching their favourite comedy films and getting steadily drunker with each witty one-liner, but while his mind repeated the words over and over, they had still never made it out of his mouth.

There was another time when Ellen had cried on his shoulder, opening her heart and letting out her frustration at being unable to save a family pet who had been run over outside its home. He had held her while she'd wept, never wanting to let her go. He had been about to say the words, then, right on the verge, but … he couldn't. He just didn't understand it.

What he did understand, and he wished that he didn't, was why Ellen was so obviously peeved at his hapless efforts with his phone a few moments ago. Almost four months of blissful yet agonising silence from Angie had recently ended with an episode that no one else in the world except her would be capable of pulling off, and though it was the last thing he wanted to do in the world, Graham had been forced to reveal the full sorry tale of his past relationship to the woman he was desperate to have a future successful relationship with. And Angie, it appeared, had some catching up to do.

At first, Ellen had been remarkably calm when confronted with the unfortunate truth about Graham's ex-wife. She had done her best to assure him that she understood; that she believed him when he told her there wasn't the slightest remnant of feeling still there on his part, aside from an inconvenient bad habit of feeling responsible for her, a habit which he explained he was trying his utmost to kick. And Ellen's easy-going reaction had seen his affection for her grow even stronger.

But like everyone, he supposed, the woman had her limits. Her patience had visibly worn thin as Angie had upped her game, launching herself back into Graham's life like a bat out of hell and ignoring his attempts to reason with her. At first, he tried to make her appreciate that he would no longer be responding to her crises, and later he succumbed to bad-tempered outbursts in which he channelled every ounce of frustration and resentment he had been harbouring for years and laid into her over the phone, thinking and hoping each time that the ferociousness of his words might sufficiently drive home the message. It seemed not.

He had toyed with the idea of blocking her number, but that had lasted all of one day before something in the back of his conscience had noisily rebelled against the move, and he had relented and removed the barrier.

Ellen had shirked off the first few episodes, comforted by the very public no-nonsense approach that Graham had taken when the calls and texts had begun to be a source of discontent between him and her, but as the days and weeks went on and Angie showed no signs of letting up, Ellen's frustration had started to seep out. Graham had done something that he had made a silent promise to himself that he would never do, and lied to her. A lie of sorts – he told her that he had blocked Angie from calling, messaging, even making contact with him via social media, which he almost never paid attention to anyway. He had left out the part about subsequently unblocking the number that had caused him so much inconvenience and was now threatening to drive a wedge between him and the best thing that had happened to him in ages. He had regretfully realised that he was powerless to give up on Angie altogether. Perhaps, he considered, he was as much of an addict as his ex-wife was. Angie was addicted to drugs; Graham was addicted to her. And he couldn't decide whose habit was the more dangerous.

He reached out for Ellen's hand as she continued to stare ahead, focused intently on one of the most beautiful and poignant sections of Act Two. She didn't bat him away, but neither did she turn to him and smile, or grip his fingers in a conciliatory gesture. She continued gazing at the stage, her pulse fast in her hand, and Graham understood that tonight would definitely not be the ideal night to pop his burning question.

Chapter Eleven

Graham
Then

Graham was positively itching for Angie to come home. He had been picturing the look on her face when he broke the news.

She would be just as excited as he was, he was sure. She'd be surprised, but in a good way, and he thought her eyes might even well up a little. She probably wouldn't all-out cry - that really wasn't her style – but he could just see her, smiling appreciatively at him, cupping his face in her hands and whispering a heartfelt 'Thank you' in his ear.

Unless ...

No. He swatted away the doubts that peppered his mind. This was a nice thing that he had done. A sweet, caring, romantic gesture, that Angie would appreciate. What was there to be doubtful about?

After two years of marriage, of full-time, occasionally punishing jobs, a long, drawn-out house purchase and a painful heart-to-heart over the dashed hopes of children featuring in their future, Graham's inherent romantic nature hadn't become dampened in the slightest. He adored Angie not a fraction less than he had when he had fallen in love with her as a doe-eyed student.

They had lived through some challenges during their years together. Naturally. What couple didn't experience ups and downs? But hand on heart, Graham could say that there had never been anything so serious that it had threatened to burst the bubble they had fashioned around themselves.

Had Graham harboured dreams of becoming a father? One day, perhaps. He had never given it much thought, other than to assume that it would just happen, because that was the way the world worked: you grew up, got married, had kids. Yet, if he was truly honest with himself, the sense of loss that he had felt when Angie had pleaded with him to respect her decision had been palpable.

That was silly, he had scolded himself. Ridiculous. How could he yearn for something that he had never had? How could he possibly grieve for a child, or children, that had never been born, and would never be born? Angie was all that he needed, he reminded himself. They wouldn't go on to have a family, and for sure a part of him would always feel a little sad about that, but they would be a unit, the two of them. They had vowed to each other and all the witnesses at their wedding that they would be just that: a tight, solid unit. And that was alright. In fact, it was better than alright – to be married to the woman he loved with every fibre of his being was better than Graham could have hoped for.

The two years since she had walked down the aisle to meet him had been the best of his life. All those people who said that marriage was hard work, that things changed once the rings were on and the ink had dried, were clearly doing something wrong. There was nothing to it.

Why, then, was his mind suddenly conjuring up red flags?

'What are you up to?' Angie joked, materialising before he had the chance to deliberate any further and making him jump in surprise. 'Nothing dodgy, I hope,' she joked. She laid her car keys on the worktop and came towards him wearing a lazy smile. 'As you requested, m'lord.' She handed him a heavy bag of groceries, and let her lips linger on his for a few seconds. He accepted the bag from her and smiled when he viewed the contents.

'You're a star,' he praised her, removing the six-pack of Budweiser bottles and the family-sized bag of his favourite kind of crisps, and retiring the carrier bag to their designated resting place – the third drawer down, underneath the hob. He had called her at work and asked her to pick up a few things on her way home, in preparation for the hotly-anticipated football match that he was planning to plonk himself in front of in a couple of hours (another reason why their relationship was often so effortless – Angie indulged his love of football. He had a suspicion that she genuinely enjoyed it). He drew her into a hug, resting his weight against the kitchen counter.

'Nope, nothing dodgy,' he answered, 'but I do have a little surprise for you.'

He thought he felt her body tense underneath his hands, but the tremor passed so quickly that he couldn't be sure it had even happened. The doubts of a few moments ago powered back, and he felt a growl of uncertainty in his gut. But it was too late now. The cat had been partially let out of the bag, and to try to put it back in would be messy.

'Oh?' she asked tentatively, keeping her face nestled into his chest and her arms clasped at his back.

That was not the response he had hoped for. This was not how this was supposed to go. Women were supposed to love surprises, weren't they? Although, now that he came to think of it, he had never tested this premise before. Why was that?

Graham felt beads of sweat appear on his forehead, his pulse hurrying a little faster than usual.

'Yeah, I've booked a little trip for us,' he explained cautiously, resting his chin on top of her head.

She jerked her head up swiftly, her face neutral. 'Where to?' she asked, almost accusingly.

He looked into her eyes, wishing now that he could take back the words that he had been so eager to say. What was that he was seeing in there? Panic? Fear?

59

'Newcastle,' he blurted out, surprised to note that for some reason it sounded like a dirty word when it reached his ears.

She detached herself from his arms and moved away to the other side of the kitchen, sliding her hand across her forehead as though she were trying to will the thoughts inside to fall into some kind of order.

'Why would you do that?' she asked him, her tone inferring a far more serious crime than he had committed.

Graham took a moment to consider how best to reply. 'I … I just … I wanted to take you away for a few days. I thought it would be romantic. You could show me where you grew up, and we could—'

'I thought I had made it clear,' she cut him off, 'that there's nothing there for me anymore.' Her voice wasn't angry, but there was something new in there, something that he hadn't heard before. There was an edge to it that was alien to him. As a couple, they were a rare phenomenon: they didn't argue, or fall out. Well, not often. That was what made their marriage so perfect, so easy. What had he done wrong?

'Yeah, you did,' he flustered, 'but I thought it might be nice, you know? I mean, of course, I know you said you moved down here for a better life, but it's still your hometown, isn't it? I mean, you must have some happy memories of the place. And I thought maybe we could go and visit your parents' graves, and lay flowers …'

He saw the way she was looking at him, with a gaze so harsh that he might as well have confessed to being the drunk driver who had cut her parents' lives so short all those years ago. He stopped, eager to attempt some damage limitation but fearful that the worst had already been done.

She turned her back on him, and for a solid minute he stood still, bewildered, torn between wanting to go to her, and giving her space to work through whatever it was that he had so unintentionally incited in her. Eventually she turned to face him again, with a weak smile that was grudgingly painted on, for effect. She reached out for him and resumed her position in his arms. Graham was taken aback, but he didn't dare question the move.

'I'm sorry,' she whispered, speaking into the soft fabric of his shirt. 'It's just that I don't like to go back there. It's just too painful. Everything bad that happened in my life happened there.'

He patted her back soothingly. 'It's okay,' he assured her, wrong-footed by the temperamentality of her mood in the last few moments. 'I'm sorry. I'm such an idiot,' he conceded, holding her tight. 'I should have realised. I just thought it would be nice for you, you know? Nostalgia and all that.'

She raised her head and placed her finger softly across his lips to silence him. 'You are not an idiot,' she corrected him. Her face broke into a soft smile. 'You're lovely,' she told him. 'You're lovely and you did a lovely thing. It's just … too much. I hope you can understand.'

Graham nodded, and brushed her hair away from her cheek. 'Of course I do,' he replied, quite convinced that he didn't, not totally.

He didn't hold out much hope of recovering any of the cash that he had paid out, but that wasn't really a concern in the grand scheme of things. He had opted for a cosy, family-run bed and breakfast on the outskirts of the city as opposed to a bog-standard hotel chain, so the price of the room for two nights hadn't broken the bank. It was non-refundable, however.

But the financial penalty didn't bother him. What made him feel uneasy, fearful almost, was the severity of the reaction that he had just borne the brunt of. Had he been a complete idiot? How could he have misjudged the situation so badly? He held her close, and she seemed content to just stand there with him, each of them lost in their own thoughts as silence descended on the kitchen.

Graham trawled through the conversations that they'd had in the past, of which he now realised there had been shockingly few relating to her past in general. He was searching for vindication; hoping that some titbit of information might present itself from the depths of his memory and provide some context that might explain why the mere mention of going back home had sent Angie into such a state.

The obvious answer was straight-forward: as she had said, the worst times of her life had played out there. Her family had all perished there, and who could blame her for associating the place with the depths of her grief?

She could see no future for herself in her home town, she had explained to him when they first met, which he had accepted without question. She had dreamt of 'escaping', for a very long time, and her acceptance to Kent had been her ticket out of a place that in the end, she nurtured no affection for.

Yes, that was the answer, he concluded. Of course, he had been a complete idiot for suggesting that she return to the town she had been plotting to get out of as soon as she was old enough. In his mind, going there would have been a trip down memory lane, an exercise in nostalgia, in making new memories with him to overshadow any negative ones that she may still harbour from before. He tried to imagine how he would feel if the tables were turned, and the mere thought of his own parents enduring the same fate as hers made him wince in pain.

'I'm so sorry, my love,' he told her, hugging her even tighter. 'Forgive me.'

She pulled back a little, enough to meet his eyeline. She was smiling. It was though their lives were a movie, and the scene had been rewound by five minutes, to the point where she had handed him his beers, before he had put his foot in it.

'There's nothing to forgive, my love,' she told him, her demeanour perky once more. 'Anyway, the game will be on in a bit. What will we have for dinner?'

She stepped away and opened the door of the fridge to investigate the options, and Graham gave a light shake of his head. The freak-out had passed, it seemed, as quickly as it had been triggered, and everything was back to normal, back to the way it usually was.

But in the back of his mind, he knew there was something not quite right. Something had panicked her. Something about home. And he wanted to know what it was. But to find out, he had to figure out a way to make her open up and tell him. And based on the evidence of the past few minutes, he suspected that might not be a straightforward thing to do.

Chapter Twelve

Graham
Now

'I'm sorry, Gray, I really am.'

His mind flashed back to the previous evening, when he had been forced to digest those same exact words from Ellen. The woman he had been sure he was falling in love with.

Ellen's admission hadn't come as a total shock – how could it? But it had still knocked the wind right out of him, like a jab to the solar plexus. It was over, she had told him, unwaveringly. He had pleaded with her, tried to make her agree with him that to throw away what they had together was madness, but through her tears she had told him that it was all too much to deal with. It was clear that he would never be able to commit to her, not truly, she had pointed out. They were over. And she was sorry.

Hearing those words now from Angie, yet again, he found himself debating whether he believed that either one of them was telling the truth.

Maybe women were all the same. Maybe you could be the nicest, most well-meaning, selfless guy in the world, just trying to do right by everyone, and it still wouldn't be good enough. Maybe you could jump through hoops, and bend over backwards, and put your own wants and needs to the back of the queue, and still end up on the receiving end of those words. Those fucking useless, meaningless words.

Maybe nice guys really did finish last, after all.

He was being harsh on Ellen, and he knew it. She had given him the benefit of the doubt plenty of times. Maybe too many times. Maybe he had convinced himself that she would just always be okay with it, because of how she felt about him. As it turned out, she wouldn't.

He was being harsh on her, but only in his mind. He was allowed to be angry at her in there. He was allowed to feel like he was the one who was hard done by. He was allowed to ball his fists, and grind his teeth, and feel like he could punch a wall, when he was alone. Which he now was. Again. Courtesy of Angie. Again.

'Let me stop you there, Ange, before you go any further,' he said, holding up a hand to halt her flow of excuses. 'Before you feed me all your bullshit, and you beg for understanding, and then forgiveness, just stop, okay? I didn't come here to listen to any of that shit.'

She looked surprised, which angered him even more. He kept his head though. He had to. Once he was home, he could vent his frustration as much as he wanted: verbally, physically (he had a punching bag in his garage that he used for exercise, when he felt motivated – he could pummel the shit out of, if it came to it), but whilst he was in her presence, he had to keep it under control. The strength of the urge he felt to slap the sheer self-destruction out of the woman, once and for all, scared him a little. A lot, in fact.

He blew out a long breath. 'I'm only here to tell you that this is the last time. I know, I've said it before, and I've always gone back on it. More *fucking* fool me.' He emphasised the expletive, the word feeling good on his lips. 'Well that's all in the past now, Angie, exactly where it should have been right from the start, when I signed those papers to set myself free.'

'Gray—'

'Don't!' he yelled, raising his voice for the first time

since he'd entered her house. He held up his hand again, to reinforce his point. 'I mean it this time, Angie. You have fucked up my life one too many times, and now it's over. We're done. Do you understand?' He didn't wait for her to reply. 'In fact, here, maybe this will help you to understand,' he said, making her flinch as he reached suddenly into his pocket and pulled out his mobile phone. She watched, bleary-eyed, as he tore apart the phone, with no apparent regard for dismantling it safely. 'Here, do you see this?' he demanded, holding the tiny SIM card in front of her face. She could only nod her affirmation. 'This is you and me,' he told her, tossing the card on the floor and stomping on it. The cracking sound underneath his shoe made her wince, and a tear rolled down her cheek as she watched him jump up and down ferociously on the shattered pieces that became of it.

He stopped after several seconds, his face red from exertion and emotion. He reached down and gathered up what he could from the floor, the components now barely more than dust.

'You don't contact me anymore,' he warned her, holding the debris in his hand, letting her see what had become of the item that signified the only link she'd had with him. 'You can't contact me anymore, you get that right?'

She stared at him, her eyes flitting nervously, like a child being reprimanded.

'Tell me you get that, Angie,' he roared, making her flinch again at the loudness of his voice.

'I get it, Gray,' she answered, in a soft whimper.

He stared at her for a moment, as though debating whether he needed to labour the point any further. He hadn't even intended to smash up his SIM card – his temper had run away from him. He was thankful that he hadn't gone so far as to jump up and down on his phone, or his resolve not to get violent with her would have been tested even further.

'No, you don't,' he said ruefully, finally looking away

from her tear-stained face. 'You never did. You never will.' He stuffed the remnants of what used to be the nerve centre of his phone into his jacket pocket, and made for the door.

This time, Angie didn't try to stop him. This time, he wasn't even tempted to look back.

Chapter Thirteen

Graham
Now

'I'm telling you, man, that won't be the end of it,' Irish Eoin announced confidently. 'I mean, Matt Damon's got a good few years left in him. Did you see the bod on him at the beginning there? Give it a year. Two, tops. Jason Bourne'll be back, I'm telling you.'

'Bloody hell, mate. Checking out his "bod", were you?' Owen teased, making air quotes with his fingers.

The others laughed, and Colin gave Eoin a hearty, brotherly slap on the back. As hard-core fans of the hugely popular, fictional CIA-assassin-turned-good-guy movie franchise, the friends had reneged on a Friday night pool session for the most recent, hotly-anticipated resurrection of Jason Bourne, and they were unanimous in their praise for the movie.

Graham had taken much coaxing, in light of the fog of gloom that he had been encased in following the severing of ties which had taken place between him and both Ellen and Angie (Ellen having been the one to initiate the severing, whereas finally cutting the cord that had bound him to Angie had been done of his own volition), but he was glad he had paid heed to the three leery, good-natured bullies who had appeared at his front door earlier, with promises of two hours of heart-stopping car chases, side-switching and good, honest-to-God hand-to-hand combat, followed by a few pints in the cinema bar. He had enjoyed the film, but more than that, he had enjoyed having some fun company.

On the orders of Colin, he suspected, none of the men had mentioned either of the women who had made their own very distinct imprints on his life in the not-too-distant past, and at points he found himself so engrossed in their chatter or in the movie that for periods of several moments he didn't so much as think about either Ellen or Angie.

When his mind did wander away from the shootouts and the double-crossing playing out on the screen, it naturally drifted firstly to Ellen, and he would feel a wave of regret wash over him at the thought of what might have been. He had tried calling her a handful of times, hopeful if not confident of a reconciliation, but when she had failed to respond after the sixth attempt, he had reluctantly conceded defeat.

His feelings were erratic, flip-flopping between guilt over the times that he had failed to live up to his promise to expel Angie and all her inconvenient, over-bearing drama from his life, and conversely a deep sense of injustice that Ellen clearly hadn't felt strongly enough for him to give him the benefit of the doubt, to trust him.

The more he thought about it, the more convinced he became that the aggravation generated by Angie's omnipresence (as significant and soul-destroying as it had been) probably didn't fully answer the question as to why Ellen had seen fit to bring the curtains down on her relationship with Graham after only five months. Five months which had been, for the most part, truly enjoyable, immensely satisfying and, Graham had dared to think, the beginning of something special. At least for him, they had been.

From the first time he had introduced Ellen to the guys, he had been on the receiving end of regular jibes that he was 'punching above his weight'. That he had 'really fallen on his feet', and (from Irish Eoin), had 'bagged a stunner'.

He had laughed away their comments, overjoyed to simply warrant the attention of and actually be dating a woman so much more attractive than him, chalking their observations up to the typical banter that flows between friends. They didn't mean anything by it, he knew. They were happy for him.

But when the laughter inevitably died down and he was left, in quiet moments, to pore over his deep-rooted insecurities, the jokes would echo inside his mind, stirring up a storm of anxiety. Of course, he was the lucky one in the relationship, that was plain for all to see.

Ellen was gorgeous, a stunner indeed. He was … average, he supposed.

In recent times, when he had reluctantly attempted to gauge his overall attractiveness, he tried to picture himself being the subject of one of those cringe-worthy reality TV shows, where unsuspecting members of the public have a microphone thrust into their faces, and are bombarded with awkward questions about the poor, sad subject of the show standing in front of them.

'Madam, just a minute of your time, please, if you don't mind. Great, thank you. Now, could you tell me, how would you rate this man's looks, on a scale of one to ten? Five? Ooh, that's a bit harsh, isn't it? (Laughs, winks into the camera.) Okay, well this might be a moot point now, but would you date him?'

A five was probably about right, Graham guessed. How could he know? The face he saw staring back at him in the mirror was perfectly agreeable, even at the ripe old age of thirty-six and three-quarters, but really, how could he possibly have a clue as to how to go about rating how attractive it was to others?

He had been told that he was good-looking, in his younger days, and it had greatly amused Angie to make him blush by bestowing praise on him, particularly when they were amongst company, back in the good old days. He was her 'beautiful man', she would tell him, ruffling his hair to make it look 'sexy'.

When he was inclined to be fair on himself, he concluded that he hadn't changed dramatically since his twenties. Aside from the random grey flecks that clung to the edges of his hair and the first signs of a slight paunch that he had made a silent commitment to getting rid of, thirty-six-year-old Graham Pike bore a striking, undeniable resemblance to twenty-five-year-old Graham Pike. But maybe that wasn't saying much, he told himself, when the doubts chorused in his mind.

What did he really have to offer a woman like Ellen? She was successful, miles ahead of him in terms of professional achievements. She was focused, and driven, and lived for her work. Graham lived for the hours away from work, when he could switch his brain off from the dull, repetitive tasks that by now he could do with his eyes closed, having done the same job for more years than he wished to concede. It didn't cause him any grief and was reasonably well-paid, but he hadn't exactly set the professional world alight during his career.

Ellen was well-travelled, knowledgeable about other countries, other cultures. She went in search of new horizons. She spoke French and Spanish, and a little Italian.

Graham had been to the Costa Brava several times on holiday with Angie; he had lain on a sun lounger and read a novel until it was time to eat, drink, and enjoy the entertainment on offer. His only other venture outside the UK had been a trip to Tallinn once, on a stag weekend. He struggled to do so much as order food in any other language.

As he tallied up Ellen's obvious qualities versus his own perceived deficiencies, his fears only gripped him even tighter, and the added complication of Angie, hovering constantly on the periphery like a demented wasp, could only degrade his worth even further. And it hadn't taken long for his fears to be confirmed.

'It just isn't working, Graham,' Ellen had told him remorsefully.

Raking over that moment again made his stomach muscles contract until he began to feel strangled, and a sickening murmur of regret would appear, rising up through his body until it left a sour taste in his mouth. When the bile appeared, his mind was hard-wired to go to Angie, and the regret would turn to anger, lighting a fire inside his chest that burned like persistent indigestion.

'Jesus Christ, we've lost him,' he heard Irish Eoin say, and realised he had zoned out for a few moments, walking without paying attention to where he was going, on auto-pilot as he wove his way through the streets, not hearing a word of what his friends were saying.

'Hey, Earth to Pikey!' Owen yelled, curling his hands around his mouth to amplify the sound.

'Yeah, okay, I'm here,' Graham laughed. 'What is it? What do you want?'

Colin put a hand on his shoulder. 'We're trying to decide where to go, you muppet,' he joked. 'Blackfriars or Maggie May's?'

Graham shrugged, assessing his desire to stay out much later. He debated the pros and cons in his head for a second, and decided that in a contest between sinking a few pints with his mates and sitting at home, sulking and feeling sorry for himself, pints and pals won hands down.

'Blackfriars every time, for me, mate,' he answered decisively. 'Your average punter in Maggie May's is about twenty-five, if you're lucky.'

'Exactly!' Irish Eoin cried, far more animated than the two pints he had drunk in the cinema bar accounted for. 'That's why we should go there!'

Owen shrugged indifferently, leaving Colin with the deciding vote. He took a moment to mull over the appeal of each venue, and then pointed to his left, towards Blackfriars.

'You can go on the pull some other night, mate' he told Eoin, whose disappointment was instantly plastered across his boyish features. 'Preferably when we're not around to watch you crash and burn.'

The other men laughed, on the move again towards the homelier of the two pubs.

'Hey, I'll have you know, the younger girls can't get enough of me,' Eoin protested, sounding genuinely aggrieved at the slight.

'What happened to Whatsherface?' Owen asked. 'I thought you were loved up.'

'Oh yeah,' Colin concurred, as the men reached the door of the pub. 'Iona, wasn't it?' He turned to whisper to Graham as he opened the door and let the others go before him. 'I remember because I thought it was fucking hilarious,' he told Graham. 'Eoin and Iona. You couldn't make it up!'

Graham laughed along, struck by the ease and the detachedness with which Eoin went on to explain to them how he had, for a very brief period, been under the impression that he had found his soulmate in the lovely Iona. A dark-haired, pale-skinned and naturally beautiful (Eoin's unusually detailed description) yoga teacher from Aberdeen, she had caught his attention on one of his rugby nights out, and for three whole weeks they had embarked on a whirlwind romance, only for Eoin to realise (for approximately the thirtieth time in his adult life, by Graham's calculations), that he wasn't looking for a relationship, and call it off.

A part of Graham wished he could be more like his friend. The difference was – and it was quite a stark difference – that he really, truly, did want to be in a relationship. A successful one. But if he couldn't make that work, he sure as hell would have loved to have the ability that Eoin had to bounce back from a failed romance as though it had caused him no more inconvenience than ripping one of his rugby shirts. In fact, Graham suspected that finding a tear in his kit would probably wound Eoin far deeper than any woman ever had.

'Pints all round?' Graham asked, knowing that there was as much chance of his friends switching from their usual tipples – Carling or Kronenbourg, depending on the pub – as there was of Ellen bursting through the door of Blackfriars, shuffling through the throng of bodies and throwing her arms around his neck, whispering in his ear that she loved him and wanted to give it another go.

He allowed himself a little ironic chuckle at the notion, and even though it still hurt, he was heartened to realise that the dull ache he had been feeling since they'd broken up had dissipated ever so slightly. At least he was able to think of her and force out a laugh, albeit a weak, mirthless laugh.

The feeling of disgust that appeared when he thought of Angie wasn't so easily set aside. He brought his phone out of his pocket to check for missed calls or messages, his actions driven by habit, muscle memory. There was no way that Angie could make contact with him now, since the wrecking of his old SIM card (an act which had caused him significantly more inconvenience than he had anticipated, and had left him mobile phone-less for five days while his provider used snail-mail to furnish him with a replacement), but even looking at the phone itself invoked a reflex that set his teeth on edge. Maybe it would be best if he got a new one of those, too.

He put the phone away, scolding himself for failing to rewire his brain sufficiently to keep Angie out of it. He had resisted it before, for reasons he now felt at a loss to explain, and his refusal to kick her to the kerb had cost him more than he should have been willing to pay. But there had been a shift in his perspective, he knew. He no longer wondered about her, or worried that she might be in dire straits, in need of his help. He had turned a corner in his life. The well of his kindness had run dry, as far as Angie was concerned. There was nothing but resentment rushing around his veins when he pictured her face.

Chapter Fourteen

Angie
Then

'Well, if it isn't my boy,' Iain Pike announced, his smile illuminating his whole face. At fifty-seven years old, he was still in possession of a stunningly well taken care of set of teeth, a full head of luxurious brown hair, and as much charm as anyone could ask for. 'And you, my love,' he said, landing a fond peck on Angie's cheek, 'look exquisite.'

Angie smiled warmly, and patted her father-in-law's arm. 'Thank you,' she answered. 'You scrub up quite well yourself!'

'It's great to see you, Dad,' Graham beamed, drawing his father in for a firm hug. 'Angie's right. You're quite the dapper-looking gent tonight.'

Iain laughed, and a rich, warm sound echoed around the large room. 'Your mother thinks I overdid it a bit,' he told them, lowering his voice conspiratorially, 'but wait until you see her outfit. The words "pot" and "kettle" came to mind.' He chuckled again, and Angie felt herself begin to relax.

What had she got herself into such a tizzy about, anyway? She adored Iain and Pam. Most likely, their friends and neighbours, or whoever else they had invited along to their anniversary shindig would prove to be equally adorable; little carbon copies of two of her favourite people in the world. And yet she couldn't shake the apprehension that she felt about coming here tonight. A niggling feeling of impending doom that had shaken her awake that morning like a bucket of cold water being tossed over her.

Her stomach hurt all the way up to the top of her ribcage, as though a balloon filled with trepidation had been inflated in there, and was applying pressure to every organ that surrounded it.

She hadn't dared let on to Graham how she was feeling. What would she say, anyway? 'I can't shake the feeling that something bad is going to happen tonight.' She couldn't tell him that. He was almost as excitable as Iain clearly was, and had been all day long. And in spite of her anxiousness, she loved him for his unwavering enthusiasm, for that trait that he had inherited from his father, to always focus on the sunny side of life. His positivity radiated from him like rays from the sun itself, and she forced herself to soak it up like he was her vital source of vitamin D. If anyone could brighten the eternal darkness that festered inside her, it was Graham. And there was no way that she was going to let her fears take over and spill out, spoiling his evening. Everyone's evening.

She gave Graham's arm a little squeeze, taking reassurance from the firmness of the muscle she could feel through his shirt. He was her rock. Even if she couldn't always be strong (and lately it felt like the strength she had worked so hard to build was starting to erode at an alarming rate), Graham could. He would.

But she didn't need him to prop her up tonight, she told herself. The nerves she had experienced earlier had been nothing more than a brief wobble. It happened, now and again. But she was fine now, amongst people who loved her. There was no need for her to give in to the anxiety that was brewing up in her mind, clouding her perception.

'Pam!' she gushed earnestly, as her mother-in-law appeared at her husband's side, dressed in her best and looking effortlessly glamorous as always. 'You're beautiful,' Angie told her, choking back a sob that came out of nowhere.

The occasion was getting to her, she could feel it. The Pikes were celebrating their thirty-fifth wedding anniversary. Thirty-five years of love, devotion, and, as Graham had occasionally opened up to her, periods of difficulty, both financially and in terms of Pam's health. And here they were, the two of them, dressed up to the nines and surrounded by their nearest and dearest, proving to the world that they were an unbreakable unit, an indestructible couple. Jealousy and sadness surged through Angie's body in equal measure as she mentally fast-forwarded thirty or so years in her own life and saw a scene far, far removed from the one in front of her.

'Oh, so do you, my darling,' Pam returned, sweeping Angie into a tight hug. A hug that Angie was loath to check out of.

'Mum, you're stunning,' Graham announced, and stooped to kiss Pamela on the cheek.

'Oh, you're kind, the two of you,' Pam said, waving away the compliment with her hand. 'I'm just glad you could be here. I know it's not exactly the kind of do you young things would choose to go to on a Saturday night, but—'

'Oi, less of that,' Iain joked, draping his arm over his wife's shoulder. 'It's going to be a hell of a night,' he promised. Angie reflexively winced at his use of the word 'hell' and hoped no one had noticed. 'We've hired a proper disc jockey and everything,' Iain carried on, pointing to the far side of the room where a man dressed in jeans and a Rolling Stones t-shirt was grappling around with his array of audio equipment. 'And there are a fair few dancers in here, I'll tell you,' he chuckled. 'You'll be amazed when you see little Alfie Bedford start cutting a rug. Little bald fella, wouldn't say boo to a goose, you can barely hear him when he speaks. But when he gets on the dance floor... Well, you'll see.'

Pam nodded her confirmation of her husband's assertion

and the pair exchanged affectionate gazes, their obvious adoration for each other so cute that it was almost too much for Angie to bear.

'I'm sure it'll be a great night,' Graham concurred, laughing along. 'We're happy to be here, aren't we, Ange?'

'Of course,' Angie replied, hoping to convince the others, if not herself. But her voice was strained. 'Drinks, dancing, the happy couple looking a million dollars, what more could we ask for?'

'Bloody right!' Iain agreed emphatically. 'Now listen, we're duty bound to go and do some mingling, so you two grab a drink, and enjoy yourselves. Oh, and Ange, save me a dance for later.' He winked and the pair headed off into the crowd, hand in hand, like teenagers.

'Will do,' she answered belatedly, a sinking feeling befalling her as she realised that leaving early in the proceedings wasn't looking like it would be a possibility. She hadn't planned to suggest too early an exit, but she had hoped that braving the three-course meal and perhaps an hour or so afterwards might suffice. She wasn't sure she had it in her to stick around for the dancing, that would no doubt carry on into the small hours of the morning. She couldn't pinpoint exactly what it was that was lodged in her tummy, sending ripples of discomfort all over her body, but she had no trouble deciphering the message it was trying to send: You shouldn't be here. Get out of here, fast, before it goes awry.

Before what goes awry? she felt like asking out loud, as though her own intuition might suddenly develop a speaking voice and explain to her the reasons why she had a horrible feeling that the evening was cursed, destined to take a turn for the worse. It didn't, and in the absence of any sound advice to the contrary, she allowed herself to be led across the room by Graham, as he spotted a family friend that he wanted her to meet. She clung to him for dear life, repeating in her head the mantra that she had invented out of necessity when her life had been thrown into disarray as a youngster: Just get through this. You can do it.

Chapter Fifteen

Angie
Now

She hadn't wanted to believe it. Even though she had seen it with her own eyes, witnessed the unadulterated hatred that flared in him and seeped from every pore, she hadn't wanted to concede that he would stick to what he had said that night. Evan after all the times she had hurt him – really hurt him – in the past, he had never come so close to lashing out at her as he had that night.

She still couldn't begin to consider that it might be true. That he was gone from her life now, and he was never coming back.

He had terrified her with his behaviour, but the danger of physical violence wasn't what struck fear into her heart. For all his ire, the notion that he might finally snap and swing for her had buzzed in and out of her mind in a fraction of a second, and her flinch had been unfounded. No, what scared her were the words that had come flooding from his mouth. Words that she had been waiting for, expecting to hear for years, if she was honest with herself. But as the years had passed and she had tested him beyond the tolerance of a lesser man, and those words had remained locked away, shoved down deep inside of him in a place that she knew he fought so hard not to go, she had lulled herself into a false sense of security.

He hadn't cracked yet, in all this time, in spite of all

the harm she had inflicted on him. Did that mean that he never would? Did that mean there was no limit to the man's understanding, to his kindness, to his faithfulness? She had come to comfort herself that that was exactly what it meant. And her regular pushing of his buttons had become a twisted game, a challenge.

Until that night.

What was left for her now? Nothing, was the undeniable answer to that question. There was no place for her in the world. There never had been, at least not as an adult. Even though she had managed to find Graham, and to feel those stirrings of something akin to happiness, looking back now she could see, it had been clear that she was living on borrowed time.

Playing the role of settled, happy, 'normal' Angie for so long had been nothing short of exhausting. Applying that intricate mask each day and taking the utmost care not to ever let it slip, had only condemned her to be a prisoner to her past. Hardest to bear of all though was the fact that, in Graham, she had found someone who was truly everything she could ever want. The devastating irony was that if there was one person that she could have considered opening up to, laying herself and her demons bare, it was Graham. But she had known from day one that he could never be that person.

With him, she had developed a persona that she could use to truly disguise herself.

She was transformed; she was the woman she had always wanted to be, and the woman that Graham had apparently been looking for. Confident, affectionate, laid back. Someone who trusted her man to the moon and back, who cherished their time spent together and loved him unconditionally.

Someone who waded easily through life, who unfailingly lent the voice of reason whilst others around her were losing their heads over minutiae that meant nothing in the grand scheme of things.

Graham could never know that the woman he slept beside each night, and kissed awake each morning, was a fraud. Nothing more than a skilful actress.

During the seven years when the world had been rosy, when the artificial bliss she had created for herself had played cruel tricks on her mind, let her wonder whether perhaps the real thing could one day be within reach, she had managed to maintain the pretence. She had faltered a couple of times, made silly slip-ups, but they were rare. None of her moments of weakness had laid bare anything so significant that they had achieved any lasting harm. Out of context, without the spark to ignite the curiosity to scratch below the surface, there was nothing particularly concerning about her reluctance to go back to her home town, or to speak of her family, or her early years. She had won the lottery and her prize was a man she steadfastly adored, but underneath the outward elation breathed a fear, a certainty, that her house of cards was destined to fall down around her ears, and she was just waiting for the gust of wind to come along which would topple it over.

For seven years, she had managed to conceal the truth from Graham, and in a certain way, from herself. As surely as her happiness had continued to grow with each victory, each day undiscovered, dread would build up at twice the pace, each day adding another pebble of anticipation to the pile, until the pile eventually grew too high to be contained any longer.

When it finally came, her unmasking had been more devastating than she could have imagined. Well now, the curtain had fallen on the Graham and Angie Show. There would be no more happy times to come. There would be no more kind words, no more smiles that did something to her deep inside, no more shared celebrations. They certainly wouldn't be taking the trip of her dreams on their tenth wedding anniversary.

Now with the recollection of Graham's violent annihilation of his SIM card playing in front of her eyes like a movie clip stuck on repeat, there was barely any room left over for storing memories of the past, the embers of those seven good years.

Chapter Sixteen

Graham
Now

'So, can we assume that tonight spells the end of the *Pikey's nothing but a miserable bastard* era?' Colin asked, now that Eoin and Owen had disappeared on a mission to track down some darts from somewhere, a mission they had not anticipated would be necessary given the presence of the dart board in the pub.

Graham gave a rueful smile. 'Vital signs are good,' he replied, feeling slightly better about the state of his world as his fourth drink of the night entered his bloodstream.

'That's what I like to hear,' Colin answered, although his smile was tight. There was an elephant in the room, that neither man was in a hurry to acknowledge.

On some level, Graham wondered whether it might be a good thing, if Colin were to start firing questions at him, giving him license to pour his heart out about everything that had gone on in the past few weeks. Ellen. Angie. The ends of two very different but equally upsetting eras. He knew that Colin would be armed and poised to aim a few home truths at him, and Graham would be ready and willing to hear them. Maybe what he was looking for was closure. And maybe he would get that if he talked everything over with Colin, bared his soul.

But on the other hand, a voice inside his head was begging him never to lend a thought to either of the women, ever again. It spelled out the benefits of enjoying a carefree night in the pub with his friends, chatting about inane, unimportant things, like who might emerge victorious from the board when (or if) Eoin and Owen returned and challenged them to a darts doubles match. He was relieved to have Colin take the decision out of his hands.

'So, listen,' Colin began, 'it's Jenna's birthday next week, and she and Liz have got it into their heads that you'll want to come to the party – you being her godfather and all.' He rolled his eyes as though he was appalled by the idea. 'Now, of course, you don't have to come – believe me, if I could get out of it, I would – but I promised I'd ask. And not to lay the guilt trip on you, or anything, but Jenna actually really wants you to be there.'

'Really?' Graham asked, surprised but heartened by the revelation that Colin's eldest daughter apparently held him in such high esteem as to warrant an invite. 'She said that?'

'Hm-hm,' Colin replied. 'Miserable bastard era aside, you've always impressed with the gifts, apparently. What can I say?' he shrugged. 'She's ten. She's shallow.'

Graham smiled, revelling in the sensation of being appreciated. Even if it was just for his seemingly-impressive present-buying skills. For the longest time, he had banned himself from acknowledging how much he had lamented not becoming a father. Like so many other emotions he'd been lugging around with him, the disappointment had lain dormant in the pit of his stomach, inactive but not gone, like a benign tumour biding its time before ultimately transforming into something sinister. Being asked to be Jenna's godfather had been the highlight of a very devastating decade, and as he had held her at the altar, promising to take care of her should anything befall her parents, that little kernel of regret had swollen up and burst open, taking his breath away just as he was about to make an undying promise to always be there for her.

He could have argued harder, pled his case when Angie had made hers seem like the only voice that mattered in the decision-making process. The end result, he knew, was destined to be disaster. On a larger scale than the devastation that had already clouded their lives. What hope would a child of theirs have had? Damned from the beginning, born to a broken mother, a shattered family. The poor kid would have known more heartache than it could ever have deserved. As much as it pained Graham to admit it, abstaining had been the right thing to do. But that didn't mean it didn't hurt like hell, to cradle Colin's child in his arms and know that he would never know the joy of holding his own.

'Of course, I'll be there, mate,' he declared confidently, accepting Colin's invitation. 'Wouldn't miss it for the world.'

Chapter Seventeen

Angie
Then

It was his voice that she recognised. She would know it anywhere – it was the voice of her nightmares.

'No,' she whispered, blaming the two glasses of champagne she had drunk far too quickly for making her imagine things. She had hoped that the fizz might have been a boon to help steady her nerves, but the bubbles had gone straight to her head, clearly. She was hearing things, hallucinating even. Think of your worst fear often enough and it's bound to come true. Her nerves were getting the better of her even more so now that she was giddy from the alcohol, making her heart beat faster, making her invent things that weren't really there.

But then she heard it again. Closer this time. Chillingly close.

It was him. Unmistakably. She didn't have to turn around to see, to verify. She couldn't, even if she wanted to.

He laughed, and the sound transported her back in time, to a place she would have given all that she owned to have erased from her memory, if such a procedure existed. She froze on the spot, feeling as though her blood had begun to run cold in her veins. Her mind was screaming at her to move, fast, anywhere, but her legs refused to play the game. And then another laugh, familiar too, shook her alive. Graham. Talking to him. Laughing with him. Behind her.

Close. Almost upon her. Calling her name.

She forced her legs to move, desperate to break into a sprint but only managing a laboured, breathless walk, struggling through a throng of smiling, partying people, who seemed to be clubbing together to block her at every turn.

'Ange,' she heard from behind her. 'Ange, come back, there's someone I want you to meet.' Why did Graham's voice sound different? It was the words he was saying, the gravity of their meaning. Like he was issuing a threat.

Dark thoughts flooded her brain, her skin glossy with the sweat of fear and paranoia. Did Gray know? Had he brought her here tonight, knowing that he would be there? Had her husband, the only man she had ever felt safe with, been stringing her along all this time, patiently waiting for the right moment to enact a big, public reveal?

Please god, no.

She shook her head, refusing to entertain the thought. It was coincidence, that was all. It had to be. A fucking horrible, devastating, heart-breaking coincidence.

'Hun, where are you going?' Gray called after her worriedly, catching up with her and grabbing hold of her elbow.

'Don't!' she yelled through gritted teeth, swatting him away. He looked stunned, as did the older man whose back she had inadvertently slapped with her wayward hand. 'Sorry,' she whispered to the stranger, turning away from Graham and resuming her quest to make it to the exit. She had to be outside, in the fresh air. If she had to breathe one more lungful of the toxic atmosphere that the man's sheer presence had invited into the room, she felt like she might die.

'Ange, what the hell?' Graham asked, perplexed.

She reached the door and threw it open, gasping for breath as she stepped into the night.

'Hun, look at me,' Graham pleaded, his voice loaded with concern. He laid his hands on her shoulders. 'What's going on? Are you alright?'

She tried to regulate her breathing, recognising that she was on the verge of hyperventilating if she didn't manage to calm herself down soon.

'Gray,' she whispered, her eyes filling with tears, her hands reaching out to him like a child clutching their security blanket.

'Shh, shh,' he soothed, drawing her in close to his chest. 'Just take deep breaths,' he told her, willing her to calm down. 'It's alright,' he assured her, gripping her tightly. 'You're alright. Just breathe, okay?'

She nodded, her tears now accompanied by loud, hacking sobs, her shoulders jerking up and down as they came in waves. Over a decade of repressed emotion was suddenly flowing out of her as though a tap had been turned on, and the torrent was so powerful that it left her unable to speak.

Several minutes passed before she felt able to communicate again, exhausted from the outpouring of sadness that several of the nicotine-loving partygoers had nosily witnessed while they loitered outside, sucking hungrily on cigarettes.

Graham sensed her reclaimed composure and leaned back, studying her face for answers. 'Better now?' he asked, his brow furrowed in concern.

Angie nodded, wiping away the worst of her tears from her face with her hand.

'Here,' Graham said, unfolding his pocket handkerchief and helping to clear away remnants of the foundation and mascara that had mixed with her tears to create unsightly streaks. He let her be for a moment, bursting to know what had caused her dramatic exit but careful not to push her too soon. She had the look of a frightened animal about her, as though she had found temporary shelter but still feared for her life.

'Ange—'

'Just hold me, Gray,' she pleaded. 'Just for a minute. I can't go back in there right now.'

He was about to protest, confused and curious, but his features creased and he swallowed his questions, pulling her close again.

Her eyes were open this time, and without intending it her gaze connected with a figure dead ahead, who was staring straight at her. She gasped, but didn't look away. She clasped her hands tighter around Graham as the figure emerged from the shadows, wearing a sickeningly familiar, warped smile on his face.

Chapter Eighteen

Angie
Now

How could it be that she had never thought of doing this before? She had to have done, surely.

She wracked her brains, impeded by the cocktail of drink and drugs that was working on her, aiming to send her high as a kite but also conspiring to hurtle her towards rock bottom at the same time.

Had there really never been a single time when she had considered it? That much was hard to believe. So hard that she suddenly felt compelled to garner evidence to the contrary.

'Pen, pen,' she muttered, committed now to performing an in-depth analysis to support her theory.

'Pen, for fuck's sake!' she yelled angrily, as though she were barking orders at an incompetent lackey. But there was no one else around. She was alone, in her sitting room, listening to Adele's *21* album at a volume that her neighbours were unlikely to endure for much longer without complaining. The inevitable ire of Mr and Mrs Colson, the sweet but occasionally intolerant couple from upstairs, was of no consequence to her. She had more important things to think about than neighbours reaching the end of their tether with her. Like proving herself wrong. Or right. She wasn't quite sure which she was trying to achieve. Or whether it mattered. The drugs were really starting to take hold of her now.

'Aha!' she exclaimed, holding up a blue biro whose cap was missing, as though it was the most significant discovery of the twenty-first century. 'Now paper,' she added, grabbing one of the unpaid bills that had been stacking up on her kitchen counter to use as writing material.

She felt a jolt of twisted excitement about what she was about to do. Not just about the analysis that she was armed and ready to attempt now that she had acquired the appropriate materials, but more so about what was going to come after. The main event, as it were.

Her heart made a sprint, and reflexively she cried out, 'No!', praying for it not to end this way. She hadn't done all she needed to do yet. She needed more time. Not a lot more – her task would be done by sunrise – but just enough to put some things in order. It wouldn't be fair to take her before she was ready to be taken.

She rode out the worst of the palpitations, taking deep breaths and sitting at ease while she waited for them to pass. The sensation wasn't new – she had felt like her heart might break free from her chest many times before, worse – but it had never scared her before. This time, it scared her for the most perverse of reasons: on the night that she was preparing to die, she didn't want to die too soon.

She took a gulp of water and settled herself on the floor, kneeling and resting her elbows on the coffee table. It was an uncomfortable position, but aches and pains would cease to be an issue soon enough.

That time, she wrote, in shaky handwriting. That life-changing, soul-destroying period of her young life that had broken her beyond repair. She forced herself to go back there, safe in the knowledge that her nightmares would be redundant in a matter of hours. Had she really made it through seven whole years of his vile, evil abuse without once wondering whether she had the courage to end it all? She must have done, she conceded, tearing up at the revelation. She had possessed an inner strength back then that she couldn't recognise, and certainly could not summon now. In the depths of her despair, she had once seen a flicker of hope, and she had clung onto it as though it was a part of her that was surgically attached. No one could take that hope from her, back then, and it had got her through the worst of times. Killing herself had not so much as entered her head.

But if not then, surely there had been opportunities for the seed to be watered during the following years.

Immediately after Graham found out, for example.

The first time she saw the heartbreak on his face.

The first time he walked in on her fucking another man in their home (not the first time she had done it, but the first time he had caught her red-handed, as it were).

When he had left her the first time.

When he had divorced her.

When he walked away without looking back, each and every time thereafter.

No? The booze and the drugs were conspiring to mess with her mind. She was so certain that the life she had lived couldn't possibly have lasted thirty-six years without her making at least one attempt to put herself out of her misery.

She stared at what she'd written, struggling to focus, unable to decipher her own illegible scrawl.

'Bullshit!' she screamed, hurling the pen and paper at the wall, disappointed at the futility of the action as they fluttered pathetically to the ground, the sound of the collision of the plastic and plaster drowned out by Adele's powerful, mournful voice as she belted out *Set Fire to the Rain*.

Angie hummed along, joining in with the lines which resonated deep inside, forcing tears to the edges of her eyelids.

... And I threw us into the flames.

When it fell, something died, 'cos I knew that that was the last time.

She slumped onto the sofa, grabbing handfuls of her hair and covering her face with it. Annoyingly, she began to question whether she had made the right decision. Only a few minutes ago, it seemed, her mind had been made up. She had banished all the doubts that had surfaced at the inception of the idea, locked them away in the back of her mind and thrown away the key. But now they were trying their damnedest to escape; creating an ungodly din inside her head, as though they were pounding on the walls of her brain, demanding to be set free.

'It has to be now,' she told herself out loud. There was no time left for trawling through her thoughts, scrambling for justification for what she was about to do, searching for answers as to why this time, of all times, was the deal-breaker. Why, after all that she had managed to survive in the past, this was the point in her life where she had reached the point of no return. It just was. She had simply had enough. She could not go on.

She tried to recall what the other things were that she had wanted to do, her final acts, but she couldn't think straight for the incessant banging that continued inside her head.

It took her a few seconds to realise that the noise didn't just exist inside her skull. It was the sound of someone knocking heavily on her door.

'Oh, fuck off,' she spat, her voice lost in the cacophony of sounds that filled the room. There was no more time to waste. She couldn't handle the noise any longer. She reached for the first bottle, and twisted off the cap.

Chapter Nineteen

Graham
Then

He drove with the window down, thankful for the cool breeze that cut through the humidity of the night. Thankful also for the fact that he had been so occupied with chatting and catching up with his parents' friends, colleagues and the many neighbours that they had garnered over the years, that he had barely had the chance to take two sips from the glass of champagne he had been carrying around with him since shortly after they had arrived, and was still in a fit state to drive. Legally he was, at least. Whether his state of mind was conducive to a safe journey home, was up for debate.

He was glad of the breeze because it helped to keep his temper under control, wafting in and dropping his temperature in those moments when it would threaten to rise up and fill his cheeks with the blush of anger. Anger that he fought hard not to give in to, but that he was finding it increasingly hard to suppress. Especially now that Angie appeared to have recovered from her 'trauma', and had dozed off in the passenger seat, seemingly at peace.

'You what, love?' He winced as he thought back to the look on his mum's face as she checked what she had heard: that they were leaving. 'Oh.' Her disappointment was evident, but she wouldn't make a big deal out of it. It wasn't her way. Her way was to be concerned.

'She is alright, though, isn't she? Poor love. Are you just going to take her home then?'

'Yes, I think it's for the best,' he had grudgingly admitted. 'I'm so sorry, Mum.' He had hugged her for a good long moment, gutted at being forced to run out on an event that had meant so much to them. All of them. He wanted to assure his mother that he would take Angie home, see her tucked up in bed, recovering from whatever it was that had spooked her, and rush right back to the party. But he had the good sense to make no such promises.

'Oh, now, don't you worry about it,' Pam had answered, wholly genuinely. 'You just tell her we're thinking about her, alright? Tell her we hope she feels better soon. And remember, if there's anything you need.'

'I know, Mum,' he'd told her, feeling horribly guilty on Angie's behalf. 'You're the best. Tell Dad I'm sorry I didn't get the chance to say goodbye, will you? I can't see him anywhere.'

'I will,' Pam had replied. 'I'm pretty sure he's sneaked off for a cigar with that Charlie Portman. You know, the fella you were talking to a little while ago.'

'The guy from the golf club?' he'd asked, remembering that he had been about to introduce Charlie to Angie when she had run off so unceremoniously.

Even when he had returned to the car, finding her locked in from the inside and shaking like a leaf, she had refused to tell him what was wrong. She had apologised profusely for being the reason they were leaving, less than an hour after arriving, but there was nothing he could say to convince her to spill the beans.

And as always, he had gone along with what she had asked.

'Just take me home, please, Gray,' she had urged him, and like a mug he had agreed. And now she was asleep. And he was pissed off.

'We're home,' he announced loudly, turning off the engine and removing his seatbelt. There was no sympathy in his voice. For the moment, he felt as though he had run clear out.

Angie stirred, opening her eyes wide and staring at him uncertainly for a moment, before realising where she was. 'Oh, thank God,' she answered, undoing her own seatbelt and opening the door.

Graham stayed put for a moment, watching her as she hurried towards the front door of the house, rifling through her handbag for her key. 'What the hell's gotten into you?' he asked, but she was already out of earshot, the car door slammed shut with a heavy thud behind her.

After a few seconds, she realised he wasn't behind her, and turned to see what was holding him back.

'Gray, what are you doing?' she asked him, her voice panicked again, like it had been in the car park. He reluctantly got out of the car, his eagerness to know what was causing her to behave this way waning, slipping away. He didn't want to be here, at home, dealing with God knows what kind of dramatic episode that his wife was determined to embroil him in. He wanted to be back at the party, with his family, having a good time and celebrating what his parents had achieved. He longed for the simplicity of the things he was missing out on: food, drink, conversation, fun. Why was he here, at nine o'clock at night, about to embark on a probably futile attempt to break through his hysterical wife's maddening wall of secrecy?

He rubbed his temples, feeling weary at the thought of what he was walking into.

She could be odd sometimes, could Angie. He had only recently started to really let it in, and for the most part had managed to retire it to the back of his mind, but in light of tonight's showing there was no denying it. It was like a placard suddenly being waved in his face, that said: 'Something is not right here! And you're a prize idiot for not realising it sooner!'

Now that there was the possibility that he might find out just what that something was, he wasn't sure that he wanted to know. Part of him wanted to go in there and shake her until everything that was a mystery about her came pouring out, like confetti spilling to the floor, but at the same time there was an opposing force at work, telling him that knowing everything might not be a good idea.

He gingerly entered the living room, finding her pacing, and crying.

'I think you should sit down, Gray,' she stated, keeping her eyes away from him.

Graham sighed, his heart suddenly several pounds heavier, as though it had been filled with concrete. 'Okay,' he said, taking a seat on the couch.

Chapter Twenty

Graham
Now

What a difference a day could make. A few hours, even.

There wasn't an anti-depressant in the world, Graham would have asserted in that moment, that could work more effectively than the playful, at times downright immature, antics of his pals, when it came to making his heart feel lighter.

Darts had been sequestered by Irish Eoin, who through a happy coincidence had remembered that one of his rugby pals lived three blocks away from the pub, and was bound to have the necessary equipment they were searching for. An owner of some adequate darts, Darren in fact was. Happy to see two leery, loud impostors appear at his door demanding to borrow said darts when his kids were trying to sleep, he had not been, reportedly.

Nonetheless, the darts had been handed over, and the leery, loud men had returned to the pub like victors, over-excited at the spoils in their hands and the thought of kicking off a tournament.

'No pressure, mate,' Owen teased, as Graham assumed his place at the ochey, aiming for double-top to claim victory in the final game of the night. Most of the other pub-goers had already cleared out, and the bell had rung for last orders ten minutes earlier. Graham deliberately took his time, rhythmically swinging his arm in a practice movement, inviting groans of derision from the others.

'Get the bloody hell on with it!' Irish Eoin yelled, his words slurring together. His rugby-honed build afforded him a slightly higher tolerance level for alcohol than the others, but tonight he had pushed his limits, and was beginning to sway as he sat perched on a bar stool that barely looked sturdy enough to hold his considerable weight.

'Don't rush me!' Graham volleyed back, wholeheartedly hoping that his shot hit the right spot. Winning this game was the sole focus of his life for the next few seconds. He came close to letting go of the dart several times, pulling out of the shot when he realised that playing it would signal the end of the game, and the end of the night. The pub was about to close, and he and his friends were about to be turfed out, to make their way back to their homes, separately. And he didn't want that to happen. He didn't want this night to end.

'Yes!' he yelled loudly, clenching his fists in a victorious gesture as his dart hit the intended spot, while the other three voiced their unhappiness, and reached for their jackets.

'Yeah, yeah, well done,' Owen congratulated him sarcastically, evidently not far behind Irish Eoin in the inebriated stakes.

'Time for a taxi,' Colin announced, slapping Graham on the back.

The streets were busy and the queue for the taxi rank enormous, as was normal on a Friday night in the centre of town.

'Fuck this,' Owen grumbled, stuffing his hands into his pockets.

'Could be a while,' Colin said, stating the obvious, but none of them had much choice but to endure the wait. Each of them lived a few miles away, and with ten or so pints in their system and a diminished sense of direction and safety, walking could not be considered a realistic option. Colin and Graham would share a cab, given that they lived the shortest distance from each other, and at a push Irish Eoin and Owen could do the same, but at the very least the men were in need of two cabs, in a queue that contained probably eighty people. 'To phone, or not to phone, that is the question,' Colin muttered.

Graham checked his watch, which told him that the time was nearing one o'clock in the morning.

'Hmm, tricky one, mate,' he answered. 'Liz isn't the wait-behind-the-door-with-a-rolling-pin kind of woman, is she? On the other hand, she might have your bollocks for earrings if you roll in at two without so much as a text message.'

Colin tapped a finger to his temple as if to acknowledge Graham's sageness, and pulled out his phone to send a grovelling text.

Graham looked around at the other people in the queue, a mixture of young couples, groups of friends, and older, most likely married pairs, who brought to mind his mother and father, and the impressive social life they had continued to pursue well into their early sixties. For a second he remembered that he had aspired to exactly that with Angie: to grow old together; to enjoy their retired years by living life to the full, doing the things they had always done and always wanted to do.

A sharp pain cut through the force field and the mellow mood that the alcohol had created and he felt a lump in his throat, and a brief second of regret.

'Pity,' he whispered, quietly enough that no one round about him could hear.

Chapter Twenty-One

Angie
Then

Why did he look so mad? His face hadn't looked like that earlier, when he had consoled her, soothed her fears in the way that he had always been so accomplished at. He had been her rock, just like always, scooping her into his arms and whispering assurances to her that everything was going to be alright. He had made her believe it; he was so damned convincing. For a short, sweet time, she had dared to believe that everything really was going to be fine. But why had such a change come over him since then? Why, now, did he have a face like thunder?

Not right now, she pleaded silently. Not in the very moment when she was poised to unveil the truth that she had guarded with the ferociousness of a lioness protecting her cub, from the moment they had set eyes on each other. To conjure the strength to do what she was about to do, she needed Graham. The real Graham. Her Graham, ready and willing to prop her up, to hold her hand. How could she go through with one of the hardest moments of her sorry life and spill out her secret to this angry, hard-faced man that sat in front of her, wearing a look that said he would rather be anywhere else?

Chapter Twenty-Two

Graham
Now

'Shhh!' Graham hissed at the kettle, as its whistle echoed loudly around the kitchen. He crumpled with childish laughter at his own silly gesture, revelling in being so delightfully drunk that he found it hysterically funny to yell instructions at an electrical appliance, and even funnier that it appeared to comply.

He made himself a cup of instant coffee, adding three sugars as though he were on a mission to make absolutely certain that sleep would not feature in the next few hours of his life. Imminent sleep was not a concern, anyway. He had arrived home with a lightness of heart that he had not experienced for a long time, his sides aching from having laughed so much at the antics of his daft, wonderful friends. Having to wait an hour and a half for a taxi and finding his wallet considerably lighter than it had been when he had left the house earlier hadn't so much as made a dent in his happiness.

On account of his newfound high spirits, he had also developed a sudden, urgent need to finally get around to watching the last few episodes of *Sons of Anarchy* on Netflix, so that he could enter into discussions about the finale that the rest of the boys had already watched, and had been unable to mull over freely in Graham's company so as not to lay down any unwanted spoilers.

In his inebriated state, he took longer than usual to ascertain the commands required by his 'smart' television to enter into Netflix mode, cursing its over-complicated menu and half-a-second time delay between his depression of the relevant button and the action being replicated on screen.

Before settling down with his coffee, ready to commence viewing, he glanced at the clock, wondering briefly if he would have the stamina to last the four hours or so that it would take to get through the final episodes.

It was three o'clock in the morning.

Chapter Twenty-Three

Angie
Then

'Don't be mad at me, Gray, please.'

Angie's anxiety grew as he kept his eyes averted from her, rubbing them with his right hand while his elbow rested on the arm of the couch. They were red around the edges by the time he saw fit to look at her again.

'Just tell me what was so important that we had to leave my mum and dad's anniversary party, will you?' he demanded, his tone empty of sympathy. 'Just tell me why, on the one night that I really, really wanted – no, *needed* – to be there for my family, you choose to run out on me like you're having some kind of manic episode, leaving everyone standing there, gob-smacked, wondering what the hell is wrong with you?'

He left no time for her to respond before carrying on.

'Then, to make matters worse, you clam up; refuse point blank to even tell me what the problem is! I mean, Jesus, Angie, you ran out like you thought the place was on fire, for Christ's sake! Care to explain that to me?'

She was shocked into silence for a moment, ill-equipped to deal with the frustration that was spraying out of him in jets. She studied his face, his body, looking for traits that were familiar to her: patience, understanding, empathy. She was distraught to find none of them as she watched him cover his face with his whole hand now, the sound of his exasperated sigh reverberating against his skin.

'I will explain,' she told him, her voice weak and unsure. 'I will explain everything, I promise.'

He looked up, scepticism etched on his features.

Her mind was awash with questions of her own, like how the fuck did that evil bastard even know the Pikes, never mind be close enough to them to be invited to their celebration? But she had no time to think right now. She had to act. She didn't want to, but she had to.

'And I'm sorry, Gray,' she said. 'You have to believe me, I'm so sorry for ruining your night, and for running out on your parents like that. You know I love them to bits. I just … I couldn't stay there.'

Graham stood up quickly, making her flinch and knocking her slightly off-balance with the surprise.

'Yeah, you told me that, sweetheart,' he said, frustrated. He said it less confrontationally than before, more like the Graham she knew but still with a hardness in his eyes that made him seem like a different person. 'But what you haven't told me is why?'

He stared at her as though he thought he might find the answer in her face, and she looked away, feeling unclean and uncomfortable under his gaze as she contemplated saying the words.

She was hot, uncomfortably so. Where was the heat coming from? It was October, for goodness' sake. She had shivered from the cold when they had stood in the car park, clinging to Graham for warmth as well as stability and comfort. Now she touched her forehead and found it clammy. Her throat itched with a sudden, overwhelming thirst and her tongue took on an immovable quality, lurking inside her mouth like a lazy slug.

Or maybe it wasn't her tongue that was the problem. Maybe the problem was that the words were just too hard to say.

There had been occasions when she had come close, in the past. Do-or-die moments when she had been forced to weigh up the risk of opening up her rotten, festering can of worms against the very real risk of Graham baulking and retreating from her everyday unreasonable behaviour; her requests, her demands which were direct products of her toxic secret.

The pain that registered in his eyes when she had decreed that they should live out a childless marriage had brought her perilously close to opening the floodgates, for better or for worse. He had tried to shield her from it, to absolve her of the blame that lay firmly at her door, by insisting that her words hadn't cast deep, irreparable lacerations into his heart, but Angie knew him too well to blindly accept the assurances that came from his lips and ignore the truth that lay in his eyes.

For a moment he had been silent. Gobsmacked, she had assumed. Reeling from the revelation that his 'perfect' woman (as he had believed) was unwilling to bear him a child. Not unable – she could never bring herself to tell a downright lie of that magnitude – but simply unwilling. Not interested in sacrificing her body, their closeness, their freedom, she had told him. Not prepared to commit to a lifetime of putting a child's needs first, over their own; of making another human being the centre of her universe when the only person she saw fit to occupy that position was Graham. Half-truths. Omitting the critical reason that she couldn't bear to bring a new life into the world.

He had nodded silently, accepting her well-rehearsed rhetoric without offering a counter-argument. He had considered trying to talk her round - she could see the cogs inside his mind working, trying to find the words to change her mind - but the exercise had been ultimately futile, the words out of reach. And she had felt her heart splinter inside her chest at the ease with which she had shattered his dreams. What was left of it, anyway.

The temptation to take him in her arms, to press his bewildered head to her chest and release the poison that had been eating her up for most of her life had risen up inside her as though it was bile, almost spilling out. She had tried, as hard as her limited reserves of courage would permit, but the distance between her lips and the world she had to henceforth survive in was just too far a journey for the words to make.

'Angie!' His impatient voice cut through her reverie, startling her back to the present, to the matter at hand. To the moment she had been dreading since the moment she had first felt herself drawn to the kind, gentle face of the man who would become her husband.

'I was abused.'

Seven years. Seven long, torturous years of wondering, planning, rehearsing, what she would say and how she would say it, when she finally let the darkness inside of her creep out. Gone. Disregarded, in an instant, as she simply blurted it out like the phrase was a tough piece of steak caught in her throat, choking her, and Graham had tapped her on the back and sent it flying out.

'By my uncle,' she qualified her statement, suddenly overcome with an urge to get it all out as quickly as possible. Now that the earth around her had shattered, she had no choice but to tell her whole story before the ground swallowed her up entirely. She owed that much to Graham.

'My mum and dad were killed when I was a kid, I never lied to you about that.' She stifled a sob at the mention of her parents, whom she had loved so much, knowing that if she allowed the tears to escape there might not be any way of stopping them. 'I was seven. And they really were killed in a car accident - some fucking drunk driver rammed them off the road.'

She could sense Graham taking a seat out of the corner

109

of her eye, as though his legs had become weakened by what he had heard a few moments ago. She couldn't turn to look at him. She couldn't digress from the path that she was on now, no matter what catastrophe it might lead her towards.

'Both of my grandfathers had already passed on by that point, so my only living relatives were my two grandmothers and my uncle, my mother's brother. He still lived at home, you see – a thirty-two-year-old man. With my gran, on my mum's side. My other gran was infirm – multiple sclerosis put her in a wheelchair in her thirties and she had gone into a home when my grandfather passed - so there really wasn't much in the way of discussion about where I should go to live. I went to stay with my granny Denholm, and my uncle still lived there.'

She struggled not to gag at the use of the proper, benign term, that betrayed no hint of the evil that lurked inside the man.

She risked a glance towards Graham, and instantly wished that she hadn't. He was dumbstruck, as she had always anticipated he would be, once the truth was let out. She couldn't be sure that he had heard anything beyond the phrase that had irreversibly changed both their lives, but she carried on, knowing that she would never again be able to gather enough strength and composure to go through all this again.

'My gran was a gem of a woman, bless her. She was never the same after ... what happened to my mum and dad. How could anyone be? No mother should ever have to bury their child, whether that child is three or thirty years old. But she tried her best. She'd been a widow for most of her adult life, and had only a meagre pension to survive on, so we didn't have much. But she tried.'

She broke down, helpless to stop the tears from coming this time.

'Ange ...'

Graham's voice sounded far away, like there was a wall of glass between the two of them. He got up from his chair slowly, reluctantly, and stood awkwardly beside her, debating whether or not to reach out and touch her. He finally stretched out a hand and laid it on her shoulder, tentatively, as though he feared she might burst into flames at his touch.

'No, don't touch me, please, Gray,' she pleaded, not knowing what she should do with his kindness. If she were to surrender to his embrace, she would lose herself to him, and her courage would be gone. The time for shying away had passed.

He jerked his hand away, half-dejected, half-relieved, she thought. Would he ever want to touch her in earnest, ever again?

She wiped away her tears with her hand, annoyed with herself for capitulating. *It's what the bastard would want*, a small voice in her head reminded her, and it worked like an anaesthetic, numbing her tear ducts into temporary redundancy. Graham returned to his seat, the movement in his body minimal, as though it too was stunned so much that it was not able to function as it usually did.

'Anyway, my gran didn't last too long, as it turned out. She'd had a bad heart for quite a few years, and I think the stress of it all got to her, in the end. She was gone before I turned nine. And after that it was just me and him. Lawrence.'

It had been so long since she had dared even to think of him that she wondered now whether she had even got his name right. If felt alien to her when she heard her own voice saying it out loud.

Lawrence. That couldn't be it, could it? Lawrence was the kind of name that an all-knowing, kindly doctor had. Or a smart, driven lawyer. The kind of name that was befitting of a man worthy of occupying the role in this life of son of Benjamin and Nancy Denholm; the kind of man who was deserving of being the only brother of Jane Denholm,

Angie's mother. It was not the kind of name that should belong to the evil, twisted monster of a man who had stolen his niece's innocence and dragged her through a childhood of hell. Except that it was. She was certain of it.

'Yes, Lawrence,' she said out loud, concluding the battle in her head to determine whether she had remembered correctly or not. 'I suppose I had always considered him to be something of an oddball, even when I was too young to really understand. I didn't have any other aunts or uncles, so I didn't really have any frame of reference, but it was obvious to me that he was nothing like the other adults in my life. Thinking back on it over the years, I've remembered bits and pieces, little fragments of memories. My dad voicing his concerns about 'Larry's behaviour' and my mum trying her best to defend her brother, but a little too half-heartedly.

'He was a slime ball. A degenerate loser who had never amounted to anything and never would. He hung around my gran like a desperate leech, bleeding her dry and pulling the wool over her eyes. When it ended up just me and him, I ...'

She broke down, defenceless now against the onslaught of tears. 'I ... I ... He was there, Gray. I saw him. Tonight. You were talking to him.'

'Shh, shh,' Graham soothed, catching her just in time as her body failed her and she began to slump to the floor, as though the effort of breaking her silence had drained her of all her strength.

'Don't cry, my darling,' he pleaded, as tears streamed down his face.

Chapter Twenty-Four

Graham
Now

He woke suddenly, confused at first about where he was, and why there were men with guns, facial scars and intimidating tattoos on the screen in front of him, and a loud knocking sound coming from behind his head.

'Shit,' he muttered, reaching for the remote control and muting the sounds of violence that were, he now realised, booming unnecessarily loudly from his television. He hadn't been able to stay awake anywhere near as long as he had planned, even in spite of the caffeine and sugar combination he had imbibed before embarking on his box-set marathon. He remembered making it through one whole, fantastically dramatic episode, but beyond that he had no clue what had gone down in the world of the Redwood Original Motorcycle Club. Other than more violence – that was a given.

The knocking continued, more urgently now, and he tried to steady himself, sensing his hangover starting to kick in before he had even made it all the way to sobriety. His legs didn't seem keen to obey his instructions to take him to the front door, but he eventually made it, catching a glimpse of himself in the mirror along the way and noting that he looked as done out as he felt. 'I'm too old for this,' he chastised himself, as he opened the door.

'Graham Pike?'

Two tall, uniformed policemen stood in front of him,

their hats in their hands.

'Yes,' he answered, noting that his voice was a little hoarse from all the laughing he had done earlier.

'We have your name listed as next of kin for a Mrs Angela Louise Pike, is that correct?'

If his legs weren't already unsteady enough, the police officer's serious tone was enough to send a tremor through them, and he let his body lean against the wall for support.

'What's happened?' he asked, his voice thick with anxiety.

The police officers exchanged a look.

'You are Mrs Pike's next of kin, then?' the officer who had spoken originally asked.

'Yes,' Graham answered, wondering if there was any chance that he might still be asleep, and in the midst of a bad dream. The pain in his head felt real, as did the fear that had him in a tight grip, making him feel like he was running out of air. But then, he'd felt pain and fear in dreams before, many times, and this felt different, more real. If this was a nightmare, he willed himself to wake up. Soon.

'Mr Pike, we need to tell you that Mrs Pike has been taken to hospital and is in quite a serious condition. If you'd like to come with us, we can take you there.'

It was the other officer who spoke this time. He was younger than the other man, by quite a few years, Graham guessed. He had a softer voice, a more soothing tone. Much newer to the force, probably. Less hardened to the reality of the constable's job.

This was no dream, Graham realised.

'What ... what's happened to her?' he managed to ask.

The officers exchanged glances again.

'It appears,' the older man began, 'that Mrs Pike deliberately overdosed on painkillers. She was taken to the accident and emergency department at the Queen Elizabeth Hospital, and is being treated at the moment. That's all we know, at this stage.'

'Oh, fuck,' Graham said, sliding his back down the wall until he was seated on the floor, his elbows on his knees, his head in his hands. 'She's my wife. My ex-wife.'

'Mr Pike, would you like to come with us?' the second officer asked. He squatted down beside Graham and put a comforting hand on his shoulder. 'We can take you to the hospital now.'

Graham didn't answer. He stared ahead, at nothing in particular, trying to make sense of his thoughts. The officers' words resonated in his mind, piling on more agony each time they were replayed.

Serious condition. Deliberate overdose. Accident and emergency.

'Mr Pike?'

'I'm coming,' Graham replied, accepting the young officer's offer of a hand to help him get back on his feet.

'Let me just grab my keys.'

Chapter Twenty-Five

Angie
Then

'I thought we could go out tonight,' Graham suggested tentatively, tossing a hopeful glance in Angie's direction. She didn't answer. She was facing the television, seemingly engrossed in the teatime news. 'Colin and Liz were thinking of having a barbecue, seeing as it's a lovely night. What do you reckon?'

She turned her head to look at him, wearing a look of disgust, as though he had suggested that they spend their evening raking through the neighbours' bins for food scraps.

'You go,' she told him categorically, and repointed her gaze back towards the television screen.

Her response was sadly unsurprising, but it nonetheless struck a blow to Graham's already fragile emotional state. He rubbed at his temples, a habit that he had picked up in the six months since his marriage and his life had been blown to pieces. He was running out of ideas.

He was trying to be understanding and, above all, patient. But just how was he to be expected to come to terms with the fact that the woman he had married was essentially gone? That in her place had arrived a woman with no desire, nor willingness, to play a meaningful role in their relationship, or even in his life?

It wasn't just about physical intimacy – of which there was not so much as a hint, anymore – although that was, naturally, a factor. It was about the lack of enthusiasm, the lack of effort that Angie demonstrated. The lack of any will to keep fighting, to keep rising above what had happened to her, the way she had seemingly managed to do for the entire time he had known her. Until that night.

Why didn't she feel free now, unshackled by the burden that she had carried? Why couldn't she at least try to rediscover the courage, the determination that she'd possessed during the time they had shared, and allow him to show her that knowing about her past didn't change the way he felt about her?

'Because now that you know, things will never be the same between us,' she had told him, shutting him down coldly. 'How will you be able look at me the same way, knowing what you know? How will you ever be able to touch me, without thinking about him, about what he did? No. We had a good run, Gray. The happy years I had with you were more than I could ever have hoped for.'

Graham was stunned. It wasn't supposed to be like this. They were supposed to be at their happiest right now, settled into their love and their marriage like a favourite shoe that's been worn in to the optimum level of comfort. They were supposed to be ticking off adventures as they went, filling those photo albums with cringeworthy snaps of this holiday and that weekend away. Suddenly, Graham was no longer stunned; he was angry.

'So, what you're saying is, that I don't even get a say in this? That I don't even get the chance to prove to you that I am the man I always promised you I would be? For God's sake, Angie, haven't you been paying attention all these years? I love you. You are the most important thing in the world to me. And nothing, NOTHING, can, or will ever change that. Don't you understand?'

She had thrown him a look that made him feel sick to his stomach, a cold, disdainful look that gave her face a hard quality that he had never been aware of before.

'So, what, you're going to save me, is that it?' She had sneered at him, unkindly. 'Well, good luck, Gray.' The bitterness dripped from her words. 'You're going to need it.'

'I will,' he assured her. 'If you'll let me; I'll do whatever you need me to do. Just tell me.'

And he had tried. If there was a possibility that she could be saved, if she wanted to, he would be the one to do it.

While he had refused to give up, always understanding and tolerant of her dark moods, her harsh words which were never warranted, her decision to emotionally check out of their marriage, she had capitulated. She had continued to work, but the job she had once enjoyed became nothing more than a means to an end for her. She rarely spoke at home, other than to berate Graham for his 'overbearing' concern. She positioned herself as far away from him as possible when they lay in bed, and often waited until he fell asleep before switching off the television and taking her place at the edge of the bed they had once shared so lovingly.

He had floated the idea of her seeing a counsellor, or at least a doctor, but his suggestions had been met with the same scorn as everything else he dared to say. He had sought guidance from books he found at the library; from the internet; from a friend he had known to suffer from manic depression at university.

There was no miracle cure, of course, but for any of the suggested coping mechanisms he had read about to work, the sufferer had to be willing to at least give them a try. And Angie didn't want to do that. She steadfastly refused.

His attempt at trying to bring some normality back into their lives, by suggesting they go to their friends' barbecue, had failed spectacularly. He found himself watching her as she sat listlessly on the couch, her face blank as the colours on the screen lit up her face. She wasn't paying attention to the news, after all, he concluded. She was simply looking anywhere but the road he was on.

Chapter Twenty-Six

Graham
Now

The roads were quiet, owing to the time of day, and yet the journey to the hospital seemed to go on forever. Graham cursed every red light, every give-way that sacrificed even half a second, and he had even considered asking the officer to switch on the emergency light in order to get them there a little bit faster.

But as the car made its turn into the hospital car park, the realisation hit him that actually, he didn't want to be there at all. He would rather be anywhere else, about to do anything else, other than to walk into that building and be met with the consequences of his actions.

The journey in the car had only taken fifteen minutes, but in that time Graham had accused, tried and convicted himself of the crime of driving Angie to attempt suicide. He had left her with no hope, no reason to carry on, and if she were to die, he would have to live with the self-indictment that he had been culpable for her death.

He wished Colin were there, to tell him that he was fucking insane to be thinking such a thing, that he had done everything that could reasonably be expected of someone in his position. He had tried, desperately, to help her, to love her, and to encourage her to forgive herself for whatever it was that she thought she had done wrong. He tried to remind himself of those truths, but they wouldn't stick. His own words, spoke with such ferocious anger, from that fateful day when he'd told her that they were finally over came back to haunt him, drowning out any rational argument that he tried to make.

'This way, sir,' the younger police officer guided, opening the car door for him and gesturing towards the illuminated Accident and Emergency department sign to his right. Graham's stomach lurched, and for a second he thought he might throw up the beer he had drunk earlier, but he managed to compose himself. He took three gulps of fresh air, and followed the officers inside.

'Take a seat here, Mr Pike,' the older policeman instructed. 'I'll go and ask for an update.' He went off to look for a health professional to speak to, while the young officer took a seat beside him.

'Did you find her?' Graham asked him, picturing the scene.

The officer cleared his throat. 'We received a call purporting to a disturbance, a noise violation. We attended the property and there was no answer from inside, so we forced entry. We found the ... Mrs Pike unconscious, and called an ambulance.'

Graham noted the official tone and language used by the man, as though he were presenting an official statement to a superior officer, or perhaps to an avid audience in a courtroom.

'So, the neighbours called you about the noise?' Graham sought confirmation, keen to understand every detail.

'Yes,' the officer answered. 'The neighbour in question was waiting for us to arrive. He said he'd been banging on the woman's ... Mrs Pike's door for the best part of an hour, on and off, but that she wasn't responding. It was then that he decided to call us. He was also the one who told us where we could find you.'

Graham nodded, trying to digest what he'd been told. 'Mr

Colson,' he said quietly. 'He's a good man. He tries to look out for her, you know? He and his wife. None of the other neighbours give her the time of day, although I suppose you can't really blame them.'

The young officer arched his eyebrow inquisitively.

'Angie's not the easiest person to get along with, or live next to,' Graham explained, letting out a tired sigh. 'I got into the habit of apologising for her behaviour, trying to make amends, but eventually they all started giving me the cold shoulder as well.' He shrugged. 'Like I said, you can't blame them. All they wanted was a bit of peace and quiet.'

The officer gave a curt nod.

'So, I take it you're divorced?' he asked.

'Five years,' Graham replied.

'Were you still in contact with her?'

Graham closed his eyes, his last words to Angie flashing before them once more.

'On and off,' he admitted, looking at the floor. 'She would call me sometimes, to help her out, if she needed it. She didn't cope too well on her own.'

A lump began to form in his throat as he eked out the words. *And yet, you walked away from her,* came the accusation that only Graham could hear.

The officer simply nodded again, and Graham tried to quell the notion that the man was judging him, putting two and two together and coming up with the same result as Graham's own conscience.

'You don't know!' he wanted to yell. 'You can't understand until it's you, until you're the one in the situation, sacrificing your own life trying to help someone who just doesn't want it, who refuses to accept it!'

The return of the other officer broke his train of thought, and he instinctively jumped up from the uncomfortable plastic chair he'd been sitting on, desperate for news.

'There's nothing more to report at this stage,' the

policeman told him, holding out his hand in a 'calm down' gesture.

'What did they say?' Graham asked anxiously. 'Is she conscious? Has she said anything?'

The man gave a sigh, as though he was irritated by Graham's questions. 'Like I said,' he said grumpily, 'there's nothing more to tell at the moment. She was unconscious when she was brought in, and the doctors are working hard to ... reverse the effects of the drugs in her system.' He paused for a second, and lowered his voice when he spoke again. 'It's possible that she may have taken other drugs, as well as the painkillers, and an empty bottle of vodka was found at the scene.' His face took on an expression of sympathy for the first time. 'Do you have any information that might help the doctors, Mr Pike? Any idea what kinds of drugs she might have taken?'

Every word hit Graham like a punch to the gut, although in reality he wasn't surprised to hear that a cocktail of poisons was at work inside her body. Why hadn't he anticipated this? For God's sake, she was as unstable as a person could possibly be! If she had been arrested for any reason and thrown into the cells, she would have been on suicide watch around the clock. Why hadn't he had the presence of mind to suspect that she might do this?

'She drinks,' he admitted. 'A lot. I don't know for sure what other drugs she might have taken, but there were times in the past when I suspected she was doing coke. I couldn't say for sure though, it was just that she was really jumpy and edgy a lot of the time.' He paused, and took a deep breath before continuing. 'I can't believe that she would ever sink so low as to do heroin – I doubt she could afford it, for a start – but again, I can't say for sure that she didn't. She never had any marks, you know? When I went to see her, I never noticed any track marks or anything. I don't know.'

Graham felt like it was he who was on drugs, unable to

form a cohesive thought or string together a sentence that made complete sense. He hadn't wanted to believe that Angie could be a fully-fledged junkie, but had he simply anaesthetised himself to the truth? The booze, he had learned to make his peace with, as hard as that was. He knew why she drank, and a part of him couldn't blame her for seeking out the blissful oblivion that the alcohol offered. But hard drugs? He knew she smoked weed – the horrid smell had clung to his nostrils and his clothes on those occasions when he'd been in her flat for even the briefest amount of time – but was she a coke-head? Or worse, was she a heroin addict?

It was all too much for him to take, and he made a beeline for the exit, gasping for breath. His stomach finally relented to the storm of anxiety and fear that was gathering momentum and he vomited at the side of the road. The policemen had followed him out, and asked him if he was okay, but he waved them away, craving distance away from their accusing stares and conspiratorial glances.

He took a seat on a bench just outside the door, and covered his face with his hands. With his eyes closed, nothing could detract his attention away from Angie. Images of her flooded his brain, but not the image of her as she was now: the skinny, damaged shell of a person she had morphed into. The images that flashed before his eyes were memories of a golden period in his life, when he had believed that his love for Angie, and her love for him, could weather any storm that may come their way.

He saw her squinting at the sun, her hair floating on the breeze on the day they first met. He saw her smiling, radiant in her wedding dress, stretching up on tiptoe to whisper in his ear that they had just enough time to make love before the ceremony. He saw her swimming in the sea on their honeymoon, her skin golden from the sun. He saw her grinning at him from the side lines, cheering him on when he had agreed to take part in a charity football match with colleagues from work. He saw her the way she was, the way she used to be, before her pain had flowed out and consumed her. Before shame had become the only emotion that she knew how to express.

'Oh God,' he whispered, tears flowing freely now, as the first, tepid rays of sun began to pierce through the dawn sky. 'What will I do? What will I do if she doesn't make it?'

There was no one around to answer his question. He continued to cry, praying all the while that he wouldn't need to find out the answer.

Chapter Twenty-Seven

Angie
Now

'Do you feel up to seeing a visitor, Angie?' Rachel, the red-haired, kind-hearted nurse whose face had been the first thing that Angie had seen when she had re-opened her eyes the day before, asked her.

Still suffering excruciating pain in her throat from having a tube inserted to pump the drugs from her stomach, Angie weakly mumbled, 'A visitor? Who?'

Rachel smiled warmly. 'A charming young man by the name of Graham,' she explained. 'He's been hanging around here for three days, asking to see you. Someone you know?'

Angie took a moment to reply, her mind working overtime, trying to understand how Graham could have known that she was in the hospital, let alone why he of all people would be loitering around the corridor, waiting for her to wake up.

'My ex-husband,' Angie croaked, taking a sip of her water to lubricate her throat. 'He really wants to see me?'

Rachel seemed intrigued by the question. Her inquisitive look quickly gave way to another knowing smile. 'He really does,' she answered. 'He's something of a permanent fixture at the desk. To be honest, my love, you'd be doing us a favour, if you let him in.' She laughed, and Angie instinctively mirrored the action, as best she could manage.

'What should I tell him?'

Angie pondered for a second. Her mind had been flushed along with her bloodstream, and it was clearer than it had been for years. The sensation was oddly unsettling.

She was lucky, the doctors had told her. Lucky that old Mr Colson had been sufficiently pissed off about the music blaring from her flat to call the police. Lucky that she hadn't been able to remain conscious long enough to ingest the number of pills that it would have taken for her to finish herself off. Lucky that she hadn't choked. So much good fortune, she thought to herself with an ironic smile.

Then why didn't she feel lucky? Why did she feel like waking up in the hospital, surrounded by kindly doctors and nurses, and having Graham waiting in the wings, worrying and caring about her, was the last thing she wanted? Or deserved.

'Tell him he can come in,' she finally declared, with far more conviction than she felt, and Rachel nodded.

'Will do,' she said, and slipped out of the room.

Angie felt her pulse increase as she waited for Graham to enter. She downed the rest of the water left in her plastic cup, and poured a fresh cup from the jug on the portable table beside her. She would've much rather waited until her throat was healed, and didn't feel like there were shards of broken glass in it any time she swallowed, but this was a conversation that she might have only one chance to have. And this time, there was no sense in putting it off. Look how that had worked out for her, in the past.

'Hi,' he said, his voice filling the small room. He looked tired, she noticed. Some more lines had appeared on his face since the last time she had seen him, and she wondered whether they had come about in the past few days, like the grey-flecked stubble that graced his chin, making him look older than his years.

'Hi,' she replied, only just managing to be heard.

Graham sat down gingerly in the chair beside the bed.

'How are you feeling?' he asked, sitting forward, his hands on his knees.

'Not great,' Angie answered honestly, and attempted a smile.

Graham sat silently for a moment, his eyes roving as though he was trying to make sense of his surroundings, as though the scene he had stumbled upon was not what he had been anticipating.

'I was so worried about you,' he said finally, his voice cracking with emotion. 'I thought ... I thought I was going to lose you.'

His eyes began to redden, and Angie felt the same rush of emotion inside herself.

'I'm sorry I put you through this,' she said, the pain in her throat surging with the additional effort required. She took another gulp of water. 'I never wanted to hurt you, Gray,' she continued. 'I haven't been thinking straight for a long time, as you know.' Graham nodded, but didn't speak. 'I got to thinking that the best thing for everyone would be to ... well, you know.'

Graham reached for her hand. 'That was never what I wanted, you know that, don't you?' he implored. 'Angie, not for a second did I think that you would go and do something like this. If I had known you were having those thoughts, I'd ...'

'Please,' she said, holding up her free hand to stop him. 'Gray, none of this is your fault. None of it. I made some bad decisions, and you got hurt, and you have to believe me, that is the last thing I ever wanted.' She freed her left hand from his and brought it to his face. 'You're the best man I have ever known,' she told him, her voice hoarse again. 'And now that I'm finally thinking clearly again, I want to tell you all the things I should have told you a long, long time ago.'

A flicker of fear crossed his face, and she tried to allay it with a smile.

'I'm truly sorry, Gray,' she told him. 'I'm sorry for all the terrible, unforgivable things I did when we were married. I'm sorry for clinging to you, even after you came to your senses and left me, and for ruining every chance at happiness you've had since then.'

He looked surprised to hear her acknowledge something he had thought was beyond her comprehension.

'I'm sorry that you had to find out about this,' she carried on, her voice labouring, 'and that you had to waste three more days of your life worrying about me.'

'Don't say that,' he urged, but she cut him off.

'And I want to make a promise to you.' She brought her other hand to his face now, and looked straight into his eyes as she spoke. His expectant look melted her heart. 'This is the last time, Gray. You're free.'

'What do you mean?' he asked, edging back. She dropped her hands.

'I mean, I'm setting you free. I've had a wake-up call, and I intend to listen to it. I can't keep going the way I was going, living my life like I was nothing, worth nothing. And I can't keep relying on you to mop up my mess. You were right, before, when you smashed up your SIM card.'

Graham winced at the shameful memory, keeping his eyes closed for a second.

'You can't keep being there, rushing to save me whenever I need you. I never had any incentive to change, when I knew that you would always be there, that you would always bail me out. It was like I knew I could just go on fucking up and it wouldn't matter. You would still be my safety net.'

She had to stop to take another drink of water, coughing through the last few words of her admission.

Graham sat silently for a moment, analysing what she had said. He looked hurt.

'So, you're saying this is my fault?' he asked incredulously, retreating back in his chair and returning his hands to his knees.

'No,' Angie countered quickly. 'I'm saying that I was using you, Gray. You were a crutch to me, a parachute for whenever I got myself into a mess that I couldn't get out of. And I'm telling you that I will never do that to you again. You'll never have to hear from me, or see me, or clean up after me ever again.' She tried to pull off a smile, but it didn't quite work. 'Don't you see?' she asked. 'This is what you wanted. This is what's best, for both of us.'

Graham looked away from her, staring idly at the chart above her bed. She had managed to fuck up yet again, she feared. She had managed to make her words come out all wrong, in a way that seemed to have hurt him once more.

'Gray, listen—'

He stood up quickly, aborting her sentence.

'No. You listen, Ange,' he told her, raising his voice. 'I've been to fucking hell and back the last few days, thinking that you were going to die, and that it would all be my fault, because I rejected you, because I abandoned you. How do you think that made me feel?' He didn't pause for her to respond. 'But then, you don't think, do you? You never think about anyone but yourself.' Angie stayed silent. She had no means to contradict him. 'And now this.' He let out an ironic laugh. 'I'm the one to blame all right, but not for leaving you, no, for being there for you! What am I, eh? An enabler? Is that what they call it? Jesus Christ, you are something else.'

Rachel poked her head around the door, wearing a concerned expression.

'Is everything alright in here?' she asked, directing an accusatory glance at Graham.

Graham looked at her for a second, then looked at Angie, whose eyes were pleading with him not to do this, not to bring their issues to the attention of the entire ward.

'Everything's fine,' he said, forcing himself to be calm. 'I was just leaving.'

'Gray—' Angie started, but he was gone, stepping past Rachel in a flash, without looking back.

'Are you okay?' Rachel asked, clearly concerned.

'Yes,' Angie answered, letting out a long sigh. In a strange way, she was. She felt more okay than she had in a long time.

Part Two

Chapter Twenty-Eight

Graham
July

The benefits of living in a small village were plentiful, as Graham had found out.

Small, peaceful neighbourhoods. Quiet evenings. A sense of community camaraderie. But the best part of two decades spent living in a large, bustling town had left an indelible mark on Graham.

Maidstone was never going to win any prizes for being the most attractive place to live, but it had everything you could want or need; it could rival any city. Shops. Bars. Restaurants. Noise. Sometimes, Graham thought to himself, that was all he craved. Some noise. Living out in the sticks, where the most noteworthy news of a week was who had won the Friday night quiz down at the Dog and Bear, excitement and noise were hard to come by. And so were friends, he had found to his dismay.

It had been his choice to move, to uproot his life and relocate to a sleepy village not far from Ashford, and he hadn't yet doubted that it had been the right thing to do. The problem, however, was that his closest friends were now a twenty-six-mile round trip away, and what with Colin and Owen committed to the hilt with their families and Irish Eoin committed to his own narcissistic lifestyle, opportunities for the group to spend time together were as rare as scandals in the village of Elham.

There were people in the village whom he had come to think of as friends: men he had shared a drink with, women who frequently expressed a desire to take him under their wing as the resident single person and make him feel welcome at any gathering. But the comfortable companionship offered by his new acquaintances could not rival what he'd enjoyed for so long with his boys.

Colin, to his credit, had surpassed himself in the best friend stakes when the chips were down. On the morning that Graham had been confronted with Angie's outpouring of truth, Colin had rejigged plans with his family in order to pick him up and take him home. He had managed to put his personal feelings towards Angie aside and sympathise, both with her and with Graham, the poor bugger who had once again been left behind to deal with the trauma that her compulsions had caused.

Inexplicably, Colin had spent an hour or so arguing the case for Angie – perhaps it was just the lawyer in him – whist Graham tried to cut through his disgust and disbelief to digest what he had just heard in her hospital room.

'Can you believe it?' he had yelled, still incandescent with rage thirty-five minutes after storming out of her room. Colin had driven in silence, playing his role as a sounding board effectively. 'I'm the one who's been running to her, pandering to her all this time, and I'm the one in the wrong! Me! I hang around for days, praying for her to wake up, worried sick about her, feeling guilty as hell for leaving her in the first place, and she basically tells me to fuck off!'

He had looked at Colin for a reaction, clearly expecting him to echo his incredulity and spout some vitriol of his own about Angie, like he had done on so many occasions before. Colin stared ahead, intently watching the road, his face impassive.

'Is it me?' Graham had asked, dumbfounded.

'I don't know what to tell you, mate,' Colin had answered

135

reluctantly. 'I mean, the way I see it, this is the best thing all round, for everyone. Isn't this what you wanted, for her to stop relying on you? From what you've said, it sounds like she's finally behaving rationally, doing the right thing. Don't you want to be free of her?'

Graham considered his friend's questions, his head aching from the sheer burden of the past few days. He'd had barely any sleep, so tightly wound he was with nerves, and had spent every waking hour pacing and praying that everything would be alright.

Was he right to feel aggrieved by Angie's decision? Or was there a more logical response that he should be clinging to, one where he should be feeling a rush of pure relief right now, and the sense of closure that he thought he had been yearning for?

He had held his head in his hands as his stomach growled loudly, reminding him that his eating pattern had gone the same way as his sleeping pattern the last few days – downhill.

'I don't know,' he'd whispered, surprising himself with the honesty.

Colin shot a glance at him for a second before turning to face the road again, looking equally as taken aback by the revelation.

'You don't know if you want to be free of her?' he prodded. 'Or is it that you don't believe she really means it? You've got to ask yourself, though, why would she lie now?'

'She wouldn't,' Graham replied quickly, convinced of her trustworthiness, this once. 'I do believe her. I just can't believe she's got the nerve to make out that I've been the one holding her back all this time, like somehow she might have been better off if I had told her where to get off right from the start.'

Colin sighed wearily. 'Is that what she said?' he asked, frowning, although he didn't wait for a reply. 'If you ask me, mate, it doesn't really matter now. All that shit from before is in the past where it belongs, and what matters now is that she's giving you license to move on, to untangle yourself from her. I'd say that's a good thing. Actually, I'd say that's probably the best fucking news I've heard in years!'

Graham sighed heavily, his eyes drooping with the weight of three days' worth of missed sleep and the burden that had caused it.

'You're right,' he admitted, as Colin pulled into a parking space and killed the engine. 'It's just ...'

'Hard? I know, mate. Of course it is. But you'll feel better once it's sunk in, I'm sure of it. It's raw right now. It's like someone being released from prison, having to readjust to life without restrictions on where they can go, what they can do. It will take a while for you to get used to being able to live your own life without having to look over your shoulder all the time.'

'You're right,' Graham had repeated, letting his head fall against the headrest. 'I'll feel better after a shower and a sleep.'

'Better' had perhaps been a little ambitious, however once he'd taken a shower, wolfed down some well-filled sandwiches to appease his grumbling stomach, and slept for a solid nine hours, he had awoken with a different perspective on things. The pain of having had to see Angie like that, so frail and damaged in her hospital bed, with machines and wires and life-preserving liquids all around her, would take some time to drift away. As too would the hurt that he found hard to shake, of being rejected so spectacularly, although Colin's words had gone some way to convincing him to snap out of it and see the situation for what it really was: an opportunity. A chance to get his life back.

But there was something new, something he dared to think of as exciting, in the mix of emotions he felt when he had got out of bed the next day. There was optimism.

137

There were the beginnings of a re-awakening taking place, of a realisation dawning on him that he had choices ahead of him now. He could choose to make changes in his life, if and when he wanted to, where he had been reluctant to before because he had felt bound to keep one foot rooted deeply in the past. He could move, if the fancy took him, to a new house that held none of the memories of his previous life that his Maidstone place did, and had no connection with the difficulties he'd gone through. He had options, and that felt new to him. And it felt, dare he admit it, good.

The move to Elham had come about not long after he had made a long overdue visit to his parents, staying with them for a weekend at their insistence. He had told them everything, dropping in facts that he had withheld from them for years because he hadn't wanted their memories of Angie to be clouded by the harsh truths of what had transpired during the latter years of their marriage and beyond. He had cried on his mother's shoulder like he was a child again, and had soaked up every ounce of the comfort and solace that flowed freely around his childhood home, like a weightless gas that floated on top of the air they all breathed. And when his father had casually remarked that perhaps a change of scene might be on the cards, he had clung to the idea like it was a lifebelt keeping him afloat, not daring to let it go until he had parted with a small fortune to fast-track the paperwork and pick up the keys of his new cottage, in his new village.

His first breath of country air had acted as a form of detox, the most effective kind of all. One cleansing breath was all it had taken to begin to rid his body, and to an extent, his mind, of the debilitating toxins that had been hindering his progress in life. Toxins that had clung to the air, to his clothes, had pervaded his nostrils, when he had lived in the town where he and Angie had shared their lives. Memories that needed to be expunged, if he had any hope of salvaging anything worthwhile from the ashes of the era he hoped had now come to a complete and irrefutable end.

He had made a new start, including a new job (although, sadly, not a career change – under-writing was a depressingly transferrable skill) in Ashford, and two months in, the change seemed to be paying dividends.

He dared to believe that he could reclaim some of the happiness that he had once had. Not with Angie, of course – not necessarily with anyone, since he had taken himself off the romantic market for the time being – but he reminded himself that he'd been a happy, positive person before he met Angie. Surely, he had it in him to be that person again. He was prepared to give it a damn good try, anyway.

And it seemed to be working. His days were easy: a fifteen-minute commute was all it took to get to work, which he found comfortingly familiar, if not enthralling. Evenings in his cottage were spent reading, a lost pleasure that he was very much enjoying rediscovering, or cycling, a new pleasure that he had become steadily addicted to. He could pop in to see his parents on his bike jaunts, and frequently did, taking full advantage of his mother's need to feed and coddle him. His life was simple, if a little monotonous. It was lacking in two things: drama, which he could not have been gladder to be finally rid of, and company, which he had to admit he was beginning to feel the absence of.

He called Colin, letting the phone ring six times before giving up. It had been a long shot, but worth a try. It was Friday night. A time of the week that, despite his improved disposition, proved tougher than any other. In time, he knew, Friday nights would come and go the way they always had; just another period of time in amongst all the rest. But for now, the memory of that one fateful Friday night was just too raw.

He checked the time and the colour of the sky, deliberating whether it was too late for a bike ride to clear his head. He decided not, and quickly changed into his cycling gear, giving himself a metaphorical pat on the back for having immersed himself in a hobby which not only helped with the detoxification process, but had already helped him to shift a little of the weight that had begun to feel uncomfortable around his middle previously. It had helped quite a bit, actually, he realised, as he caught sight of himself in the mirror on the way out.

His exposure to the sun on his outdoor pursuits had produced a healthy glow on his skin, and he couldn't remember a time when his eyes had looked so bright. He was looking better than he had in a while. And feeling better, too. He smiled at himself, and was surprised to see the face in the mirror wink back at him.

Chapter Twenty-Nine

Graham
August

'I'm thinking of getting a dog,' Graham announced, twisting the cap off a third bottle of Budweiser. He had invited Colin, Liz and the girls to his new home to enjoy a barbecue, intent on making the most of the lingering summer.

Jenna's face lit up, only to immediately fall again and for a frown to sweep across her eyebrows.

'Dad says we can't have a dog,' she grumbled, launching a disgusted look at Colin.

Colin threw a similar glance at Graham, as though to say, 'Cheers, mate'.

'We've talked about this,' he reminded Jenna. To Graham, he said, 'What do you want to do that for? Don't you know how much work is involved in having a dog? It's a pretty big responsibility.' He was making the point for his daughter's benefit, but Graham knew that this was a conversation that had taken place many times in the Anderson household, and that Jenna's desire for a pet was unlikely to be dampened, no matter how often or how severely Colin tried to over-exaggerate the implications. Liz shook her head good-naturedly – Graham also knew that Colin's wife was often caught in the middle: absolutely not averse to becoming a dog mummy, but so far unable to make any dent in Colin's steely resolution that it was never going to happen. No, it wasn't that he was scared of them, he had insisted repeatedly. He had simply had a less-than-pleasant experience at the hands of an un-muzzled German Shepherd as a youngster, and didn't trust them. Any of them. The entire canine species.

'I'm thinking of the kids,' was a much-used line of his.

Graham smiled conspiratorially at Jenna. 'Yes, I'm aware that they take a lot of looking after, but I think I'm up to the job,' he explained. 'Just think, there's so much open space here.' He gestured with his arm towards the vast expanse of land which lay beyond his cottage. 'The dog could run around in the fields, and it would be great company for me. I mean, I suppose there could be some weekends when I could use some help taking them for really long walks, but I think I might know someone who would be willing to help.' He gave Jenna a tiny nudge on her elbow.

Jenna's face brightened again, and Colin narrowed his eyes. Graham knew his friend was calculating whether Graham's plan was as beneficial for all concerned as he was making it out to be. Or whether he had been publicly, shamelessly undermined.

'I think it's a brilliant idea,' Liz chimed in, and the realisation appeared to dawn on Colin's face that this might not be as impromptu a chat as his wife and guest would have him believe; rather that he was being ganged up on by two people who should know better. Liz answered Colin's disapproving look with one that he was familiar with, an expression of innocence that said, 'What?' and directed a smile at Graham. 'What kind would you get, Gray?'

'Will you get a puppy?' Jenna asked, before Graham could reply. 'Or a rescue dog? It's best to get a rescue, you know, Graham. There are so many poor dogs in shelters, just waiting for a nice owner to come along. In fact, you should probably get two, because if you only get one, it'll probably get lonely, and it might bark a lot when you go to work. And sometimes they can have this thing called separation anxiety ...'

142

'Okay, sweetie, I'm sure Graham will figure out all the details,' Liz interrupted, half a second before Colin could get in there. Jenna was a bright, inquisitive young lady, and when she got started on a topic, often it took some time and effort to reign her in.

Graham laughed, amused and impressed by his goddaughter's knowledge and obvious interest in the subject. 'That's really good advice,' he told Jenna. 'I was thinking that I would adopt a rescue, but I think I should probably start out with just one for the moment, and see how we get along. Two might be a little bit overwhelming in a small cottage like this, especially if I was to adopt a Labrador or something.'

Jenna seemed appeased by his reasoning, and smiled at the prospect. 'I love Labradors,' she announced. 'Mum, can I use the iPad? I want to look up the Dogs Trust website and see if they have any Labs who need new homes.'

'That's enough, Jenna,' Colin said tersely. 'Graham will choose his own dog.'

Jenna looked glumly to her mother and then to Graham, who shrugged and said to Liz, 'I don't mind if you don't.'

Liz looked torn for a moment, as Colin rolled his eyes, acknowledging that he was outvoted. 'Okay,' she conceded, 'but remember, this is Graham's dog we're talking about, alright? Don't be getting yourself attached, and having a go at your dad for saying "no" again.' She winked at her bemused husband, and retrieved her iPad from her canvas bag. 'Be careful.'

'I will,' Jenna answered sulkily. 'I'll go and use it indoors. Is that okay, Graham?'

'Of course,' Graham answered. 'There's more pop in the fridge; help yourself if you're thirsty.'

Jenna loped off into the cottage via the back door, her shoulder-length hair swishing as she ran, an excited spring in her step.

'Well, thanks to you two Judases, that'll be at least six months' grief lined up for me,' Colin huffed.

Liz laughed. 'Oh, don't be such a miserable bugger,' she teased him, nudging him on the shoulder. 'This is a good thing. Once she's got her surrogate, she won't have to keep pestering you for one of her own.'

'Or,' Colin began, raising his index finger to make a point, 'she'll be so enamoured with Graham's new mutt that she'll be even more eager to get one of her own. Yep, mark my words,' he warned, 'you, my friend, have whipped up a shitstorm of grief for me.' He pointed accusingly at Graham. 'Thanks for that.' His tone was serious, but the sentiment wasn't hostile. Graham merely grinned, shirking off the reproach. Colin drowned his apparent sorrows in the last of his bottle of Corona, leaving a sorry-looking slice of lime at the bottom amongst the last drops.

'It's not my fault you're such a miserable bugger,' Graham retorted, echoing Liz. 'And I don't think you've got anything to worry about. This dog of mine, when I do get it, will keep her occupied for a while, and then once she turns thirteen, I'm sure it won't be long until you'll have bigger fish to fry than her asking for a dog.'

'So, it's *when* now, is it?' Liz asked, keen to gloss over the insinuation in Graham's comment before Colin could run with it, shuddering a little at the thought of having a teenager on her hands in the not-too-distant future.

Graham rested his head against the back of the chair and sat in contemplation for a moment. 'Why the hell not?' he said, with a victorious smile. 'It's almost the law in the countryside, anyway. I think I'm the only one in a ten-mile radius without one.'

'I think it's a great idea,' Liz stated. 'I think it's just what you need. And you know what they say. Dogs are proven chick magnets.' She winked at Graham this time, and he smiled coyly.

'Well, I can assure you, that's the furthest thing from my mind right now,' he insisted. 'And besides, I'm pretty sure that all the women within a ten-mile radius are taken as well.'

Colin snorted derisively, still sulking and seeming a little bit tipsy from the four lagers he had put away. Liz was the designated driver for their journey home, and was working her way through a bottle of Schloer grape juice. 'Your new perfect life not quite all it's cracked up to be then?' he asked snidely.

Liz drew daggers at him. Graham looked surprised for a second but shrugged it off.

'It's been a great move for me,' he retorted. 'I wasn't complaining,' he added, directing this to Liz, who nodded. 'Women are off my radar, that's all I'm saying. For a while at least.'

'Just don't leave it too long,' Colin quipped. 'You're not getting any younger, you know.'

'But he is getting fitter,' Liz countered, a mischievous glint in her eye. 'Maybe you should think about getting a bike,' she teased, 'if these are the results one can produce.' She gestured towards Graham and his somewhat improved physique, and he felt a flush of embarrassment.

Colin looked between his wife and his friend, clearly peeved. 'Oh, fuck off,' he said, prompting his tormentors to erupt with laughter.

Chapter Thirty

Graham
September

'He's how old?' Graham asked the shelter worker, pointing towards the Shetland Sheepdog who was wagging his tail excitedly at him, pacing at the edge of his enclosure, which Graham couldn't help thinking was pitifully small.

'That's Roger. He's ...' The woman checked the details. 'He's six, we think. He was brought here by a neighbour when his owner died, and we weren't really given any information. Six is the best estimate the vet could make.'

Graham nodded pensively. 'Roger?' he asked with a curious smile.

'I know,' the woman said with a soft laugh. 'He doesn't look like a Roger to me. Do you, lovely?' She looked to the dog, whose ears pricked up at the cheery tone of her voice. 'In spite of the slightly dodgy name, do you think you could be interested?' she asked Graham.

Graham took a second to deliberate. 'He sure is a handsome boy,' he admitted. 'What's his temperament like?' He wanted to make sure that whatever dog he went on to adopt would be a good match for Jenna and little Amy, when they came to visit.

'Good as gold,' the woman replied. Graham squinted at her name tag, noting that her name was Sheila. 'Shelties as a breed can be quite highly strung,' she was explaining, 'but Roger here is an absolute sweetheart. He doesn't like a lot of noise, and he would be better off in a house where there are no small children, but he's always very well-behaved. We think he's possibly had obedience training at some point in the past.'

Graham nodded again, heartened by what he was hearing.

'They really are very bright dogs, Shelties,' the woman added. 'He will definitely need lots of walks and physical exercise, but he'll need mental stimulation as well. Plenty of games. Fetch, hide and seek, and so on. Would you be leaving him on his own for long periods?'

Graham did a quick calculation in his head, deducing the probability of him being able to make it home during his lunch hour on weekdays, if required.

'Not too long,' he answered, confident that with a bit of effort he would be able to fit in a ten or fifteen-minute walk in the middle of the day, as well as a longish one before work, and as much exercise as the dog could wish for most evenings. 'Three or four hours at a time would probably be the maximum.'

It was Sheila's turn to nod, although Graham was concerned that her expression contained a trace of suspicion. Perhaps it was a reflex, a natural reaction. It was her job, after all, to make sure that the animals who left her care went on to be housed with decent, trustworthy people. From what he had heard, many of the souls had already been through a lot in their lives, and for the staff, he thought, it must be imperative that the dogs and cats they cared for went to homes where they were sure they would never have to suffer ever again.

'Well, that should be fine,' she conceded, seemingly on board with Graham's proposed schedule.

'And I don't have any children,' he told her, surprised not to feel the twinge of regret that he usually experienced whenever he had reason to say those words. 'It's just me at home. And he would never be stuck for exercise. I plan to

147

recruit him for my current fitness regime.'

The woman smiled, and Graham got the sense that she was warming to him, trusting him a little more.

'Would you like to meet him?' she asked, and Graham nodded enthusiastically.

'Absolutely,' he said, trying not to get too carried away, in case something went wrong along the way and he found himself disappointed. The last thing he wanted was to fall for this dog, only to be left broken-hearted if for some reason it turned out that he was unable to re-home him.

'Hello, Roger,' he greeted the exuberant dog, who immediately showered him with affection, his tail a furry blur as it wagged ferociously. Graham knelt down, and Roger began licking his face, visibly excited at the prospect of a new friend.

'Roger, calm down, darling,' Sheila urged him, gently patting his head. 'Mr Pike doesn't want to be walking out of here covered in your hair and drool.'

Graham laughed, practically rolling around the floor now, letting Roger take the lead. 'It's fine,' he insisted. 'He's just excited, aren't you Rog?' He looked to the woman. 'I think I'm sold,' he told her with a broad smile. 'Can we get the process started?'

'Of course,' she replied, smiling cautiously. 'We'll need to arrange a home visit – it's standard procedure – and we can take it from there. He's already been neutered, so he'll just need a check on any vaccinations that he might be due. All in all, he seems to be in very good health.'

'I can see that,' Graham observed, as Roger continued his elaborate welcome. 'I think I'm going to have a little live-wire on my hands.'

'He does calm down, eventually,' the woman advised. 'He obviously likes you. Dogs are usually very good judges of character, you know.' She flashed him a pleasant smile, and Graham wondered for a second whether there was a possibility that she might be flirting with him. She was younger than he was, by probably five years or so, and now that he was paying attention, he couldn't deny that she was conventionally pretty. Her auburn hair was tied up, perching lazily on top of her head, and she seemed to be wearing no make-up, allowing the freckles on her face to show themselves in all their glory. He snuck a glance at her left hand while she made some notes and noticed that she wore no rings there.

She's just being nice, he thought to himself, dismissing the idea of any flirtation. He was here to pick out a dog, not a prospective new love interest. Although, he had to concede, in a frighteningly short time he had well and truly fallen in love with the furry, feisty, full-of-beans canine that he was currently play-wrestling with. Hook, line and sinker. He would try out a new name for him, though, he decided. Roger conjured up an image of an old, grumpy man, or a cartoon rabbit. The name really didn't fit with the ball of energy and fun that was bounding around in front of him.

'When shall we arrange the home visit for?' Sheila enquired.

'Are you able to do evenings?' Graham asked. 'Or weekends? I'm usually home on a weekday by half past five at the latest, and any day would be fine. As soon as possible, really.'

Sheila smiled again, and this time Graham registered her straight, white teeth. 'You're quite taken with him, aren't you?' she remarked, observing his enthusiasm with amusement. 'It's a good job. Roger seems quite keen on you, too. Let me check what times we have available,' she said, and disappeared to her desk.

I could see myself being quite taken with you, too, he thought to himself, suddenly feeling as though today might be a day for throwing caution to the wind and going after things that would make him happy. 'What do you think, buddy?' he said to Roger, thinking it was probably best to take one step at a time. 'Do you fancy making Casa Pike your new home?'

Roger tipped his head to the side inquisitively, and Graham's heart melted at the gesture.

'Deal,' he said, unable to contain his happiness. He hadn't known what to expect when he had chosen this privately-run, charity-reliant shelter to come and check out, other than what he had read online: that the staff worked tirelessly to re-home cats and dogs of all breeds and backgrounds, and that there were several pooches just waiting for someone to come along and offer them a safe, secure forever home. Someone just like Graham.

He had felt a little overwhelmed when he'd walked in at first, taken aback by the sheer volume generated by the excited, undoubtedly anxious animals vying for his attention, but when Roger had caught his eye, he had felt something click. This was the dog for him, he'd told himself, and the rest was on the way to becoming history.

'How does Wednesday evening at half past six sound for you?' Sheila had returned, minus the clipboard she had been carrying earlier.

'Sounds good to me,' Graham replied, feeling a little flutter of disappointment that he would have to make it through four whole days before he could hopefully set the wheels of Roger's adoption in motion.

'Great. Well, we have your address and your telephone number, so unless anything changes, we'll see you on Wednesday.'

Walking back to the car, he could have kicked himself for not asking what Sheila meant by 'unless anything changes'. Was there a chance that someone else could come along and swoop in, and adopt Roger from right under his nose? No, he told himself, that was ridiculous. In all likelihood, Sheila had simply been pointing out the obvious: that even the best laid plans sometimes went awry. Graham could get held up at work, and not be able to make the appointment, for example. The staff carrying out the home visit could find that their car didn't start on the night, or that a tyre had suffered a puncture. There could be an emergency at the shelter, requiring all hands on deck.

He suppressed a shiver of dread at the thought of anything emergency-like taking place at the shelter, realising that in the space of just under an hour, he had gone from potential pet dad to someone who loved 'his' dog so much that the thought of anything happening to the precious creature had his heart in a grip of fear.

The next four days were unexpectedly excruciating, and brought to mind thoughts about how he might have coped as an expectant father, had his life been permitted to take such a course. Perhaps it was the lack of pressure (and, if he were honest, stimulation) at work that allowed him so much scope to daydream, but keeping Roger out of his mind for any expanse of time proved a struggle. During quiet moments he ran through a list of possible names to try out, keen to find one which much better suited his boy than Roger.

He didn't care for the traditional ones. *Shep. Fido. Rover.* He wanted something different, something that could capture and accurately portray all of the little dog's personality, of which there was much. By four o'clock on Wednesday, he had deliberated over dozens of potential contenders, and had narrowed the choice down to just two. Now, all he had to do was prove to the adoption people that he was a suitable, dependable candidate to take over the duty of care for the little cutie.

He felt butterflies in his tummy, the likes of which he hadn't experienced since he was a much younger man, as he waited for the two deciders of his fate to arrive. Mercifully, they didn't keep him waiting, arriving at a little before half past six, and he could hardly contain his excitement as he ushered the two women into his home, offering them tea, coffee, soft drinks, wine, or any other kind of beverage they could possibly ask for. He was pleased to see that Sheila was one of the assigned assessors, and breathed out a sigh of relief when he retreated to the kitchen to follow through on his offer of a cup of tea.

The women ran through a list of mandated questions, a couple of which had already been covered with Sheila a few days earlier, but Graham didn't mind. They asked to take a brief look around the cottage, and the garden, and to see where Roger was likely to sleep. They took notes as they went, making Graham nervous, and by the time they left, it felt like the beers in the fridge were calling his name, offering to do what they did best and calm his nerves.

'We'll be in touch,' Sheila had assured him, with a smile that hinted that the deal was sealed. Graham hoped. Still, he didn't want to get ahead of himself. Now that he had whipped himself into a frenzy, making the acquisition of this dog the single most important focus of his life, the prospect of it all falling through was one he dared not think about.

It took less than a day for him to be put out of his misery, and the fist-pump gesture he made in the office upon receiving the call with good news had drawn some amused glances. The first thing he did after he hung up with Sheila was call Liz, and ask to speak to Jenna, who was equally as overjoyed about the new addition. Amy was still too young to understand, but he hoped that she would feel the same way about his new fur-baby as Jenna did, and inherit Liz's affection for dogs as opposed to Colin's deep suspicion for them.

Three hours later, he was kitted out with a starter pack (toys, bed, bowls, leash, box of food), signed up to a fully-comprehensive pet insurance policy, and ready to be a dad for the first time. He had already broken his own rule and bought a book on canine psychology, and had picked up some useful tips that he was dying to test out.

'Come on then,' he said, as the object of his affection trotted happily alongside him. 'By the way, you're not called Rog anymore, kid,' he announced as they reached the car, having made up his mind between the remaining two options on his list in the last few seconds. 'Your name is Charmer.'

Chapter Thirty-One

Graham
October

'How about this one?'

Liz screwed up her face to demonstrate her disapproval. 'Nah,' she answered, 'too girly. This one looks better.' She picked up a grey-coloured coat with navy trim, and Graham had to concede that it was a much more apt selection than the red one he held in his hand.

'You're right,' he admitted. 'You see, this is why I need you here.'

Liz smiled affectionately. 'You do realise, Jenna is going to be furious when she finds out about this. Telling her is all on you, I'm afraid.'

Graham winced. 'Yeah, I'm not looking forward to that part,' he told her. 'But I'm afraid this couldn't wait until she gets back. If he still had knackers, the little guy would be freezing them off right about now.' He placed the fleece-lined coat in his shopping basket and continued along the 'outerwear' aisle.

Liz let out a laugh, then covered her mouth as though she were ashamed of seeing the funny side in poor Charmer's somewhat delicate plight.

'She's back on Friday,' she explained, a fact which Graham already knew. 'Are you sure doggie fashion advice is the only reason you asked me out here?'

Graham continued to browse, pretending that he hadn't

heard the accusation.

'Graham?' Liz softly touched his shoulder to get his attention.

'Not exactly,' he confessed, his face flushing a little at being found out. He turned to face her, and she folded her arms across her chest, a habit she had picked up from eleven years of perfecting the art of extracting the truth from her offspring.

'I do need a bit of advice,' he began, 'but not about doggie fashion.'

'I suspected as much,' said Liz, with a knowing smile. 'Who is she?'

'You know me so well,' Graham remarked, grinning bashfully. 'Let's pay for this and grab a coffee,' he suggested, glad to have secured a dapper-looking garment for Charmer as a side-effect of his plan to get Liz alone and glean some female perspective from her.

'I really shouldn't,' Liz protested, as he laid down a blueberry muffin for her, along with her coffee.

'Of course you should,' Graham countered. 'It's winter. You're supposed to eat more in the winter. You need it for insulation, you know?' He bit into the raspberry cheesecake muffin that he had bought for himself.

'I think that's polar bears you're thinking of,' Liz retorted. 'Not so much of a problem for us humans, when you've got supermarkets on every corner and petrol stations that open twenty-four hours a day. And anyway, it's not winter yet. The clocks haven't gone back.'

Graham shrugged, and continued to eat. 'Bugger it,' he replied, clearly enjoying his sugary treat.

'So, tell me everything,' Liz urged him, relenting and taking a bite of the muffin. 'Jesus, that's good.'

Graham smiled. 'Told you so. Well, her name is Sheila. She works at the shelter where I adopted the boyo from. She's twenty-eight, unattached, no kids, and, well, that's everything.'

Liz took a sip of her coffee, cursing when it burned her tongue. 'That is not everything,' she pointed out. 'What's the situation? Are you dating her? Do you see a potential future with her?' She lowered her voice and leaned in closer. 'Has she been back to the cottage yet?'

Graham laughed embarrassedly. 'The situation is, we've been out a couple of times, for dinner, and we plan to do it again, so yeah, I suppose you could say I'm "dating" her.' Liz rolled her eyes at the air quotes he made with his fingers, a pet hate of hers. 'Do I see a future? I don't know, is the answer to that one. She's lovely. She's kind, she's funny, she's a positive person...'

'But?' Liz enquired.

'What makes you think there's a *but*?'

'Well, because you called me and asked me to drive the fifteen miles, or whatever it is–'

'Thirteen,' Graham interjected.

'Whatever,' Liz waved away his correction, 'you asked me to come all the way out here and now we're getting fat on cakes and sugary coffee while you try to work out what it is you want, so I'd say there was always a pretty good chance there was going to be a *but*.'

She took another drink from her cup as though she was in need of it after her monologue, and cursed even louder than before as the hot liquid caught her by surprise again.

'You got me,' Graham conceded, grateful for Liz's no-nonsense approach to calling out his procrastination. He gave a heavy sigh, loaded with frustration. 'I'm just no good at this stuff,' he said, wondering if there had been a point in his life when he had ever felt truly confident about interacting with the opposite sex.

Angie had come to him, in the beginning, making the first move, taking the lead whilst sensing, correctly, that he was more than happy to follow. Her confidence had rubbed off on him, spurred him on; her keen interest in him and the occasionally over-the-top affection that she showered him with when times were good had given him an air of invincibility, which he had begun to lose long before he had finally called time on their marriage.

Devoid of desire for a very long time after the divorce (his 'dry spell' had become the unfortunate hot topic of conversation amongst the guys, and although he had insisted it was very much of his own volition, he had been ecstatic to eventually bring it to an end), he had shied away from relationships. Even meaningless encounters were out of bounds, because the legacy of Angie's infidelity had numbed the part of him that had once craved affection and intimacy as though they were as crucial as food or drink in keeping him alive. Even his all-too-brief foray back into the world of romance with Ellen had come about as a result of her overt willingness to demonstrate that she was interested in him, that night in the pub. Not once in his life had he ever approached a woman, chatted her up, and 'pulled' her, in spite of the fact that in Irish Eoin he had a friend who could do those things with his eyes shut and his hands tied behind his back, and frequently offered up his services as Graham's wing-man. Graham just wasn't that kind of guy. Apparently, he was the kind of guy who held back and let the twenty-first century female be the one to take the reins. But for how long could he continue down that path? Sheila was a nice woman. A good woman. And he *was* attracted to her. How could he break out of his self-imposed shell and show her that he was worthy of her time and affection?

Liz laid her hand on top of his, and offered him a sympathetic smile. 'You've been through a lot,' she reminded him, as though she had been reading his mind whilst he was silent. She refrained from going into further detail. 'You've had some bad luck in your time, that's all.' Graham gave an incredulous look, and she corrected herself. 'Okay, shit

157

luck,' she agreed. 'Unbelievably shit, bordering on fucking horrendous luck,' she qualified. Without the children around to hear and chastise her, having the freedom to swear at will felt good. 'But you're in a good place now, right? This woman doesn't need to know about anything that went on in your past, and for the first time ever, you don't need to worry that it'll come back to bite you on the arse.'

Graham still hadn't quite accepted that Angie wasn't going to suddenly burst out from the shadows and throw a proverbial spanner in the works at any moment, but he dared not admit to Liz what he feared.

'I suppose,' he said. 'But sooner or later, we're bound to have the conversation about how come we're both still single, aren't we? And what do I say then?'

Liz rolled her eyes, as though she were dealing with a child.

'You just tell her that you were married, it didn't work out, you got divorced. End of story.' She retrieved her hand and sat back. 'For all you know, she might have a similarly murky past that she doesn't want to talk about, anyway. And if you're wasting time on your dates talking about each other's past relationships, then you're doing something wrong.'

Graham's face softened as he soaked up the simplicity of what Liz had pointed out. She was right. Why the hell would he and Sheila want to get bogged down in conversation about their past exploits? Maybe the subject didn't have to come up at all. Maybe they could just be two people who happened to be single, for no other reason than because neither of them had found the right person yet.

'You're right,' he said. 'I knew you would be on hand with just the right words.'

'It's nice to know you only want me for my advice,' Liz teased him, blowing on her coffee to cool it before drinking it this time.

'And your sparkling company, of course,' Graham assured her. 'And talking of sparkling company, how is that belligerent bugger of a husband of yours? He's still not taking my move very well, is he?'

Liz sighed and rolled her eyes again. 'He is not,' she concurred. 'He's mad at you, like a bloody kid. Moving away, "getting Jenna all hyped up about that bloody dog" – his words – and the fact that you've lost weight while his waistband seems to be expanding as though he's eating for two. You've really done a number on him.'

Graham didn't detect any hostility in Liz's voice – in fact there was definite amusement at her husband's childish behaviour – but it bothered him to think that a wedge had been driven between him and his oldest friend. After surviving years of disagreements over Angie, and working so hard to maintain their friendship through those hard times, it concerned Graham that they now seemed to be drifting further apart. He made a mental note to make a peace offering. He hadn't expected the issue of Jenna and the dog to be such a divider, thinking that Colin would come around once he realised that nothing would change in real terms, other than perhaps Jenna bringing home some stray hairs on her clothes after a visit to the countryside. But perhaps Graham hadn't made enough of an effort to put himself in Colin's shoes and see the situation from his point of view. Colin was an experienced father, after all. He lived to provide and care for his family, and Graham winced inwardly at the notion he'd put undue pressure on his friend. He would call Colin soon, and arrange a proper mates' date with him. Put things right.

'I'll make it up to him,' he pledged to Liz. 'Thanks for doing this,' he said. 'For coming out here, and talking sense like I knew you would.'

Liz smiled affectionately. 'Any time,' she replied. 'Are you feeling a little better about things now?'

'A whole lot,' Graham answered honestly. 'I've got Charmer to back me up, now, don't I? A proper little wing-man, he is.'

'Hmm,' Liz murmured. 'Well, I'm glad you're feeling a little more upbeat. Seeing as you've got to break the news to Jenna that we went clothes-shopping for your wing-man without her.'

Graham chuckled at the absurdity of the situation. 'He could use a few different coats to choose from,' he explained, thinking on the spot. 'She never needs to know.'

Chapter Thirty-Two

Graham
November

The night that Graham had been dreading for weeks had arrived. Charmer, he had been pleased to discover, wasn't skittish by nature, but there was no way of telling how he might react to the loud, prolonged banging noises that were due to start sounding off any time now.

It was the scariest night of the year for many dogs, Graham had read. And cats. All animals really, seeing as there were despicable bastards in the world who seemed to think it was entertaining to subject them to torture when freely-available explosives and naked flames were suddenly *de rigeur* for one night of the year.

Graham's plan was simple: draw the curtains. Play some soothing, atmospheric music – a Max Richter album – at a volume which he hoped might obscure the worst of the explosive sounds from the living room whilst at the same time not alarming poor Charmer unduly. Additionally, he would make a fuss of the little guy. His favourite squeaky chew toy, in the shape of a rolled-up newspaper, was past its best already, so Graham had bought a brand new one (a rubber chicken this time), which he would unveil at around nine o'clock, when the village's organised fireworks display was due to get underway. That way, he hoped, Charmer's attention would be so captured by the noisy piece of rubber that the background noise wouldn't even seep into his consciousness. That was the plan, anyway.

Graham checked his watch, hoping that his schedule wasn't about to be thrown out of whack by some rogue detonation before he had the chance to initiate his scheme. It was only a quarter to eight, too early as yet to bring out his arsenal of defence weapons. He flopped himself down on the couch, and waited for Charmer to join him. In a matter of seconds, the dog followed suit, and rested his head wearily on Graham's lap, flashing him a look that seemed to convey, 'Finally! I've been waiting for you to do that for ages!' It was a hard life, lazing around all day.

Graham absentmindedly stroked the dog's ears, his mind drifting to Sheila as he pondered the rest of his evening. He wished she were here, tonight, giving him advice and perhaps even offering to stay, and steer him through his first fifth of November with a canine companion in tow.

He stared ahead at the fire as it roared higher with every gust of wind that tried to tempt it from the top of the chimney. Another attempt at finding a human companion had gone begging, and this time, for the first time, he was struggling to figure out where he had put a foot wrong.

He had taken Liz's stellar advice, and recounted very little of his past forays into the realms of romance. He had been polite but firm when he had explained to Sheila that his failed marriage was something that he didn't like to talk about (Sheila had broached the subject, to his dismay), and had avoided asking her any probing questions about her own history.

He had treated her well on their dates, all seven of them, affording her attention and respect. There were no interruptions, no 'pressing matters' that he had to dart off and attend to, and no awkward phone calls that had to be fielded.

He hadn't tried to kiss her, loath to jump in too soon and ruin whatever it was that seemed to be blooming between them. Even when Sheila had pressed her lips tenderly against his when he'd dropped her home from the local pub on what turned out to be their last date, he had drawn on all of his reserves of restraint and bade her goodnight at her front door, preserving his status as a gentleman, a man who knew there was more to a relationship than just the physical side, and who was prepared to spend some time getting to know her before jumping into bed.

Perhaps he had answered his own question about where he had taken a wrong turn, he suddenly thought, as the fire crackled loudly, almost angrily. Charmer lifted his head inquisitively, but found nothing to be perturbed by and went back to dozing, enjoying the closeness of Graham and the massaging of his ears.

Perhaps, Graham considered, he had waited too long to make a move. He thought back over the dates he and Sheila had been on; what they had done together, what he had said. Had he actually shown her that he was interested in her? Had he told her she looked nice, or that he liked her perfume, or that her hair was pretty on any particular night? Not that he could remember. He had been so focused on trying not to rush things, not to screw it up by being his usual self, that he had seemingly left the poor woman believing that he was in the market for nothing more than a friendly chat and a partner for the pub quiz. No wonder she had politely brushed him off when he'd asked her to accompany him to Ashford for lunch. Following his outward display of indifference when she kissed him (whilst inside he was sorely tempted to respond with gusto), there was a chance she had begun to suspect that he was gay, he thought to himself, with a wry chuckle.

'Another one bites the dust,' he muttered, hearing the song in his head, glad to at least have his buddy Charmer to cosy up to on the cold evenings. And that was no hardship, not by a long chalk. His decision to quell his loneliness with a four-legged friend had been one of the best he could remember making in decades. Far from being 'a lot of work', as Colin had initially tried to convince him, the feeling of companionship and of importance that came from Charmer treating him like he was the centre of his universe far outweighed the responsibility involved, and the hardship of having to brave the outdoors in the harshest temperatures to allow him to do his business.

Perhaps that was all he needed, he mused. A loyal, loving companion who never failed to make him smile. Perhaps women, or more accurately his relationships with them, were a part of his life that should be filed away under 'Been there, done that, ballsed it up'.

'Looks like it's just you and me, buddy,' he said to Charmer, giving up hope of an unprecedented visit from Sheila, from whom he had heard nothing in over a week, in spite of three friendly, yet breezy, text messages.

He had a six-pack of beers chilling in the fridge, having felt more optimistic about the potential for having company when he'd shopped at Asda in Ashford (Sheila enjoyed a bottle of Budweiser as opposed to a glass of wine – he knew her well enough to know that), and decided that an evening in, with Charmer snoring contentedly beside him, a listen through of *The Blue Notebooks* followed by a leave-your-brain-on-standby movie and a few beers, was not the worst Bonfire Night he could imagine.

Chapter Thirty-Three

Graham
December

'It'll just be me again this year, I'm afraid,' Graham confirmed to his mother, who tried but failed to conceal her sigh of disappointment over the phone.

'Oh well, not to worry, love,' she recovered. 'The main thing is that you're coming. And all you need to bring is yourself.'

'Let me at least chip in for the meal, Mum,' Graham insisted, replaying a debate that took place between him and his parents every year. Without fail, Graham had been trying for decades to slip a few quid to them in order to contribute towards the more than adequate spread that they put on, and without fail, when he returned home on Boxing Day, the cash would have miraculously made it back into his pocket. He had exhausted many methods of concealing the notes in places he felt sure they (he suspected his father as the culprit, in truth) wouldn't notice, intending to send a victorious text message the following day advising them where to find the money, but his dad was a wily old fox. How he managed to seek the offerings out, Graham didn't know, but he did, every single time. He either had the nose of a bloodhound, or there was a network of hidden cameras following Graham around the house.

Turning up with additional food was not the answer either, as Iain and Pamela invariably filled their table with a meticulously-planned order from Marks and Spencer, which was delivered to their door on Christmas Eve. Bringing any more food into a house already packed to the rafters with turkey, vegetables, wine and chocolate would simply be a horrendous waste. Graham tried to compensate in other ways, such as offering extra special gifts for both of them, but the pair were so stubborn in their insistence that there was never anything in particular that they wanted or needed that he invariably had to go with his gut and hope that what he ended up buying them went far enough to demonstrate his deep appreciation of them, and all that they did for him.

'No, I won't hear of it,' Pamela warned him, predictably. 'And don't be going overboard with the gifts, the way you always do,' she added. 'We're a couple of old codgers now, we don't need anything fancy.'

Graham laughed at the familiarity of it all, thinking that the content of this phone call could have been pulled from any one of the identical conversations he'd had with his mother in all the years he'd been returning home for Christmas Day.

Going back there alone was not a new experience, but this year, his single status somehow seemed more pronounced, more significant than before. This year, as perverse as it seemed to think it, the fact that he no longer had to consider the threat of Angie disrupting his day made him feel sad, in a pathetic sort of way. Even though he had spent many of the last few Christmas days cursing her for her bloody inconsideration, and apologising profusely to his parents for having to inevitably devote time to dealing with her drama, the fact that he would be uninterrupted this Christmas day brought home to him the harsh reality of his life: that no one needed him. No human, at least.

Charmer was excited about spending a day at his grandparents' house, on account of Graham having spent days whipping the dog into a frenzy by promising biscuits and maybe even some turkey and trimmings, if some happened to 'fall' from the table. He had no real confidence that Charmer knew what he was talking about, but he had learned that if he himself acted excited enough and spoke enthusiastically enough about any topic, Charmer would mirror his exuberance.

He had taken the week off in the run-up to Christmas, something he couldn't remember having done for years.

For his first task, he spent half a day in Ashford, shopping for Colin, Liz, and the girls, clueless as always about what to get them. He resorted to calling Liz to ask for advice, again, and armed with her instructions he was able to acquire the items in good time, in spite of the heaving shops. He couldn't resist picking up a little stocking filled with treats and toys for Charmer, and smiled like an idiot when he handed over the cash for a medium canine-sized Santa hat, complete with flashing bauble.

It took the best part of a day for him to finally get around to finding, unravelling and re-constructing his long past its best Christmas tree and decorations, and by the time he was finished, he was spent. He had intended to stash Charmer's gifts under the tree, but it quickly became clear that they were not likely to remain in place or intact if he did so, and he moved them into the coat closet until the big day.

The next day he drove into Maidstone to hand over the presents he'd bought for the Anderson family, keen to see Colin again for the first time in ages. For one reason or another, neither he nor Colin had been able to free up any time in the preceding weeks to go for a reconciliatory pint, and Graham had missed his old pal. The feeling was evidently mutual, as Colin offered him a very warm welcome into his home. Unexpectedly, he had even consented to Graham bringing Charmer along, on the condition that if the dog proved to be a disruption or showed the slightest hint of posing a danger to the girls, he would be banished to the back garden on his

167

leash, freezing temperatures or no freezing temperatures. Graham couldn't conceive of the happy, uber-friendly dog that he knew being a danger to anyone (he had witnessed him trying to instigate a game of chase with a cat, who had knocked him back disdainfully with a mere look, in that way that cats do best), but nonetheless he ran through a pep talk with him while he drove.

For his part, Charmer was entirely well-behaved on the journey, occupying the front seat happily and enjoying the sights he was able to take in as they whizzed through the country roads towards the big town.

'Now listen, buddy,' Graham began, 'we're going to see some good friends of mine, and there are going to be a couple of kids there, so I need you to be on your best behaviour, okay?'

Out of the corner of his eye he could see that Charmer had turned to him as though he was listening intently, and Graham reached out his hand and patted the dog's head. 'Yeah, I know you'll be good, mate,' he said with a smile. 'Just be yourself. Everyone'll love you. Even Colin.'

Love was perhaps a strong word when it came to Colin's reaction to having an energetic, over-affectionate creature lunge towards him, desperate to make friends with him, but he came around after a while, relaxing a little once he'd seen Liz, Jenna and even little Amy fall in love with Charmer.

'It's good to see you, mate,' Graham stated, surprised to be feeling a little nervous about coming face to face with his friend after such an unprecedented period of distance. The men hadn't fallen out, far from it, but theirs was a friendship which had been tested many times in the past, and Graham had half-wondered whether putting such a physical distance between the two of them might be the thing that caused it to finally capitulate.

'You too, mate,' Colin replied with a wide smile, pulling Graham into a brotherly hug and quashing his worries.

'How have you been?'

Graham puffed out his cheeks and then let the air go. 'Oh, you know,' he answered, 'never a dull moment with me, mate.'

Colin smiled weakly, and Graham guessed that he was probably up to date with regards to the Sheila situation through Liz. Squeals of laughter from the living room interrupted their exchange, and they went to investigate.

'Dad, look!' Jenna exclaimed. 'Charmer does tricks!'

The consummate showman, Charmer had chosen this moment to demonstrate that the obedience techniques Graham had been endeavouring to teach him had not fallen on deaf ears after all. He had simply been waiting for the right audience, clearly.

'Charmer, paw,' Jenna instructed, and the crafty little beggar duly complied, much to Jenna's delight.

Graham chuckled. 'Typical,' he remarked. 'Give him a bit of female company and he's Mr Obedient. I've been trying to get him to do that for weeks.'

Liz laughed, pleased to see that Colin's mouth was curling up at the sides, giving her hope that his long-held rule could be open to some bending, or even breaking.

Graham and Charmer spent the whole afternoon with the Andersons, and when they left Graham felt that Charmer was as disappointed to be heading home as he was. Had he made the wrong move, relocating away from the bosom of friends who felt more like family, isolating himself?

It was the time of year making him melancholy, he told himself on the drive home. It was a much-discussed fact that the festive period was a struggle for a lot of people, and he counted himself amongst the affected. That was all it was. Maybe he had even succumbed to a touch of Seasonal Affective Disorder, he considered. That was as good an explanation as any as to why he felt a bit under the weather, psychologically.

The following day was Christmas Eve Eve, and he only had his parents left to buy for. He'd spent hours pondering what he could get for them, preferring to browse online for ideas rather than venture into the shops, which by now would be insanely busy, but so far, he had come up with nothing that seemed fitting.

Perhaps a trip to the largest retail centre in the United Kingdom, which was a mere fifteen-minute drive from the cottage, was required, but the motivation to get up and go was not forthcoming.

He lazed on the couch, with Charmer by his side, feeling sorry for himself, but not totally understanding why. So, he was single at Christmas. Again. Why should that bother him so much? He had been in that very same boat for years now, and it had never affected him this way before. But then, he couldn't really explain exactly how it was affecting him. Not in a way that anyone else would understand.

There was a lethargy about him, the likes of which he hadn't experienced since the period around his divorce. A strange, uncomfortable sensation seemed to be lingering in his gut, leaving him with very little appetite, and he had to talk himself round to muster the energy to even walk Charmer. It was the damnedest thing, and he could feel it dragging him down.

Once Christmas was over, and the festivities had given way to focus for the new year ahead, he was sure he would feel better. He just needed to snap out of it, whatever this thing was that seemed to have enveloped him without warning.

He never did get around to popping down to Ashford that day, preferring instead to enjoy a day of complete rest and recuperation, in the hope that a recharge of his energy-sapped batteries might do the trick.

A phone call the following day, Christmas Eve, provided an explanation of what had triggered the sudden murkiness in his brain. But it didn't make him feel better.

Chapter Thirty-Four

Graham
January

There was something so cruel about losing a loved one at Christmas time. The sense of loss perhaps may not be felt any less violently at any other time of the year, but watching his father slip away from him at the height of the season where everyone was supposed to be in celebratory mode added an extra layer of hurt for Graham.

Christmas Day would never be the same again. His life would never be the same again. And neither would his mother, he knew. Iain and Pamela had come as a pair, since day one of their courtship. Now Pamela was a violin without a bow.

Graham's rage at the injustice of it all had come later than the pain. It had kicked in the day after the funeral, which had to take place a full eight days after his father's death due to the lack of available facilitators over the festive week. Graham had thus far managed to compartmentalise, to quarantine the anger in a dark corner in order to make it through the stomach-churning day.

Colin and Liz, Owen and Catherine, and Irish Eoin along with his current squeeze had mercifully been on hand to prop him up when required, quite literally at times. He had operated on auto-pilot for those eight days in the run-up: making phone calls, sorting through mountains of paperwork, comforting his mother as best he could. His body had learned to run on fumes, and only when he sat down for the first time at the wake did the gravity of the situation begin to sink in.

The wake was a sombre but heartening affair, with close to seventy people showing up and raising a glass to Iain, a 'fine man' by all accounts. By the time he was helped into bed by his faithful friends, having raised one or two glasses too many on an empty stomach, Graham was exhausted. Mentally and physically.

Waking with a disgusting hangover and an overwhelming urge to cry, the following morning was the first time he allowed the anger to ignite. And there were so many things to be angry about.

Eight months. For eight months they had both known that Iain was living on borrowed time, suffering from a silent but deadly disease that had crept up out of nowhere and signed his death warrant. For thirty-two weeks his mother and father had colluded to keep their son cruelly in the dark, to smile and laugh and act as though everything was normal, even encouraging him to move closer to them whilst they hid behind parental concern and a desire to have their only son at arm's length.

He had trusted them. All throughout his life, even when he had plumbed the depths with Angie, they had been there for him, standing strong, providing the back-up that he had so often sorely needed. He had worshipped them, in awe of their everlasting love and respect for one another, and of their unwavering devotion to him, their only child. He had done his best never to let the trials and tribulations of his own life demote them to the bottom of the pile. He had been a good son, he knew. Worthy of their trust. Worthy of the truth.

The fact that there was nothing that he could have done to change the eventual outcome made no difference to him. The fact that nothing good could have come of him being aware of the aggressive, inoperable tumour in his father's brain, and that they had shielded him from the horror of it only to spare him from the brutal reality, gave him no comfort at all. He had a right to know, he had told his mother at the hospital, through tears that had seemed like they would never stop falling. He had the right to make his peace with it, as his parents had apparently done, and to get used to the idea that his father, his idol, would not be around for much longer.

He had realised, mercifully quickly, that his mother couldn't handle his fury on top of her insurmountable grief. There would come a day when he would open his heart to her, and tell her how hurt he had been to hear of his father's condition for the first time only when it was too late, when there was no going back. But that day could wait.

He was thankful that he'd had the time to make it to the hospital, and to kiss his father's cheek and hold his strong, warm hand one last time, but he hadn't had the chance to say everything that he would have said, had he known that he was about to lose one of the support columns from his life.

It had been peaceful, in the end. A stroke had rendered Iain unconscious, and in the early hours of what should have been a fun, affection-filled Christmas Day, he had drifted away, as though he were merely falling into a deep sleep.

That he would never again hear his father's voice, or see him smile, was unimaginable to Graham. The harsh facts of life had been locked out, unwelcome in his mind, his parents' advancing ages failing to register as a concern. They were invincible. They were going to live forever, together. But now they weren't. And at the age of thirty-seven, Graham felt like a lost child.

The phone rang, the shrill sound piercing his ears and making him wince. He cursed the caller for disturbing him so early, shocked to find that it was already half past eleven, and that the lion's share of the morning had come and gone already.

'Hello?' His voice was gruff, having gone unused for so many hours.

'Graham? It's Sheila.'

His brain was on a lag, and it took him a second or two to connect the voice and the name together.

'Oh, hi,' he said, unenthusiastically. His lack of interest was nothing against Sheila; he harboured no inclination to speak to anyone at that moment in time.

'I just wanted to call and say how sorry I am,' she said solemnly. Her sympathy was too much for Graham. A lump formed in his throat, and he had to choke back a tear.

'Thanks', he managed, rubbing his eyes. 'I appreciate it.'

Silence prevailed for a few moments as neither of them quite knew what to say. They weren't friends, technically speaking; they had no real connection other than the fact that they had spent a few hours together a handful of times. Sheila knew little of Graham's parents, or his childhood, or the memories of his father that would go some way to helping him through his grief.

'How is little Charmer getting on?' she asked, reaching for the only common denominator that existed between them.

Graham took a look around his bedroom, realising he hadn't even noticed that there was no warm, heavy object resting on his legs when he had come to. He felt a surge of panic as he scanned the room and realised Charmer was not there, his head hurting even more as he stood up and moved as quickly as he could through the rooms of the cottage, yelling the dog's name.

'Oh, there you are,' he cried, as Charmer dutifully appeared from the living room. By this time of the day he was almost certainly in urgent need of a foray outdoors, and a meal, and Graham had to fight the urge to cry again as Charmer wagged his tail lovingly, with no sense of accusation, unwittingly piling on the guilt.

'I'm so sorry, buddy,' he told Charmer, kneeling down to accept the offer of sloppy reconciliatory kisses from his beloved pet. 'Give me five minutes,' he told him, hoping that a shower, followed by a brisk walk in the cold air, would help to clear his head a little.

He looked down at his hand, and caught sight of his phone perching precariously in it. 'Shit!' he exclaimed, remembering that he had been in the middle of a somewhat stilted conversation with Sheila before he had begun haring around the house on the hunt for his wayward pup.

'Sheila, I'm sorry,' he said. 'I couldn't find him for a sec, but he's here. He's probably peed in the kitchen, but that's my fault. I was in bed, you see, when you called. I'm just going to take him for his walk now. You don't fancy meeting me, do you?' he asked, a spur of the moment decision. 'For a coffee or something. Sheila?'

The line was dead. She had gone.

'Bugger,' he exclaimed, his guilt multiplied now that it included Sheila as well as Charmer. He would call her sometime, he decided, when he was feeling better about everything, and invite her for that coffee, just to chat. When he wasn't standing in his hallway, dressed in only his boxer shorts, shivering with cold. When he wasn't in the throes of grief, and rage, and confusion about what the future held for his mother. How she might cope without her soulmate; how she had always predicted that she would die of a broken heart if her husband were to go before her. His head felt close to exploding now, the hangover doing its unpleasant thing with a vengeance, and he opened the back door to let Charmer out for emergency relief. Graham would take him for a good, long walk, but first, he was in need of a strong cup of tea and a couple of even stronger painkillers.

Chapter Thirty-Five

Graham
February

The weather was beginning to improve, slowly but surely. He had put a halt to his downward spiral into comfort eating and re-launched his campaign to get fit and lean. His mum, whilst a veritable shadow of her former self, seemed to be coping. Not thriving. Not flourishing, nor loving her life the way Graham had known her to in the alternate universe that had existed before the twenty-fifth of December, but coping. And in the circumstances, that was something to be thankful for.

Graham had got into the habit of counting up all the positives he could tally on any given day, eager to stay strong and upbeat for the sake of his mother, not to mention for his own psychological wellbeing. Following a rocky start, a January during which he had spent almost all day, every day, feeling sorry for himself and cursing his streak of rotten luck in life, he had given himself a figurative kick up the backside and decreed that he had done enough wallowing.

Making the move to Elham had retrospectively revealed itself to be a truly inspired move, as it meant that he was a stone's throw away from his mother's house and could do his duty as a son and appease his conscience by visiting her as often as she needed. And wanted.

He called her every day, terrified that his seemingly unending bout of misfortune might have cast a cruel curse on his family, a curse that might be deviously plotting to steal his mother from him as well, at any moment.

'I'm fine, darling,' she assured him, every day. He wanted to believe her, and to an extent he did, but the worry that he was missing something, that something horrendous might pop out of the woodwork like it had done with his father, was never far from his mind. She was as fine as she could be, he convinced himself. Which was not really fine at all, but then he knew first-hand what that felt like.

Life went on, of course it did. There is an inevitability about it. But that didn't mean that he and his mother were the same people that they had been when his father had been around. There was an eerie silence to the large house without Iain's commanding voice echoing around it. There was a void much larger than the man himself had been, a torturous absence in his bed, in his favourite chair in the lounge. There had been a discussion about whether they should move the chair, or indeed get rid of it altogether, since the sight of it, empty of him, was hard to bear. It had been given a last-minute reprieve, the consensus being that it had come to be a part of Iain, an extension of him. To get rid of it would be akin to purging his memory from the house.

Graham's earlier anger had subsided, so much so that his need to admonish Pamela for holding back the truth from him had been all but quashed. Now wasn't the time to have a talk of such intensity, as it would inevitably cause a rift between mother and son, one which could only harm their relationship at a time when they both needed it to be stronger than ever. And there never would be a good time, Graham had conceded. What good could come of re-opening a wound that had hurt them both equally? No good, was the answer. His father's illness was not his mother's fault, nor her secret to tell. He had been sheltered from the truth for a good reason: to spare him pain. How could he blame his parents for that?

He had moved on slowly, rediscovering his motivation a piece at a time.

His cycling was becoming less of a hobby and more of a passion, and he had taken the plunge and signed up for the Kent Cycling Festival in September, an event in honour of the British Heart Foundation for which he would enjoy training, and the side-effect of contributing to such a worthy charity was an added bonus. The weather still wasn't wholly conducive to enjoyable training sessions, which he had planned using 'expert' guides he had found on the internet, but sometimes after a slow, sedentary day at work, there was nothing more appealing than throwing on his Lycra (he had resigned himself to the fact that the proper 'gear' was required, if he were to pass himself off as a serious cyclist) and zapping some calories out in the chilly countryside. Never content to be left behind, Charmer often accompanied him, providing fierce competition with the bike by reaching speeds on foot that Graham could only marvel at.

Considering the upheaval of the past few months, Graham was surprised to be embracing a sense of calm. Not quite contentment – he had resigned himself to the fact that he was unlikely to recover the sunny disposition he had once possessed but had clumsily mislaid somewhere along the way – but calm was good. The only thing that continued to niggle at the back of his mind was Sheila – namely the failure on his part to make amends for the way their last exchange had turned out. He genuinely hadn't meant to forget that she was on the other end of the line, especially since she had been kind enough to call and enquire after his wellbeing. But now that a month or so had passed and he had neglected to so much as offer a figurative olive branch, he wondered if there was any point in trying to redeem himself.

He reasoned that she probably hadn't given the incident much thought since then, on account of the fact that keeping in touch with Graham was unlikely to feature in her list of top priorities, but every so often he would pass by the animal shelter on his bicycle and wince with discomfort at the memory of being unwittingly rude to her and not yet apologising for it.

It was a little late in the year to be making New Year's resolutions, but recently he had developed an ethos of clearing out the untidiness that had previously cluttered his mind, and in line with that, he knew that the only way to cleanse his conscience of some of the regret that he felt was to speak to Sheila, to explain that she had simply caught him at a terrible time.

He tried calling her mobile one Saturday afternoon, having cycled past the shelter and noted that her car wasn't there. She could have walked to work, and be busy, he supposed when there was no answer, although given the weather situation and the fact that she lived a good two miles from the shelter, he thought it was probably unlikely. If she wasn't at work, and not otherwise engaged, another possibility was that she had seen his name flash up on her phone and chosen not to answer the call. And in truth, he couldn't really blame her for that.

He waited the rest of the weekend, hoping that she had simply been occupied at the time and had genuinely missed his call, and would ring back to see what the reason for him making contact was. She didn't. He was loath to call again, wondering if perhaps she was now seeing someone new, in which case taking a call from someone she used to date, albeit extremely briefly, might not go down all that well. Graham's motivation for getting in touch was completely innocent – he simply wanted to convey his gratitude for her calling and his regret at having cut her off – but he appreciated that she and her new beau, if she had one, might not be on board with lending him a platform to get those things off his chest.

He resolved to make an attempt to speak to her in person, at the shelter. At least that way, there was little chance of him putting his foot in it with regards to her private life.

Her car was conspicuously absent from the car park when he passed the shelter again on Monday, but after quickly popping home and collecting Charmer, he decided he would venture in anyway, on the off chance that she was actually on duty.

He had wondered whether perhaps Charmer might recognise his previous, temporary dwellings and revolt against going inside, for fear of being surrendered to the care of the shelter once more, but he seemed to have heeded the comforting assurances that Graham had been chanting like a mantra, and sauntered through the doors without a care in the world.

There was no one manning the reception area at that moment, but then there was no one waiting to be attended to, either. Graham debated whether to hang around or not, suddenly conscious of borrowing some of Sheila's time which could be better spent tending to the animals she cared so deeply about. He decided to give it five minutes, maximum, and if neither Sheila nor anyone else appeared, he would make for home, and make his peace with the fact that he had tried to make amends but hadn't succeeded.

'I'll be with you in just a minute,' he heard a female voice say, from the office behind reception. He could see her silhouette as she moved around inside, and could tell from her frame and her movements that she wasn't Sheila. Thinking back to the previous times he had visited the shelter, he tried to remember what the other women he had met looked like, and whether the woman behind the glass could be any of those.

He didn't think so. And yet, there was something uncannily familiar about her. Her voice, especially. He had heard little of it, but there was a flicker of recognition taking hold.

'Right, here I am,' the woman announced, sounding

harried. 'What can I do for you?'

Her eyes had been immediately drawn downwards and were focusing on Charmer, whose adorability put a fond smile on her face as she emerged from the room. It was only after she had spoken that she looked up and caught sight of Graham.

He didn't respond. Now he knew where he had heard that voice before. There was something different about it, but still, there was no room for doubt. And when he saw her, even though he couldn't quite believe it, it would have taken the surgical removal of his memory for him not to recognise her. It definitely wasn't Sheila who was working on reception that evening. It was Angie.

Chapter Thirty-Six

Graham
February

'What are you doing here?' he asked, a little too confrontationally, as Charmer rose and went to greet her, his tail wagging ferociously like the instant friend to everyone that he was.

'Well, aren't you just gorgeous,' Angie addressed Charmer, using the dog's avid attention to delay answering Graham's question. Charmer lapped up the affection that Angie was offering, ignoring Graham's irritated commands to come back to his side. He was a no-good traitor, that dog.

'Yes, yes you are,' Angie continued, keeping her eyes anywhere but on Graham, 'you're gorgeous.'

'Angie?'

'I work here,' she told him, still smiling at Charmer, but looking down as though the admission embarrassed her. 'Well, I should say, I'm a volunteer,' she corrected herself. 'I only started last week. What are you doing here?'

Graham felt angered by the question, as though there was an insinuation that he was the one throwing a curveball here. This was *his* village. *He* was the one who had made the move from the city in search of a quieter life, a better life. *He* was the one who had been through the emotional wringer during the past few months, and deserved the calm and the determined focus that he had managed to carve out for himself in the last few weeks.

The old Graham would have gone on the defensive. The old Graham would have allowed the storm of feelings that swirled around inside his body at the mere sight of her to rage out of control. But the new, calm Graham took a different approach.

'I live here,' he answered coolly. 'Well, ten minutes down the road. I adopted this little fella from here.' He pointed to Charmer, who had retreated back to his side and lay gloomily on the floor. He seemed to sense the air of discomfort that had descended on the small space.

Angie smiled. 'He's delightful,' she said, in her new voice. Everything about her seemed new, Graham decided, as he regarded her properly. Her accent seemed as though it had been watered down, like the rest of her. There was a demureness, an air of serenity about her that Graham could not have ever expected to witness. He had known two Angies in his life: one a bright, confident, sometimes outspoken woman who knew what she wanted and how to get it, and raced at full speed towards her goals. And the other a crazed, broken woman with no regard for herself or anyone around her. The woman in front of him bore no real resemblance to either of those, to the extreme that he found himself questioning whether it was really her at all.

But it *was* her. She had gained some weight since the last time he'd seen her, and although still slim, her once gaunt face now had some padding in the right places. She wore neutral colours; a dark grey V-neck sweater coupled with black jeans and black Converse trainers. Her hair was tied back, her ponytail touching the top of her shoulders. If she was wearing make-up Graham couldn't tell, but whereas when he'd seen her last, in the hospital, her skin had borne a tired, grey look, her cheeks were flushed with a healthy glow, and her eyes were bright and fresh.

'I was looking for Sheila,' Graham recovered, making the decision to get out of there as quickly as possible. 'Is she

183

here?'

'I'm afraid I don't know anyone called Sheila,' Angie answered. 'Gemma's doing her rounds at the moment; she will probably know. She's the one who took me on. If you want to hang around for a few minutes—'

'I'd best be getting off,' Graham interrupted. 'It's not important. I'm guessing she doesn't work here anymore, if you haven't come across her.'

Angie shook her head. 'Not in the week since I've been here,' she confirmed. 'Maybe her leaving is why I've been brought in. They just said there was an opening; I didn't ask for the details.'

Graham nodded. He stood for an awkward moment, willing himself to do an about turn and get out of there, away from the pressure cooker of shared experiences that the small building had been transformed into. But his body refused to move.

Angie looked at him inquisitively, as though she were waiting for him to say something more. Or to leave, one or the other.

It was Charmer who intervened, letting out a bark that broke Graham from his reverie and returned him to the moment.

'Yes, mate,' he recovered. 'We're just going now.'

'Bye, Charmer,' Angie said as Graham opened the door to let them both out. He reflexively twisted his head to face her, momentarily confused.

'You let it slip when you were calling on him to get away from me,' Angie explained, at the same time as Graham managed to join the dots in his head.

'Come on, mate,' he said, hurrying out as though the air inside the room had become unsavoury and he was in need of a fresh blast of clean oxygen. He let his breath go when he made it inside the car, feeling light-headed and slightly nauseous.

He had not been prepared for what had just happened. Perhaps, as he had long suspected, he was nothing more than a gullible fool, but he had truly begun to believe that he had seen the last of Angie, that he had purged his life of all complications, save for the unfinished business of his last interaction with Sheila.

Apparently not. He had gone to the shelter to apologise to one woman for being unintentionally rude, and had come away feeling the familiar stab of guilt for unabashedly being rude to another.

'Charmer,' he said, making the dog's ear prick up in suspense. 'how do you fancy swapping lives with me, buddy?'

Chapter Thirty-Seven

Angie
February

A blast from the past was a painfully accurate description of what had just taken place. A shotgun blast, it felt like, right into her solar plexus, sending her gasping for air. Not in front of him – she had used her learned mindfulness techniques to hold her emotions in check all the while he stood opposite her, observing her, analysing her. But once he had gone, disappeared from her life yet again in a haze of disapproval and dismay at her very existence, she'd had no choice but to register the impact.

She hadn't anticipated ever seeing him again. On the evidence of Graham's reaction, she had deduced that he had held exactly the same expectation. If she ever got the chance, which she didn't suppose she would (and, in truth, she wasn't sure that she would want it), she would explain to him that her showing up here was not an attempt on her part to track him down. Yes, she had to concede that a flicker of recognition had taken hold in her memory when the name of the small village had first been mentioned, but it wasn't until she had accepted the offer and made her way there that she had made the connection. She wondered whether she hadn't ever known the name of the place, back then, or whether she had always known, but had retired the memory along with all the others that she had been forced to leave behind in order to survive. Perhaps, she mused, her mind still had some catching up to do. It was on the mend, that was unquestionably true, but she was under no illusion that she was healed. In those moments when the darkness threatened to creep back in, she feared that it may never be possible for her to be a complete person again, that she had simply abused her mind and her body too much. But the techniques she had learned in her sessions gave her tools to help transform the doubts into opportunities. They helped her to talk herself down from the brink of meltdown, like the moment she had just made it through.

Once she had realised exactly which part of the world she had settled in, two weeks earlier, she had given the situation some serious thought, and figured that the chances of her running into Iain and Pamela were slim, so long as she didn't intentionally venture too close to the house that she could remember being warmly welcomed into many years before.

By her logic, if she wasn't hanging around the vicinity of the Pikes' home, she hadn't considered that there may be any risk of bumping into Graham. The fact that he now apparently lived in the village had come as news to her, although as she dissected every second of their interaction, she feared that Graham would be quick to believe that she had orchestrated the meeting.

In a moment of clarity, she reminded herself that it didn't really matter what Graham thought. He was no longer the focal point of her life. He had long since vacated the role of her protector, her defender; the object of her affection and her unreasonable, irrational anger. At best, she might have hoped for a civil meeting, at some point in the future; a chance to sit down and have a calm, grown-up chat; an opportunity to say the things that they wanted to say to each other in order to officially lower the curtain on their past.

At worst, she imagined that he would still be focused on the feelings that had been on display that day several months ago when he had granted her wish to walk away from her, for good. What had occurred in the reception of the shelter fell somewhere in between the two: there had been some semblance of civility, with an undertone of hostility and resentment that was impossible to see beyond. She consoled herself with the knowledge that the encounter could have gone worse, but the unexpectedness of it had thrown her. Had she been prepared for seeing his face again, she could have coached herself accordingly. She could have armed herself against the feelings of regret that were now swirling mercilessly inside her, flooding her veins with anxiety. She could have warned herself to remain neutral, dispassionate. She could have employed some self-control, and prevented herself from paying too much attention to the man who had once meant the world to her, and been the only person in it who mattered.

But she hadn't had time to whisper those words of advice to herself. In the heat of the moment, she had been helpless to ignore the visible changes in Graham's appearance that had transpired since last year. He had slimmed down, whilst conversely, she had filled out to a healthier weight. His face no longer showed the haggardness that had dragged it down when they had last met, and clung onto a summer tan, which made his blue eyes appear a shade lighter. He was looking bloody good, she thought, and a stab of something that felt like forbidden attraction jabbed at her abdomen.

'Everything alright here, Angela?' Gemma asked, returning from her walk-around, her hourly check-up of the furry guys and girls that called the shelter their home. The way the older woman doted on the animals produced a warm glow in Angie's heart, and in spite of herself, she felt the tell-tale burn of it as she watched Gemma tidy up some files on her desk.

'Yes, all good here,' Angie answered, forcing a smile. She hadn't lied. It was all good. She had been shaken a little, for just a very brief moment, but the moment had passed, and she could move on, again. She was able to do that kind of thing now; she was a changed woman.

And she had been granted the answer now, to a question that she hadn't even known she had wanted to ask: she wasn't over Graham. But she had no doubt: he was finally, unequivocally, over her.

Chapter Thirty-Eight

Graham
February

'Of all the animal shelters, in all the villages ...'

Colin's tone was jovial, which was the opposite kind of response to the one that Graham had been anticipating, all the while he had been bracing himself to drop this latest bombshell. He gave his friend a stern look to admonish him for making light of his plight.

'I'm sorry, mate,' Colin replied, disregarding Graham's glare and succumbing to laughter. 'But I mean, seriously, you just couldn't make this shit up!'

Graham was miffed for a second, but Colin's giggles proved to be infectious, and he found himself joining in. It was the first time that he had allowed himself to find anything remotely humorous in the situation, but now that he was seeing it through Colin's eyes, he had to admit, there was something hilarious in the sheer ridiculousness of it all.

The men were seated in Colin's conservatory, and looked around to see Liz peering inquisitively through the window, curious about what had them buckled over.

'What do I do?' Graham asked, once both men had got the laughter out of their systems.

Colin splayed his hands in a 'who knows?' gesture.

'Beats me, mate,' he confessed. 'What are the chances of you bumping into her again? You know, assuming your days of staking out the animal shelter are over.'

'I was not staking out the shelter,' Graham replied defiantly. 'And to answer your question, I have no idea what the chances are. We didn't get around to swapping postcodes. In fact, I don't think I uttered more than ten words to her.'

'Mm-hm.' Colin eyed him suspiciously. 'And what were those words, exactly?'

'I asked if Sheila was around,' Graham replied plainly, trying to recall what he had said to Angie three days earlier. 'She told me she wasn't; that she didn't know a Sheila. So I told her I had to go, and left.'

'So let me get this straight,' Colin said, with a mischievous twinkle in his eyes. 'You've managed to scare off the only woman in the county who was willing to go out with you, and in the process of trying to track her down, you've only gone and run into the woman you never wanted to set eyes on ever again?'

'I'm glad this is all so amusing for you,' Graham answered tightly, wishing now that he had gone with his instincts and opened up to Liz instead about what had happened, as opposed to reopening an old, poisonous wound with Colin, the one person in the world who had even less inclination to share air with the former Mrs Pike than he did.

'Oh, come on, mate,' Colin rallied, offering his friend a brotherly pat on the arm. 'You know I'm only messing with you. Sheila probably didn't run away on your account. Probably.' He winked at Graham.

'Okay, here's where you are,' he carried on, adopting a serious, lawyer-like tone for the first time since Graham had shown up on his doorstep for a spur of the moment tête-à-tête. 'You've got two options,' he declared, holding up two fingers. 'One: you take a step back in time, and let her control every aspect of your life. Or two: you move on, forget about meeting her, hope you never cross paths with her again, and if you do, well, just walk away. Sound good?'

It sounded remarkably simple when Colin put it like that,

Graham had to admit. He had been procrastinating heavily for the past few days, at pains to first of all ascertain whether he had experienced any feelings of any kind when he'd seen Angie. And then, once he had acknowledged that he had, trying to analyse those feelings and determine what, if anything, he was supposed to do with them.

'She's changed,' Graham offered by way of response. He hadn't meant to say it out loud, but the words escaped as he mulled over once more that brief, but annoyingly significant five-minute period that he hadn't yet managed to put out of his mind.

'Oh yeah?' Colin asked. 'And how would you know that, having only spoken ten words to her?' There was a familiar edge to his voice, a thinly-veiled accusation, and Graham sensed that the conversation was no longer a source of humour for Colin. Rather, it seemed, the friends were veering into familiar, well-trodden territory.

Graham sighed, feeling tired already at the prospect of inviting talk of Angie back into both their lives.

'I don't know,' he answered frankly. 'I just got the feeling that she's ... different,' he said, searching for some back-up for his claim. 'She looks different for a start,' he explained, 'as though she's sorted herself out. She looks ... normal, I'd say. It took me a second to recognise her.'

'You mean she's off the booze and drugs?' Colin enquired cynically.

'I don't know,' Graham repeated. 'It certainly looks that way, but to be fair, I only saw her for a few minutes. She doesn't have that wild-eyed, wired look about her anymore. And she's volunteering, she said, at the shelter. Surely they wouldn't let her do that if she hadn't got her act together. What do you think?'

Colin paused before answering, all traces of joviality now missing from his expression as he fixed his gaze on a bee hovering outside the conservatory door.

'I don't know, mate,' he finally replied, mimicking Graham's words. 'It sounds like you've convinced yourself. Just be careful, that's all I'll say.' He stood up quickly, retrieving his and Graham's glasses from the table. 'Refill?' he asked, and Graham nodded, both to agree to another drink, and to signal his understanding that there was no currency remaining in the subject that had dominated their evening so far.

He wasn't sure what he had been expecting, but suddenly his decision to share the details of Angie's return to his sphere of consciousness revealed itself as a misguided one. Talking about it gave the event a sense of importance, of relevance, and ensured that thoughts of Angie took prominence in his mind. And he could not allow that to happen. Whether she was different now or not, she was still Angie. And his heart couldn't survive another walk down that road.

Chapter Thirty-Nine

Angie
February

She mused at the fact that she had once considered herself a 'city girl'. Surely the noisy, smoggy, twenty-four-seven life in the heart of civilisation hadn't ever really been for her?

Was there really anything better in the world than this: waking with the sunrise, to the sound of birdsong, and the answering barks of the neighbour's dogs, who were eager not to be outdone in the early-morning chorus competition by those hollow-boned little upstarts making all the racket in the trees?

If there was, Angie wasn't in a hurry to go looking for it.

The Transitional Community house that she called home, for the moment, was a haven. During her treatment, there had been times when she'd had to battle the urge to throw in the towel and make a run for it, because seeing the light at the end of the tunnel that everyone kept assuring her was there seemed like an impossible dream. Even as the rehab began to work its magic, and she began to open her mind to the possibility that there really could be hope, even for someone as shattered as she was, she had struggled to visualise what her end goal might look like.

And yet, finally, things had worked out for her. She had left the hospital with nothing more than the clothes she had arrived in and a vague sense of what was to come next. She was to get help to get back on her feet, she knew. She could go into a 'programme' they said, a word that she would have mocked and rebelled against not more than a few days earlier, but the kindness of those strangers in the hospital had shamed the cynicism out of her, and she had listened with an open mind when they had walked her through the details, painting a picture of a normal life within reach, just like she had always yearned for.

She had been scared, that was undeniable, but it was a different kind of scared than she had felt before. She had been terrified of the judgement, first and foremost, and of having to confess out loud to the things she had done to arrive at this place, to Graham, and to herself. But there was something freeing about this kind of fear, because for the first time it seemed like there could be something positive to come out it, if only she could overcome it.

They hadn't been wrong, those kind strangers, no matter how much the old Angie had tried to creep back into her head and show them up for the frauds that she thought they were. It had been far from easy to open up, to lay bare her past and relive those low points that seemed to span forever, but it had been cathartic. By the time she had felt ready to talk she had already heard from most of the other 'guests' (another word that would have elicited an eye roll from her former self), and she had realised that there was no judgement here. There was only support, and understanding. Some of the others' journeys were arguably worse than hers. Some seemed to have lived charmed lives and still managed to be lured by the demon drugs and catapulted into chaos. But in the end, it hadn't seemed to matter what reasons they had for being there. All that mattered was that they had reached the point where they needed to be there, and the only way left to go was in the right direction.

The fear of opening up had gradually given way to fear of a more logistical nature as she had begun to ponder what would come next, once her treatment was considered complete.

She had to live somewhere, when she was released from the care of the clinic, but how would she pay for accommodation, no matter how basic? Who was going to employ her, straight out of a rehab facility, with a chequered past and a conspicuous gap in her employment history?

These were the things that played on her mind, at times halting her progress and making the mountain that lay ahead of her seem insurmountable. But as the weeks passed, and the drugs and alcohol transformed from friends or crutches that had seemed so crucial in propping her up to her sworn enemies, those obstacles that had seemed so impossible to navigate became less troublesome.

The shared house was the perfect parachute for her. A welcoming place to stay, with all the structure and support she could ask for on hand; a chance to immerse herself in the real world again without bearing the brunt of the responsibility that came with it. When her application to volunteer at the shelter had been accepted, she had felt an initial rush of terror at the notion of actually being accountable to anyone else but herself. But as the news had sunk in, a sense of elation had swept over her. She had a purpose again. A reason to get out of bed in the morning.

Her first shift had passed in a flurry of ragged nerves, deep breaths, and frantic notetaking, but the sense of achievement that had come at the end of it had taken her to the verge of tears. She had felt guilty and a little embarrassed about flopping into bed that night as though she had put in a twenty-four shift in a far more hectic occupation, but the demands on her mind during those four hours that she had spent getting up to speed with how things worked at the shelter rated as highly as anything she could recall when she was a fully-fledged, full-time member of the rat race during her twenties.

That was normal, her support team reassured her. Those

of her housemates who had made the leap before her, who were on the verge of flying the nest and returning to the world in earnest, concurred. They congratulated her on taking those all-important first few steps, and asked her what she thought of it, her new 'job'. She answered them truthfully: she loved it. Granted, four hours was not a considerable amount of time in which to form an opinion on something so pivotal in her life, but that night, when she had collapsed so unceremoniously into bed, she had not brought home with her any concerns or anxieties, like she had feared she would. Sleep had come the very moment her head had made contact with her pillow, and she had awoken the following morning feeling delightfully free of the dread that had plagued her twenty-four hours earlier, when she had whipped up a storm of self-doubt inside her mind.

The time she got to spend with the animals was therapy in itself that money couldn't buy. The expectant, adoring faces of the cats and dogs made her heart melt every day, and with the unconditional love that she received from them, she was slowly rebuilding it, a day at a time.

And in Gemma, she had found an instant friend. At sixty-eight years old, and having been left a widow far too prematurely with no family to call her own, Gemma had devoted the last twenty years of her life constructing a safe place for cats, dogs, and any other four-legged creature that happened to be in need of a bed and a warm meal.

Within seconds of meeting her, Angie's nerves had calmed from a tsunami to a mild ripple. Gemma's west country accent was soft like butter and her natural demeanour was warm, understanding, and accommodating of the fact that Angie had been absent from the workplace for a significant period. Having her support had made the transition from redundant to responsible seem easy.

Having Graham pop up in her new life had caused a wobble, but the difference between the old Angie, the woman she was before, and the new Angie who woke each day with a spring in her step and an eagerness to make the most of her day, her life, was that she was now equipped to deal with such wobbles.

'Day fifty-nine,' she announced, ticking off the latest landmark on her calendar. She stepped into the shower, smiling to herself. Fifty-nine days of sobriety was a feat worthy of a smile.

Chapter Forty

Graham
March

The arrival of spring had brought with it a noticeable increase in temperature, and while it was unquestionably a bonus not to be arriving home with forearms, fingertips and shins which felt like ice to the touch after every ride, swapping the extreme cold for a perceivably warmer clime posed new challenges.

Graham dared to think himself a 'proper' cyclist now. He had treated himself to a birthday gift of a brand-new bike – a bloody expensive one, at that. It wouldn't do to carry on his training with the trusty but past-it model he had abandoned for close to fifteen years prior to its recent foray back into the fray – not if he was serious about doing well in the upcoming race. And he was. To that end, he had doled out close to a thousand pounds on his new wheels, and all the 'must-have' equipment that came with it.

He felt like a kid again; his competitive streak was all fired up and egging him on, willing him to strive for a personal best when he took to the road in six weeks' time at the event he had heard about from a colleague at work.

His sport of choice as a youngster had been swimming, but shortly after he started his university career and other interests took over, his hobby had taken a back seat, and eventually become nothing more than a rare pursuit, reserved for holidays and those rare occasions when he found the motivation to go the local leisure centre. He hadn't paid any attention to the absence of the endorphins from his life until he had really got into his groove with the cycling.

He was nailing long distances and moderate inclines for fun now, revelling in testing his limits as he went. The improvement in his cardiovascular capabilities had pleasantly surprised him, and the overall difference in his physique continually gave him cause to be proud of his achievements.

He cycled every day now, regardless of weather, time commitments or depleted energy levels. He had gone the whole hog at the cycling store, justifying the purchase of a Go Pro helmet cam along with the new bike on the basis that he lived a reasonably modest life, and if he couldn't splash out once in a while on his new passion in life, what was he going to do with his hard-earned cash?

The regrettable downside of upping his game, training-wise, was that often his outings were not suitable for canine companionship. He allowed himself to be a little selfish a few times a week, acknowledging that having Charmer for company would inevitably hold him back from reaching his maximum output, and so he designated Charmer's walks a separate pursuit, for the most part. As obedient as he was, Charmer was still a dog, and no amount of training in the world could have prevented him from foregoing the chance to sniff, greet and explore when the fancy took him. As a compromise, Graham took him along on those days when he was effectively 'resting', enjoying a leisurely cycle as opposed to a full-on training session. On those days, Graham made up their route as they went along, finding new, undiscovered spots with pleasing ease.

This evening, the late March breeze had a chill to it, and Graham was glad of the extra warmth provided by the fleece he wore on top of his cycling vest. He had found his way to Cullings Hill, a row of houses with a gradient happily conducive to free-wheeling down to the bottom, allowing him to take advantage of the respite for his legs.

He touched the brakes as he and Charmer made their way downhill, mindful of the fact that while the village may be sleepy, it wasn't devoid of cars.

It was Charmer who made the move, far too fast for Graham to stop him. He rushed to greet her as though he recognised her, veering off course and falling into an easy stride alongside her, catching her attention almost by accident as his tail swished against her while she walked.

'Oh, hello you,' Graham heard her say, as he drew closer to the pair, his mind travelling at a much faster pace than his wheels. Another fine mess Charmer had got him into, he couldn't help thinking to himself.

'Oh.' Graham watched as the recognition dawned on her face, wondering if he would have come off better or worse if he had simply carried on cycling, trusting Charmer to follow him once he had tired of the affections of the interesting stranger. 'Graham,' she confirmed out loud, looking uncomfortable as she did.

'Sorry,' he said, bringing his bike to a halt. Angie had stopped, once she'd recognised the man approaching her, and Charmer was now rolling on the ground at her ankles, appealing for his belly to be rubbed. 'He thinks he's God's gift,' Graham explained. 'Can't see a woman pass by without putting on a show.'

Angie smiled uncertainly. Her demeanour was in stark contrast to their chance meeting at the shelter, it occurred to Graham. She appeared cornered, anxious even, making him feel bad for her. She offered no reply, but made a half-hearted gesture to stroke Charmer as he writhed around in expectation.

'I suppose it was bound to happen, eventually,' Graham said, voicing the sentiment that was flowing around inside his head. 'I mean, seeing as you're working around here now.' He hadn't intended the negative inflection in his voice, but now that he heard himself speak it was unmistakable.

'I suppose,' Angie answered, deliberately ensuring that the path her eyes followed didn't reach Graham's.

'I didn't appreciate quite how small this village is,' she conceded, with a hint of a smile attempting to play at her lips. 'I actually didn't expect us to run into each other again.'

There was no indication of how she felt about their second chance encounter that Graham was able to detect, but he was very aware of the fact that she was going out of her way to avoid making eye contact.

'Yeah well,' Graham started, 'I wouldn't have realised it was you, to be honest.' He looked to Charmer to indicate that the dog was the guilty party. 'You look different,' he told her, wondering at his willingness to prolong the conversation. His first instinct had been to make his apologies for the ambush and speed home, but it had passed unheeded, and appeared to have been replaced with a desire to keep her here, keep her talking.

His comment prompted her to look directly at him for the first time, and he was struck again by the change in her. There was less distance between them now than there had been at the shelter, and this time he could see her eyes clearly. If she wasn't clean and sober, then he was David Beckham, he thought to himself. Her eyes, her skin, her hair were no longer those of a person whose body was ravaged by drink and drugs. He had borne witness to her disturbing, concerning physical transformation enough times to appreciate that he was viewing a marked improvement, and a once-familiar feeling of gravitation threatened to make a nuisance of itself.

He made himself look away, as though her eyes carried a power. They had, once. They had captivated him and altered him from the master of his own fate to a man condemned to a life of servility. The spell had been broken, however, eventually, and Graham would be wise to keep his wits about him to make sure that he didn't fall victim to it again.

'I feel different,' Angie replied, her posture relaxing a little, her stance a little more open than it had been a moment earlier. 'I am different,' she added, more quietly. She moved her eyes towards Charmer again, who was evidently frustrated at the lack of attention he was receiving from either of the two awkward adults standing over him. She took a breath as though she was about to carry on, but seemed to think better of it, and an awkward silence ensued, with only Charmer's impatient whines shattering it intermittently.

There were questions swirling around inside Graham's head. He wanted to know what had happened to her, in the intervening months since she'd hit rock bottom; he wanted to ask how she had managed to seemingly get her life back on track, and what she was doing in Elham, living there, working there.

But the answers were none of his business. What good would it do, to know those things? The fact was, they were now part of the same small community, and with the best will in the world, it seemed unlikely that they would be able to avoid each other.

They were both adults. Angie, for her part, certainly bore no resemblance to the clingy, dependent person that he knew of old. If and when fate masterminded a further crossing of paths, they were surely mature enough to exchange civil smiles and go on with their business.

'Wow,' Graham said with a loud exhale. 'It really is a small world, eh?'

'It really is,' Angie returned, with a reserved smile.

'Enjoy your evening,' Graham offered, signalling to Charmer that their jaunt was about to re-commence.

Angie didn't answer, but even if she had, Graham would not have heard. He sped off almost at his racing pace, only slowing down when his lungs felt fit to burst. Charmer proved himself to be a more able athlete than his two-legged companion, at least over the short distance they had covered, and exuded an air of disappointment when Graham gave in to the build-up of lactic acid in his legs and carried on their journey home at a crawl.

Chapter Forty-One

Angie
March

'Angela, could I have a word with you for a moment, in the office?'

It was quarter to eight, and Angie was within touching distance of the end of her Thursday shift. On Thursdays the shelter stayed open later than any other day of the week, and there had been a steady stream of visitors since Angie had clocked in at twelve. Two of the families who had come in earlier were potential success stories in the making: a charming young couple with an adorable seven-year-old son had their eye set on Jasper, a grumpy but loveable ginger Tom who had been looking for his forever home for too long, and a mother and daughter had been spellbound by Wisdom, a gorgeous, remarkably chilled out German Shepherd whose beauty and placid nature had all but secured her a new home within only a fortnight of her being surrendered to the charity due to the death of her owner. All that was left to do was for the obligatory home visits to be carried out, and providing no concerns were uncovered, there would be two vacant beds in a few days.

Angie told herself not to fret at Gemma's request. There was nothing in the woman's tone to imply that there was any reason to fear following her into the office, but her turn of phrase invoked memories of many painful conversations that she had endured in the past.

In the months before her last employer had finally exhausted all attempts at reconciliation and 'released' her, she had lost count of the number of times that this boss or that Human Resources representative had asked if they could have a word with her.

She whispered a little prayer that this time wasn't going to turn out the way of those others, reassuring herself that she had done everything by the book in the eight weeks since she'd started out in her new post. She had been punctual, and productive, and entirely compliant with the rules which Gemma had laid down as a matter of course upon her commencement of the role.

'Have a seat,' Gemma instructed, taking a seat behind her computer as Angie came into the small room a few seconds behind her. Her smile offered Angie some hope.

Gemma battered away at her keyboard for a few seconds after Angie sat down, leaving Angie to grow ever more anxious about the nature of the meeting.

'Sorry,' Gemma said eventually, turning to face Angie once her business on the computer had been concluded. 'I just wanted to finish typing up those notes from earlier, while the details are still fresh in my mind.'

'No problem,' Angie replied, her voice croaky with trepidation.

'Anyway,' Gemma carried on, 'the reason I asked you in is that I wanted to talk to you about how you feel things are going, seeing as you've been here two months now.'

Angie felt her pulse increase a little, and the realisation of just how important her work at the shelter was to her slammed into her like a ton of bricks. She had so far managed to shield herself from the inherent pessimism that used to plague her mind to the point that she hadn't even once considered the possibility that her time here might come to an end, not of her own volition, and now that Gemma felt the need to have a discussion about her placement, she was forced to acknowledge that coming to work every day had become her number one pleasure in life.

Gemma seemed to decipher the fear in her features, and broke into a soft chuckle.

'Don't look so worried,' she said, reaching out her hand and briefly covering Angie's in a comforting gesture. 'There's nothing to be concerned about, my love,' she added, in a voice used often with the animals she cared so deeply for. 'I just wanted to ask you how you're finding it, whether you're happy here, that's all.'

Angie crumpled with relief and returned Gemma's smile. 'Oh, yes,' she enthused, 'I'm happier than I've been in a long time. I thought for a moment there I might have done something wrong, and I was terrified you might be calling me in here to tell me to sling my hook.'

Gemma shook her head and waved away Angie's concerns. 'Not at all, my love,' she assured her. 'You've been an absolute boon to have around the place. The animals love you, the visitors love you, and to tell you the honest truth, I wouldn't be without you now, my dear.'

Gemma squeezed her hand affectionately, and Angie's eyes filled with tears.

'Oh, I'm so glad to hear you say that, Gemma,' she replied, crying with relief. 'I absolutely love working here. And I can't thank you enough for giving me a chance.' Gemma held out a box of tissues and she took one, and wiped her face. 'I don't want to let you down.'

Gemma shook her head to dismiss the insinuation. 'Don't be silly, my love,' she assured her. 'Everything you've done so far has been tip-top; I don't think the place has ever run so smoothly.'

An alien sensation burned in Angie's chest, and she realised that it was pride. Pride in doing a good job, and being appreciated for it. A feeling she had known only fleetingly, as a child, and had given up hope of ever experiencing again.

'In fact,' Gemma continued, 'I was wondering if maybe you would be able to stretch to a few extra hours of a week. It doesn't have to be full time, if that doesn't suit. But what would you say to a few more full day shifts to start off with; see how you go?'

Fighting off the doubts of old that took over for a second, Angie answered enthusiastically in the affirmative, before she had the chance to change her mind. 'That sounds wonderful,' she told Gemma. 'I'd be delighted to do some extra shifts, just as many as you need.'

'Lovely,' Gemma answered with a smile. 'I'll get working on a new rota then, my love.'

Angie gathered her coat and handbag from her locker, and bid Gemma a fond farewell for the night.

The pride still simmering inside her chest warmed her sufficiently that decided she could forego wearing her coat for the short walk home, and she wished there was a way to bottle this feeling, so that she could access it again and again.

Chapter Forty-Two

Graham
April

This was no good. No good at all.

Everywhere he walked, or cycled, he thought he saw her. When he thought it was her, his heart did something that it had been forbidden from doing, ignoring the command to shut down. When he realised that it was someone else, he felt a little tug of disappointment – again, unauthorised, but what could he do to prevent it?

The inevitability of them running into each other again at some point had irked him initially, but as the weeks went on and the real Angie was nowhere to be seen (in spite of many false alarms) what began to irk him was, in fact, not bumping into her.

Only because there was unfinished business between them, he told himself. Only because there was so much water under the bridge that recently he had felt that it had come to encroach on the very structure itself, and the bridge was in danger of falling down under the pressure.

The only way forward was to orchestrate a meeting. He would insist that the two of them meet, to sit down and talk; to lay all their cards on the table, and finally lay to rest all that had gone between them in the past. That way, if they did happen to cross paths accidentally thereafter, there would be no awkwardness, no underlying tension caused by words left unsaid. They could smile and nod, and carry on along their way, merely two people who had once known each other but now had no place for the other in their life. Nor in their heart.

He could find her at the shelter, he assumed with some confidence, which was probably the more sensible option than skulking around Cullings Hill of an evening, waiting for her to materialise. He gave some thought to creating a cover story relating to Charmer, but the dog was good as gold and fit as a fiddle, and he didn't want to tempt fate by making something up to insinuate that either was not the case, just to create an excuse to visit his previous dwellings.

He concluded that it wouldn't do any harm for him to be direct about why he was visiting. All he wanted was some of her time, a conversation, a chance to thrash out all the lingering hows and whys, and reach a place that was as close to peace as they ever were likely to get. One sticking point was that he had no idea what shift patterns she would be working, and the shelter was not realistically on any of the routes he had cause to travel of a day. He would have to take a guess, based on nothing but gut instinct, and if his guess happened to be wrong he supposed that he could enquire innocently enough with the older woman who worked there – the one who had accompanied Sheila to his home to assess his suitability as an adoptive dad for Charmer.

He was an old friend, he would tell her, which was not so far from the truth that he would feel bad about misleading the woman. He hadn't had the presence of mind to take note of an address or a phone number the last time they had met, he would explain, but Angie had mentioned that she worked at the shelter, and he had popped in on the off chance that she might be there. Yes, that would work, he concluded.

He opted to take the car, feeling hopeful that if Angie were there, she would accept his offer of a lift to the nearest café, where they could iron out their dealings in neutral surroundings. He second-guessed himself as he opened the door and sat down, wondering if perhaps arriving on four wheels was being a little presumptuous and may make her feel under pressure, but he reminded himself that no matter how altered she appeared, the Angie of old was still in there, somewhere. And the Angie of old would have no qualms about telling him where to go if she had any objections to going along with his proposal.

He felt a small smile tug at his lips as he thought back to some of the occasions when Angie's strong will had presented itself when they were together, and quickly shut it down. He was going to set those residual feelings free, he reminded himself. He was on a mission to get her out of his system for good, and enjoying memories of the woman she used to be was not conducive to succeeding in that mission.

He offered a rueful smile to Charmer, who stared mournfully at him from the living room window, visibly puzzled at Graham's foray into the outside world without him, out-with the usual schedule. Both were creatures of habit, and tonight Graham was breaking his habit – and Charmer's heart, a little bit – by foregoing his 'easy' cycle and planning a different evening entirely.

Within ten minutes he was outside the shelter, and he parked where he thought he had the best chance of seeing who was inside. It was gone half past six, and there were no other cars in the car park, but he could see that the lights were still on in the reception area, and the shutter that protected the windows and front door had not yet been pulled down for the night.

Now that he was here, and the prospect of seeing her again loomed, he experienced another attack of doubt. Why the hell was he allowing himself to set off down this road again? Why couldn't he just be a normal person, and commit her to the dark recesses in the back of his mind, whether she lived within a five-mile radius of him or not? He pacified himself with the notion that this would be the final time –

after tonight, all the questions would be answered, and the closure that was within reach would see him released from his emotional prison.

He got out of the car just as she made her way out of the shelter, and they locked eyes. This time, he noticed, hers didn't immediately dart away.

'You know, I can't explain it, but somehow I thought you might be here,' she told him, with a weak smile and a tone of resignation.

'I thought we should talk,' Graham answered, taking a step closer. 'There's a café in Elham that's open until nine, we could go there if you fancy.'

Angie gave another tepid smile. 'I'm not sure a café is the best place to talk about the things we're going to talk about, wouldn't you say?'

'Good point,' Graham conceded, echoing her logic. In his mind, he had anticipated that this was going to go smoothly, flawlessly, and once it was done, each of them would go their separate ways with a lightness of heart and a glow of achievement. But now that he was standing there, contemplating what was about to be discussed, he knew it would be anything but rosy. It was bound to be messy, and Angie was right – a public place was not the right setting for them to air their dirty laundry.

'We could go for a walk?' he suggested. 'Or a drive?'

Angie raised her eyes skywards. 'I don't like the look of that,' she announced, gesturing towards the grey, menacing-looking clouds. 'A drive sounds good. If you don't mind?'

'Not at all,' Graham answered, glad that she had gone along with his preferred option. If they talked while he drove, he didn't have the option to look at her. And he suspected that keeping his eyes away from her might be an advantage in dealing with what was to come next, which had taken on a lot more significance in the last few moments than it had when he had foreseen it.

212

Neither one of them was tempted to make small talk, and the silence that filled the car while Graham navigated the narrow roads transported him back to the suffocating hush that had dominated the final few years of their marriage, depressing his mood. He had somehow expected her to take the lead, to start pouring out explanations and answering his questions that he felt he shouldn't even need to ask, but now he realised that had been unrealistic. This had been his idea. It was he who had the desire to 'get everything out in the open', and destroy the baggage that was still dragging both of them down. He would need to kick things off. He would need to unload the weight off his chest, and hope that Angie didn't stonewall him, didn't shut down the way she used to do, making him feel like he didn't exist.

Chapter Forty-Three

Angie
April

It was just like that day all over again. That miserable, stressful, life-shattering day when she had woken up feeling as though her world was about to implode. And she had been right. And this morning, that sickeningly familiar feeling had woken her, taking her breath away like a punch to the abdomen.

She had started to suspect that the day would come, in recent weeks. She knew Graham, and she could tell when they had run into each other that last time that he had been holding back, deliberately avoiding flinging himself down the rabbit hole, conscious of the wounds it would re-open. But he had wanted to, she could sense it. There was an inevitability about them one day peeling back all the layers and discussing the nitty gritty of the years that had shaped both their lives so dramatically. And that day had arrived. It scared her a little, the accuracy with which her sixth sense could pick up on impending doom, and when she had stepped out of the shelter to see him there, impatient and uncertain, she had felt that same heavy lump as before inside her chest again.

There was so much to say that she almost regretted her decision to suggest that they enclose themselves inside the car; she wasn't sure if the vehicle had the space or the suspension to hold what was sure to come flowing out, once the dam was burst.

She stole a furtive glance at Graham and noticed that, for all he was staunchly concentrating on the road ahead of him, the same impatience that she'd spotted when he saw her coming out of the shelter was there. His pulse was visible in his neck, clearly operating at a higher speed than it normally would. She averted her eyes quickly, but in her peripheral vision she was sure she caught him opening his mouth as though to speak, but putting whatever it was he was about to say on hold.

It would be down to her, she knew, to initiate the proceedings.

'Can you pull over?' she asked, knowing that it wouldn't do to have Graham focused on his task of driving while she was imparting her truths, her excuses.

She thought she saw him relax a little at this, as though he had simply been waiting for the signal. He nodded, and when he found a suitable place to stop, he pulled over and cut the engine. He sat back in his chair, staring at the console in front of him rather than at Angie.

Where to start?

'My dad died.'

Graham blurted out the news before she had the chance to decide on what she would broach first. Instinctively, her hands covered her mouth. 'Oh, Gray,' she said softly, a wave of sadness washing over her as she absorbed the words. 'When?'

'Christmas Eve.' He looked at her now, his eyes mournful, and she rested her hand on his arm.

'I'm so sorry,' she told him. 'He was a wonderful man. I'm so sorry.'

Graham nodded, and turned his head again, to look out of the driver's side window. Angie retrieved her hand and wondered how best to proceed. The air inside the car was now clogged with grief, and there was no obvious segue

215

onto the recounting of much less significant history, by comparison.

'How is your mum doing?' She had once loved Pamela like a mother, but couldn't bring herself to say the woman's name. It was as though, along with all rights she had ever had to Graham and his heart, she had lost the right to hold his mother in her affections.

'She's getting by, you know,' Graham answered, his gaze fixed on a spot outside the car. The rain that Angie had predicted had made an appearance, and Graham seemed mesmerised by the droplets that were finding their resting place on the glass.

Angie almost said, 'Send her my love,' a phrase that fondly reminded her of her grandmother, but again, it just wasn't right to say such a thing. Would Graham have told his mum that he had met her, that she was living in the same area as them now? Probably not, she decided. He certainly would not have filled her in on his plans for this evening. For a few years Angie had been a partner to be proud of, the woman Graham had introduced to his parents as 'the one'. But not now. Not for a long time. Now, she was exactly what she had been for most of her life – someone's dirty secret.

She felt a tug at her heart as she imagined Graham compartmentalising his mind, separating out everything that was good and everything that deserved to be hidden away, reminding himself that this current association with her was to be filed under 'Things that no one can ever know'. It made her feel hurt, and angry, and for a second she thought she might revert to type and do a runner, taking off at speed while Graham was lost in his solemn thoughts, proving to them both that no matter how different she may look on the outside, she was still the same, disappointing Angie that had unmasked herself when her own dirty secret had been so dramatically unearthed. She got so far as to touch her hand against the door handle and stopped. She wasn't the same Angie as before. Yes, she had done some awful, hurtful things to the man sitting beside her, and she could beg forgiveness from him for the rest of her life and still not reasonably expect to receive it, but by God, she had been through the mill herself, hadn't she! For every ounce of pain that Graham undoubtedly carried around with him, she carried double, and she couldn't ignore the fact that she had been nothing more than a child when she had endured the lion's share of her suffering. She felt her cheeks begin to flush as a kaleidoscope of memories flashed before her eyes, and suddenly the need to stay, and explain herself – and for once in her life, defend herself – was a hundred times more powerful than the need to run, and hide away once more. Suddenly the need to cleanse herself of the weight of the world that she supported on her shoulders every day of her life was the most powerful force in her body, and she threw decorum out of the window and grabbed Graham by the shoulder, forcing him to twist to his left and look at her.

'You're the one who wanted to talk, Graham,' she said accusingly, taking him by surprise not least for addressing him by his proper name. 'So, I'm here, and we're alone. Let's talk.'

Chapter Forty-Four

Graham
April

He was stunned by the sudden shift in atmosphere, but the surprise was quickly superseded by a flare of anger, and words began to flow out.

'Yeah, you're right,' he answered, matching her tone, 'I did want to talk. If I'm honest, I wanted an explanation. I wanted to know how come you just happened to turn up here, a stone's throw from my new place, looking like the picture of fucking health and serenity, considering the last time I saw you, you'd just tried to top yourself.' He shifted in his seat, facing her full on now. 'I wanted to know why all the years that I put in, being there for you, trying to help you, trying just to fucking reach you, meant absolutely nothing to you. I wanted to know where's the justice in you getting to live your happy little life now, when you've ruined every chance at happiness I've ever had?'

He felt exhausted when he stopped talking and reclined against the chair. He hadn't planned it this way – not at all. Angie was supposed to proactively offer her explanations, and her apologies, and he was supposed to be the gracious, understanding man that he was and accept them and agree to move on. He hadn't planned to erupt, and he certainly hadn't expected to hear the words that had come out in his voice. But they had been in there, festering inside of him like toxic waste, and now they were out, and he was unable to take them back. And in truth, he didn't think he wanted to. Those thoughts had been in there for a reason. He had been the cuckold, the put-upon one for so long, repressing anger, and disgust, and hurt, and those emotions had to go somewhere. And it was evident now, where they had gone. And it felt like a release to have finally set them free.

Angie recoiled slightly but recovered. 'You're right,' she said softly. 'When you last saw me, I had just tried to take my own life. Do you understand what that means, Graham?'

He didn't answer, but with those words it felt like she had just rendered his entire rant, and the reasons behind it, completely irrelevant.

'I wanted to die. I literally didn't want to be here anymore; I couldn't take the pain anymore. There was nothing left for me when you cut me off. You were the only person in the world who gave a shit whether I was alive or dead, and then you didn't. And I thought, what's the point?'

Graham had developed a thick skin over the years, a necessity when trying to mitigate Angie's behaviour, but what she had just said sliced through his toughened armour with the ease of a knife piercing the skin of a freshly baked potato.

There were tears forming in her eyes, he noticed, and he felt a familiar sting in his own.

'I didn't do it for attention, Gray,' she added, slipping unwittingly back into the informal. 'I didn't do it to hurt you.' She stopped talking through sheer necessity, as her tears suddenly took over, and Graham felt like he would volunteer to fall through a crack in the earth if one happened to appear below him.

'I know,' he managed, his voice strangled with emotion.

'No, I don't think you do, Gray,' Angie answered indignantly. 'I know that it finally got too much for you, that one day you snapped, and cut me out of your life. And if I'm honest, I don't blame you. I did make it hard for you, you're right, of course I did. I took it out on you, and I knew I was doing it, but I couldn't stop. I couldn't help myself. But what I did that night wasn't some twisted, misguided cry for help. It wasn't just another way for me to get you to come running to me, like you always had in the past.' She looked straight at him, her eyes piercing his skin. 'I was ready to die. I wanted to die.'

It was Graham's turn to cry now, and he used his right hand to wipe away the tears that were now threatening to stream all the way down his cheeks.

'But I couldn't even get that right,' Angie added, with a humourless laugh. 'And when I woke up that day, the first thought that hit me was, "Just my luck!" Pulling through was the worst thing that could have possibly happened to me.' She paused for a moment, trying to compose herself, evidently recalling the emotional turmoil of the experience she had just described. 'But when the nurses came in, and the doctor, and they were so lovely to me ... Me! All fussing and fawning, checking me over, asking me how I felt, telling me how lucky I was that I had been found in time. And at first, I hated them for it. I blamed them for bringing me back to that, that ... hell. But they didn't give up. And they were all just so bloody nice. They wore me down with their kindness, and all of a sudden, I thought maybe surviving wasn't so bad, after all.' She waved her finger at Graham in warning. 'And don't think I don't know how pathetic that sounds, Gray, because I bloody do, but for the first time in so long, there were these people, these strangers, calling me "Love", and treating me kindly, and taking care of me. They weren't looking at me and seeing Angie the drunk, Angie the junkie, Angie the loser. Or maybe they were, underneath, but the point is, they didn't make me feel like I was any of those things, anymore. They made me feel like the person who had regained consciousness was a new me, a different me; I was someone worth saving, someone worth taking care of.'

Graham wanted to dive in and tell her that she had always been that person worth saving, as far as he was concerned. He wanted to remind her that he had tried, that he had wanted so badly to be the one who looked after her, who soothed her pain once he had found out that it lived inside of her. He wanted to sit forward in his seat and grab hold of her shoulders and shake her and force her to address the fact that if she had only permitted him, he would have been the one to make her understand that it was worth carrying on, that her life, and their marriage, were things that were worth fighting for.

The emotions that were swirling around inside him were making him feel almost light-headed. The gravity of her plight, the fact that she had seen only one, dark, final move ahead of her after he had turned his back on her made him feel like the worst person in the world. But how could she sit there and make it sound as though those doctors and nurses were the only people to have ever offered her a kind word, a comforting look? Hadn't he devoted two years to trying to dig his way back under her skin again, after she had cast him out like he was some kind of parasite? Hadn't he repeatedly explained to her that no matter what had happened to her in the previous life that she had suffered through before she had met him, he wouldn't let that come between them, wouldn't stop loving her? Had he imagined those months of hell, when he had felt as though he was beating his head against a brick wall, offering her anything and everything he could give, anything and everything he could think of, only to be rewarded by her cold shoulder, her silence, and eventually her stooping as far as to invite another man into their bed when he was at work?

He suddenly needed air, and opened the car door urgently, making Angie jump in fright. It didn't matter to him that it was now raining quite heavily – he was actually glad of the cool drops of water on his skin, which felt as though it was on fire. He paced for a moment, clenching and unclenching his fists, reasoning with himself. Only a few moments ago, he had been in tears, desperately moved by the hopelessness that Angie had described. But in a matter of seconds, she had trodden all over his sympathy, exactly the way she had done that day when he had visited her at the hospital.

He turned to look inside the car and saw that Angie hadn't moved a muscle. She was staring ahead, her body rigid as though she were posing for a portrait. The droplets of water on the window made it hard for him to make out whether she was still crying or not, but her stillness made him mad.

'Why?' he demanded, re-entering the car with another sudden burst of movement that made Angie flinch once more. 'Why did you listen to them, but not me?'

Angie's head seemed to turn towards him in slow motion, and he experienced a flashback to the times when she had been so doped up that she could barely recognise him.

'What?'

'You just said that those strangers made you feel like you were worth saving. But what about me? What about when I told you that you were still my wife, no matter what that fucking scum did to you, and that nothing would come between us? What about when I begged you to see a doctor, or get counselling, or talk to me? Why didn't you listen to me, then? Why didn't you let me help you?'

Angie made a face, and let out a scornful laugh, and once again Graham was transported back to the dark days, when everything he said or did was met with a similar response from her.

'You always were such an idealist, Gray,' she said mockingly, shaking her head as she spoke. 'Did you honestly think that things could have just gone back to normal, after what I told you? No chance. You would have tried, of course you would, but it would never have been the same. You would never have looked at me the same way again; you never have.'

'Because you shut me out!' Graham yelled, raising his voice for the first time. It sounded even louder than he had intended in the cramped space. 'You never gave me the chance to go back to normal; you just decided for both of us that it was over, and how would you even know how I looked at you, when you never so much as gave me the courtesy of eye contact for the next two years?'

'You don't understand,' Angie said coolly.

'You're fucking right, I don't understand,' Graham concurred, his voice thundering around inside the car. 'I don't understand how one minute, I'm supposedly the love of your life, and then the next, I'm no better than that, that ... monster. Because that's how you made me feel, Angie.' His voice broke with hurt. 'You made me feel like I was dirt on the bottom of your shoe, the way you treated me.'

'You know that's not true,' Angie insisted, her tears making a return. 'I never thought of you like that.'

'Oh no?' Graham asked. 'Well if that's true, why didn't you want to have kids with me?'

'I told you why,' Angie answered after a long pause, looking panicked for the first time.

'No, what you told me was a bullshit story, and you know it. What was the real reason, Ange?'

She dropped her eyes to her lap.

'I'll tell you the real reason, shall I?' Graham continued, not willing to wait for her answer, 'because I worked it out a long time ago, let me tell you. You didn't want us to have kids because you thought ...' His voice tailed off, and he needed a second attempt to get the words out. 'You didn't want to have a kid because you didn't know if you could trust me not to hurt them the way he hurt you. I'm right, aren't I?'

Angie didn't speak, but when she lifted her head and looked at him, he knew he had struck the right chord, and it hurt him like the heel of a hand being thrust forcibly into his chest.

'You didn't trust me not to do to our kids what he did to you. I'm right, aren't I?' He shook his head in disbelief, as though he was being presented with the notion for the first time. In truth, the suspicion had lurked inside his mind for years like a cancer, a question that he had never wanted to know the answer to. And now he did know, and the truth felt worse than he could ever have predicted it would feel. 'So, don't tell me you never thought of me like that,' he said in a solemn voice, 'because we both know that's just another lie, in the big, long list of lies that you've told me over the years.'

He put his face in his hands, leaning forward, almost resting on the steering wheel. He let the tears run free this time, catching some and letting the rest slide down his fingers.

For several long minutes, the only sound in the car was Graham's sobbing. It was a relief, in a sense, to finally have voiced the suspicion that he had suppressed for so long, but to have it confirmed had triggered feelings of such agony that he just couldn't hold back the sobs that made his whole body tremor with emotion.

'I'm sorry.' Angie's voice was croaky when she eventually broke the hiatus, as though she had just awoken from sleep. 'I'm so sorry, Gray.'

Graham's hands remained covering his face, but his crying seemed to have abated. Angie placed her hand softly on his back, only for a fraction of a second, then opened the door and got out of the car.

Chapter Forty-Five

Angie
April

She realised she had absolutely no idea where she was, and with the rain now being driven by the force of quite a hefty gale, visibility wasn't conducive to finding anything remotely familiar that she could use as a landmark to guide her home. She began to feel disorientated and slightly panicked as she walked, dressed unsuitably for the downpour, clutching her denim jacket close to her chest and trying to keep her face downwards to avoid the rain attacking her eyes.

The noise of the wind and the anxiety that flared in her bloodstream sent her mind careering back to that night, when she had finally managed to end the nightmare of her youth and set herself free, or so she thought. She tried to transport herself there fully, suddenly desperate to remember whether she had harboured even the slightest inkling at that time that her life might turn out the way it had. Had she really run through the wind and rain that night, her limbs aching, her lungs burning with lactic acid, with only hope and determination in her heart, and that treasured photo of her parents in her pocket? Her memory wasn't the most reliable, but she suspected that she had. She could remember the feeling of relief, like having a tumour the size of her brain removed as she realised she was out of reach. She could remember the moment when she allowed herself to stop running and slumped down to the ground as though she had completed a marathon, and retrieved the photo from her pocket and wept, thanking her parents for giving her the strength to go through with it, finally. She could remember all too vividly the fear and paranoia that stalked her for months afterwards, as she projected his face onto every man in the street, expecting him to crash into her every time she turned a corner. But had she really never envisaged exactly how it might all end up; had she never considered that setting herself free didn't mean she was guaranteed a happy ending? She decided that she hadn't. She had taken her one and only chance to run, and she had succeeded. She had dreamed only of making a brand new life for herself, of shedding the old skin that felt disgustingly unclean and reinventing herself as a woman she herself had never met before. She had been so focused on immersing herself in a new world, housed in a new body, that she hadn't considered what would happen when her new skin was breached, or sullied like the old stuff. Not until she had created a life that was built entirely on lies had she begun to understand the precariousness of it, the strain involved in trying to satisfy the demands she had placed on herself as a distraught yet hopeful teenager.

She remembered with powerful clarity the feeling of wanting him dead, of wishing every day of her life that some tragedy or illness would befall him, and when that day came, she would finally be free of him, for good. But that day hadn't come quick enough. And when it did, finally, while she was in the final stages of her rehab programme, the damage had been done sufficiently that it could never be erased. When she had found out, she had tried so hard to locate the child inside of her, to let her share in the sense of justice, finally, but she had found that the child no longer existed. Sure, her pain, her trauma still lived on in Angie's soul, but when she dug deep inside to tell her younger self that it was all over, that the man who blighted her life no longer had one to call his own, she had found that the girl was gone. There was no sense of victory, no sensation of watershed, or breakthrough. The news of his death simply hovered at the edge of her adult mind, serving as a reminder that now, at least, she would never have to fear coming face to face with him ever again.

Freedom from him was like the happiness she had once fooled herself that she would one day find – unobtainable. She would never truly be free of him, and in her recent sober months she had come to attribute some – if not all – of her unsavoury behaviour to the self-loathing that had built up as she strove to find a way to punish herself for being so stupid as to think that she could.

But freedom from her was now within Graham's reach, she knew, and as she walked, she silently pleaded for him to grab it with both hands. She added yet another failure to her list, that of failing to realise that he had known all along, it seemed, about her shameful fear of having a child with him, and her stomach did an unpleasant flip as she recalled every word he had spat at her in the car. And yet, as horrifying as it was that the truth of the matter had finally been laid bare, the good that would come out of it was that the rollercoaster they had been clinging onto for so long was finally coming to a halt. There was nothing left for Graham to know now. There was nothing left of their relationship to pick at – even the bones had disintegrated to dust as he had let out the grief that he felt for the children he could have had, had he chosen a better woman than her.

She stopped walking, her lungs on fire just as they had been that night, her face numbed by the harsh wind. The similarities to that night were startling as the sky continued to darken, but she took a moment to stand still and listen carefully, and in the howl of the wind she could hear her own voice, barely more than a child: 'You don't have to run anymore.'

227

Chapter Forty-Six

Graham
April

What once would have been a hard decision for him, and one that would have left him wracked with guilt afterwards, was easy and regret-free in the moments after Angie had left the car. He hadn't looked up when she had got out, and by the time he did, he had no idea where she had gone or how much time had passed since she had thrown in the towel and run, again.

It was raining heavily, and light was fading fast, and he could have spent hours out there looking for her, calling for her, chasing after her like the doormat he had allowed himself to be, but the momentary tug at his conscience came and went as though it had never actually happened.

He started the car at the second attempt, momentarily so disorientated that he completely forgot the requirement to depress the clutch before turning the key on his first try, and pulled off with such ferocity that his back slammed against the chair as the car responded with gusto to his aggressive acceleration.

He banished thoughts of her from his mind, concentrating his energy on trying to determine where he was, and how to get home. He was super-charged with negative energy, yelling and swearing at the rain, the windscreen wipers that were not living up to his expectations, the potholes that were peppered all over the roads. By the time he reached home, he had barely any memory of getting there, as though he had been in a trance and operated the whole way on auto-pilot, his limbs doing the work while his brain took a well-earned rest.

Charmer greeted him with enthusiasm and affection that made him start to cry again, and he slumped to the floor and hugged the dog for several minutes, overwhelmed with gratitude for the love the dog radiated from his little body. Eventually Charmer began to indicate that he was hungry, and Graham dutifully followed him through to the kitchen and laid out his meal with a slightly larger topping of dry food than usual, by way of a thank you for his faithful friend's tireless support.

He padded into the bedroom, hearing his mother's voice in his head telling him not to shuffle, but he didn't have the energy to walk without making scuffing noises on the laminate flooring.

He removed his jacket gingerly, the strain in his shoulders making it a painful movement, as though he had been beaten up and every inch of him hurt when he moved. He had been beaten up, he thought. He'd had his heart broken long ago, and he'd been stupid and sadistic enough to go along and volunteer to have what was left of it trampled on.

He sat down on the edge of the bed and let the top half of his body tip backwards until he was horizontal, staring up at the ceiling. 'Be careful what you wish for' was a phrase that an annoying old boss of his used to use, and Graham could hear his voice now, gloating. Graham could only take it on the chin. He had 'wished' for answers, and now that he had them, well, his boss had been an arsehole of epic proportions, but he'd made a good point.

Graham closed his eyes, weary from the crying that had taken him by surprise in its intensity, and drifted off, trying but failing to shift the images that kept appearing as he dozed, images of the children that he would have loved to have had.

Chapter Forty-Seven

Angie
July

'Oh, I knew this day was coming, but it doesn't make it any easier. I shall be so sorry not to have you around, my love.'

Gemma wrapped Angie in a hug that made Angie well up once more, after she had only just managed to clear her last round of tears.

'Oh, I'm going to miss you so much, Gem,' Angie reciprocated, teetering dangerously close to putting a halt to her grand plans and staying put, where Gemma and the animals had made her feel, for once, like she truly belonged. 'And your parents couldn't have named you better – you truly are a gem.'

'Oh, don't,' Gemma pleaded, batting her away. 'You'll get me started again.'

Angie smiled, and took a long look around the office. 'I'd better be off then,' she said, and Gemma could only nod as she had, as she'd predicted, started to cry again. Loath to drag the sad situation out any longer, Angie picked up her holdall containing everything she was taking with her. 'I'll see you soon,' she told Gemma, and headed outside to the cab that had been waiting for her to complete her goodbyes for over seven minutes.

'Sorry about the wait,' she told the driver, who nodded grumpily and didn't offer to help with her bag.

'Where to?' he asked, once she had entered the car and

fastened her seatbelt.

'Heathrow, please,' she answered, checking in the zip compartment of her bag one more time to make sure her passport was definitely there. It was.

Chapter Forty-Eight

Graham
July

'Can I open my eyes now?'

'Not yet, not yet!' Jenna yelled excitedly, her enthusiasm making her dig her fingers a little harder into Graham's eyelids.

'Ow, ease up there just a little,' he said, reaching up and releasing her grip.

'Okay, now you can look!' Jenna pulled her hands away and Graham opened his eyes gratefully, having been forcefully blinded for the last several minutes. Now that he could see what the cloak and dagger method and fuss had been about, he felt that his ordeal was entirely worth it.

'Oh wow!' he gushed, mirroring Jenna's ecstatic smile. 'Who is this little guy? Or girl?'

The dog hadn't needed any encouragement to come to him, and was investigating the new person in the room with the same level of energy as Jenna, who was literally bouncing up and down with excitement.

'This is Bear,' she told Graham, ceasing to jump and kneeling down beside the hyperactive Toy Poodle whose tail was thumping off the floor so hard it sounded like someone beating drum. 'He's six. We got him from Dogs Trust three weeks ago; we adopted him. Isn't he gorgeous? His jaw sticks out a bit, and that's why he was at the shelter for so long, because no one wanted him, but he's totally fine, and we don't even care about his jaw, do we Mummy?'

She looked to Liz, who wore a broad smile and shook her head. 'No darling, we don't care about that.'

'That's right, because we love him just as he is,' Jenna said, scooping the tiny dog into her arms and showering him with kisses.

'Well, he's beautiful,' Graham concurred. 'And what a brilliant name, Bear. Was that your idea, Jen?'

'Hmm, no, he was already called Bear, but we thought it suited him, didn't we, Mummy? Plus, he's six, so he's a little bit old to have to learn a new name.'

'You're right,' Graham assured her, his heart filled with love for his god-daughter who was beaming as though her every dream had come true.

'Do you want to hold him, Uncle Graham? I think he likes you.'

'Well sure, if you don't mind,' Graham answered, receiving Bear into his arms. 'Just one question though, how did you get Daddy to sign off on this?'

His question was directed at Liz, who had managed to keep the news from him during several phone conversations that she had initiated to check up on him since he hadn't 'been himself lately'.

Jenna answered. 'Daddy said if I promised to take care of him, and take him for walks and everything, and pick up his poop, then we could have him, because he's only a little dog, and his coat doesn't shed, and he's really well-trained. Poodles are really easy to train, you see, aren't they Mummy? The lady at Dogs Trust told us that.'

Graham smiled as Bear wriggled in his arms, keen to make a beeline back to Jenna.

'I think he wants you,' he told her, handing him back. 'Well, this is fantastic news,' he said, rising from his chair and standing beside Liz as Jenna encouraged Bear to run after her. 'I can't believe you finally convinced him.'

'Hah, don't kid yourself,' Liz said with a laugh. 'This had nothing to do with me. She's a force to be reckoned with, that girl. And as much as he protested, I actually think he quite likes the little guy. I mean, who wouldn't?'

'He is adorable,' Graham agreed, watching Jenna plead with 'the little guy' to chase after a ball.

'I'm glad I convinced you to come around,' Liz told him, touching his arm affectionately. 'That, I will take credit for.'

Graham smiled. 'Yup, that was all you.'

'And you're doing okay?'

'I am,' Graham nodded. 'I really am.'

Liz studied his face for signs of wilful deceit, and seemed satisfied that he wasn't lying to her. The fact that he had finally given in and accepted one of her invitations to Sunday lunch after rebuking several was a good sign, even if it was unfortunate that Colin had been called into the office and wouldn't be back for several hours. It was a sign that whatever had been so obviously bothering him for the last month or so, something that he vehemently denied but which Liz knew instinctively existed, was letting up.

'Good,' she said happily, basking in the glory of having got him there and made him smile, albeit through introducing him to Bear, who was quite capable of bringing a tear to a glass eye. 'What do you say we take Bear for a good long walk, build us up an appetite for lunch?'

'I say that's a mighty fine idea,' Graham replied, his spirits higher than they had been for the past month.

Chapter Forty-Nine

Angie
July

What they said about the sun was so true. All that Vitamin D, the abundance of natural light, feeling the warmth on your skin, day after day, it was magical. But there were only two more days left, and then it would be back to the temperamental, mostly God-awful climate that the UK had to offer, and back to real life. She shuddered at the thought of it and had to slam the door shut on the barrage of worries that tried to flood into her head when she thought about returning back home. In so far as England was home – she would not be returning to Elham.

She had been contacted by a solicitor handling *his* estate shortly after he'd died, but the man's words had been white noise after she had digested the initial news, and it had come as a shock when the same solicitor had later got in touch to discuss the settlement.

She had listened, bile rising in her throat at the mere mention of his name, anger sending tremors through her body as she listened to the solicitor explaining how he had not only benefited all those years from living in her grandparents' unencumbered property, but had also managed to get his filthy hands on the savings that her grandmother had left behind, and had run up debts of thousands, funding his 'lifestyle' as a human ball of slime.

The house that Angie had once lived in, if her experience

during those years could be described as living, was to be sold to repay the debts, but then there was the matter of the remaining proceeds, the solicitor had explained.

'I don't want it,' had been Angie's reply. 'I won't take a penny of that' – she paused, unable to bring herself to refer to him as a man – 'of *his* money.'

Except that it wasn't his money. He had never earned a legitimate penny in his miserable life. He had never had a job, not even when he was young, preferring to leach off of his parents under the pretence of not being fit for work. He had been fit enough to track her down, Angie thought, the nausea returning as she remembered that night when he had made himself seen in such a vile way. He'd had no problem squandering her grandmother's cash whilst pretending to be an upstanding member of the community, cynically inserting himself into Iain's circle at the golf club once he had found out where Angie was, and had masterminded a way to get to her, slowly but surely, with maximum devastation being his end goal. As if there were no limit to the ways in which the man had been able to negatively impact her life, he had managed to tarnish her relationship with Graham's parents by using Iain in such a way, a fact that Graham had managed to ascertain from his father in a casual chat, foregoing the real reason for his enquiry into the fabricated friendship.

It was her grandparents' money, the solicitor reminded Angie. Her grandparents who had loved her, who had produced her mother whom she had loved with all her heart. Her grandmother had taken her in when she had needed a home and had tried to make the absence of her mother and father as bearable as it could ever be expected to be. It wasn't her fault that her son had turned out to be a filthy excuse for a human being. Some people were just born evil, Angie had figured that out over the course of her life.

Still, she had reiterated her stance over the phone, that she didn't want the money. It was fruit from a poisonous tree, and it would be nothing more than another cinder block around her neck if she were to take it. 'Why don't I give you some time to think about it?' the solicitor had offered, and she had agreed, having no intention of giving the matter any further consideration.

And then the horrible showdown with Graham had happened. And when she had returned to her temporary home that night, sopping wet and physically and emotionally exhausted, she had made a decision that still didn't sit easy with her, but it was the right decision. It was the best way to handle a situation that threatened to unravel everything she had strived so hard to achieve in the months since she had reached rock bottom.

There was no way she could stay there any longer, in that tiny village. No matter how hard they might try to avoid each other, it would not be possible for she and Graham to ignore the fact that they were trapped in a toxic radius. She had to be the one to leave, and to do that she had to have means, and the means, however tainted, were right there, waiting for her.

She had gone into list-making, plan-making mode straight away, scribbling through almost a whole notebook that evening, jotting down possible places to live, possible jobs she might be able to get. She had spoken to Gemma about it the very next morning, deciding at the last minute against revealing the real reason for her wanting to leave so desperately, but conveying the urgent need to do so, for 'personal reasons'. Gemma had been wonderful, as Angie had known she would be, helping her to look for jobs, and creating a CV that Angie felt comfortable sharing with the world. She was devastated at the thought of losing her, Gemma confided, but the woman had a heart of gold, and with her help the task didn't seem as impossible as it once would have.

There wasn't a chance in hell that she would go back to

Newcastle, and she ruled out surrounding areas until she had vetoed the whole of the North East. Despite the considerable size of the county, likewise Angie felt like Kent itself was too small to house both her and Graham without them risking a repeat of their accidental meetings to date. Her inheritance would give her options, perhaps even rent for six months; a year if she was lucky. And she had been lucky, for once.

She had applied for over a hundred jobs, so easy was it to click a button and fire off her new, polished CV to any number of agencies and employers advertising for staff. With Gemma's help she had focused on her recent office experience, the likes of which many of the roles were seeking in a candidate, and Gemma was more than happy to provide a glowing reference confirming what an asset she had been to the shelter.

When it popped into her email inbox, Angie had originally baulked at the invitation to attend an interview in Exeter, the distance from 'home' sending a flare of panic through her. But without taking the time to think about it she had typed a reply that said yes, she would go, and once she had pressed send, she had started to think that it was quite possibly just what she needed. Over two hundred miles and four counties between her and her recent past – the more she thought about it, the more it seemed like a fantastic idea.

The day before the interview, for which she had organised an overnight stay in a hotel minutes from the office where she was to report to at eleven c'clock sharp, she had been filled with nerves. She had begun checking out potential places to live as soon as the interview had been arranged, and had even gone to view a room in a flat not far from where she hoped she would be working, safe in the knowledge that Gemma, bless her, had transferred enough money into her account to cover the very reasonable rent for six months, to give her ample time for her inheritance money to come through.

The single bedroom was compact, but it was all she needed, and the flat itself was nice: brightly decorated, with a live-in landlord who was a single, professional female of thirty-two and had told Angie that she flitted in and out at will, splitting her time between her own flat and her boyfriend's. The room was furnished, with all the essentials, and the seventy-five pounds per week for rent and bills would be more than affordable if Angie managed to secure the Admin Assistant role she was to interview for. When the inheritance money did finally come through, it would allow her to pay Gemma back, and maybe even have something of a little nest egg, to take the pressure off a little.

On the eve of her meeting with the family-run company, she had experienced a wobble not unlike the one she'd had before her first day working at the shelter. But look how that turned out, she reminded herself. In her wildest dreams she could not have hoped to make a better friend than Gemma had come to be, and she knew that there was nothing else for it than to be brave and go for it, because otherwise, what had all those months been for?

And so, she had walked into the interview with an air of confidence that, whilst artificial, was surprisingly convincing. And despite her nerves on the inside, she had presented a very competent version of herself to the kindly mother-and-son interview team who asked her questions that she found she could answer without much difficulty at all. And she had been offered the job.

Within days, having handed over her details and been given a provisional start date of a month later, she had struck a deal with the woman who owned the flat and secured the room for six months. The ease of it all made her feel unsettled, as though it were too good to be true, and something bad would have to come hurtling around the corner to redress the balance. But the wheels had been set in motion; there was no turning back.

Within two weeks she had already transferred most of her things to her new dwelling thanks to Gemma, again, and her Ford Focus which impressively doubled as a removal van. The amount of possessions that Angie had to move didn't warrant a larger vehicle, and space was limited in her new bedroom anyway, but the pleasure of Gemma's company on the drive as well as allowing her friend to view her new digs was what was important to Angie.

'You know what you need, my lovely?' Gemma had said, as they were unloading the last of her things from the boot of the car. 'A few days in the sun.'

'Hmm, that would be lovely,' Angie replied wistfully. 'Maybe in a few months' time, if I can afford it.'

'No, you should go now, before you start. Take yourself away for a week, get yourself a nice tan, bit of fresh air, you'll come back feeling raring to go.'

Angie smiled. 'I need to start earning before I can think about it, Gem. Much as I'd love to, I just don't have the cash right now.'

'Yes, you do, my lovely.' Angie felt Gemma's hand touch her shoulder and turned to face her. 'Listen to me,' Gemma began, 'I know you, Angie, or at least I'm sure enough that I do, and I've got not a doubt in my mind that you're going to pay me that money back as soon as you get it. Now, I might be an old fool, and you might end up taking me to the cleaners for two-and-a-half grand, but I really don't think you will.'

Angie shook her head. 'Of course not, I'd never do that, Gem.'

Gemma let out a laugh. 'I know you wouldn't, my love. So, what I'm saying is, take a chunk of it and book yourself a little trip, before you start this new job. It's a big step, moving out here and starting afresh, and I know you'll be just fine, but a little rest and relaxation in the sunshine never did anyone any harm.'

'Oh, Gem.' Angie had thrown her arms around her friend, feelings of adoration for the woman who felt like a surrogate mother mixed with trepidation as the gravity of what she was attempting to pull off started to become clear.

She had taken Gemma's advice – or, more accurately, followed her orders – and booked herself on a flight to Malaga three days later. Something had sparked in the back of her mind when she was browsing the internet for budget flights and saw the sixty-six pounds deal to the Spanish city. It was perfect for her budget, and it looked beautiful in the Google images, but there was something else about it. Something about the dates she was looking at, perhaps? Her memory played tricks on her, the significance of the date dancing around the edge of her mind before running away and hiding again, leaving her puzzled and frustrated, determined to know what it was. Still, it was a great price for a direct flight to somewhere sunny, and pretty, and she managed to find a decent hotel that didn't smash her budget to pieces and had great traveller reviews. Before she knew it, and before whatever little nugget of information was prattling around inside her head could make itself known, she had ticked all the required boxes, offered up her card details, and signed herself up to a week of Andalusian hospitality.

Not until she had arrived there, and gone to the Tourist Information Office to get an idea of which part of the city to visit, had it finally come back to her.

Of course, she had forgotten.

She had forced herself to forget everything that had been good about the life she'd had before, not least the best parts of her relationship with Graham. It was the only way she could make her peace with the fact that he was lost to her forever. But being there, having made it to the place they'd promised to visit together, brought the memories crashing into her head like waves.

She couldn't go so far as to remember the girl's name,

241

but she could see her face in her mind's eye: the well-off, pampered girl who had dipped in and out of Angie's life at university as the archetypal part-time friend. The one who had taken a gap year before starting her course, and had regaled Angie with tales and photographs that made Angie's heart ache with longing.

Angie had obsessed over it for a while, she remembered. The fear was still raw, still very real, and the fragile freedom she had achieved for herself still felt as though it may be snatched away at any time. Whenever she would hear a creak in the night, or see his smile on the face of a stranger, she would repoint her thoughts to the dream setting that she had created for herself.

She would picture herself there, gazing out across the city from the highest point of the castle, her hair lifted by the gentle breeze while the sun warmed her skin. She would look down to the streets, the parks, the port, searching for her true love who would be making his way to find her, to come and rescue her. It was like a scene from a romantic movie, with the ancient castle the backdrop for the fairy tale. It was a fantasy in which she could be the protagonist, the girl who got her guy and rode off into the sunset with him. She had dared to dream all those years that her white knight would come one day, and eventually she'd had no option but to rescue herself, but when Graham had come along, she had fallen for him in a way that she'd begun to fear she might never be able to. He had become the hero of her story, and he was the perfect man for the role.

She had told him about it, not long after they were married, when the protective bubble around their love was still intact, and it seemed like there was no way that life could be any better than it already was. They were married now, the day itself having gone without a hitch, without any unwelcome guests or nasty surprises. No one had objected to her claiming Graham as her guy, and his family and friends had welcomed her as his wife with genuine affection. Their wedding night had been the stuff of dreams: the hazy, sensual love-making a change of pace from the impromptu she had initiated before the ceremony, and for the first time Angie had felt ... right.

'Say we'll go there,' she had urged her new husband, resting on her elbows beside a sleepy, smiley Graham. 'Say we'll do it, on our tenth anniversary. We'll go at sunset, when everyone else is gone or getting ready to go. We'll take a bottle of wine with us, and toast each other while we look out across the city. It'll be beautiful.

Suddenly she could see his face as it had been then, as though she were lying next to him, as close as she had been that night. He had looked at her as though she were the only thing in the entire world worth looking at, in that moment.

'We will,' he'd said softly, drawing her close to him and kissing her gently. 'I promise, we will.'

Chapter Fifty

Graham
July

He had never smoked, not really. Not since his mother had
found a half-full packet of Silk Cut cigarettes stashed in his
underwear drawer when he was fifteen and shamed him
out of ever taking up the 'filthy habit' in earnest. But he
imagined that this was how a smoker must feel when they
were trying to quit their addiction.

He had known plenty of would-be ex-smokers over the
years, some of whom had succeeded and some who had
never quite managed it, and each of them seemed to measure
their progress in terms of how many cigarettes they now
smoked per day compared to the number they used to smoke
before they had started trying to quit. 'That's me down to
five a day now,' they would say. 'I used to get through forty
a day, can you believe that? Forty!'

Graham never could believe it, because he couldn't
imagine being addicted to something so odd. What pleasure
did these people derive from sucking on a substance that
made your lungs look like they had been coated with motor
oil? And yet, millions of people did it. Billions, probably.
Even after all the disgusting images that they showed on
the packets these days, and all the campaigns on television
showing what an evil, life-ending force cancer could be,
and how smoking made contracting the disease all the more
likely. But having experienced his share of self-destructive

urges, Graham thought that he might just be able to understand where those people were coming from.

That was the thing with addictions – they made no sense. Like the gambler who knows the odds are stacked against him but believes his luck will finally change when he tosses his last chip onto the table. Or the alcoholic who knows that the booze will kill him, but thinks that nothing is worse than being sober. Or the man who can't get his ex-wife out of his system, even though she's hurt him more than he ever thought possible.

He had started measuring his progress in the way that addicts do: That's only three times today that I've thought about her; I've gone a whole night without dreaming about her.

But there was no pattern to it, no discernible improvement as the days and weeks went on. One day, he would feel like he was getting there, chalking up several hours without so much as even a stray daydream. The next, it would take all his effort just to concentrate on whatever he was doing: work, cycling, reading, to get her out of his head. It shouldn't be like this, he repeated to himself, over and over. What the fuck is wrong with you? There had to be a fault in his wiring, somewhere. Wouldn't it be so much easier if such nuances in the human brain could be diagnosed with the ease of a computer glitch in a car? 'Oh, yes, Mr Pike, I see the problem,' the doctor/mind mechanic would say. 'Let me just flick this switch here, and reattach this wire here, and you'll be right as rain!' But it didn't work like that. Graham couldn't just flick the switch. Everything he'd been through, everything he'd found out, even the things he had witnessed with his own eyes still hadn't done the trick. And it wasn't for want of trying. He had simply come to the conclusion that there was nothing he could do. She was in there, all the way down inside of him, and she was never coming out. All he could hope to do was to find a way to ignore her.

Chapter Fifty-One

Angie
July

'It's stupid, isn't it? Yeah, you're right; it's daft. Okay, I'm not going, I've decided. But wait, wouldn't it be even more crazy to actually be here, in the city, and not go? Oh, I don't know!'

Angie had played out several conversations like this with herself in the mirror in the days leading up to the date that she had almost forgotten the significance of, which turned out to be the day before she was due to fly home and begin the newest chapter of her life.

She was content with what she saw in the mirror, for the most part. There were lines that belied her age and her life experience, that she could do nothing about, but her face and her shoulders were richly tanned, and her eyes were bright and clear. She had got into the habit of wearing her hair up, away from her neck due to the heat and discomfort that came from leaving it to languish against her sweaty skin, and she had come to like the new look. She wore a plain-white vest and linen trousers with open-toed sandals, and as she debated with herself for the hundredth time whether or not to go through with her plan, she decided that if she did, she would need more appropriate footwear.

She let out a long sigh and closed her eyes, imagining what Gemma would say to her if she were there.

'You'd be a bloody fool to go all that way and not see it, my lovely,' Gemma would tell her, waving away her misgivings. 'Think about this: how will you feel if you come home and you've not gone, when you were only a neighbourhood away? You'll be kicking yourself, that's what. Get yourself a nice bottle of red and get on up there!'

It was Gemma's imaginary advice that swung it for her. 'Oh, bugger it!' she declared at her reflection, and went to retrieve her plimsolls from her suitcase.

It had been another gorgeous day, and she wished she could take the weather home with her when she returned to Exeter. She was sad at the thought of leaving the warmth and the beauty that was everywhere she looked, from the breathtaking cathedral to the stunning port, but at the same time she had begun to feel the first twinges of nervous excitement, and a little part of her wished she could fast-forward to her first day to get it out of the way.

For now, though, she could afford to take her time. And she did.

She followed the path she had treaded for the past five days, navigating the streets as though she had lived there all her life. She did exactly as the voice of Gemma inside her head had cajoled and purchased a bottle of wine along the way, concealing it in her canvas bag while she made her way to the *Paseo de Don Juan Temboury*. She could feel her pulse racing and her body temperature rising as she passed the university, knowing that she was feet away from beginning the ascent she had psyched herself up for. She began to feel heady with the heat and with nerves, as though she had uncorked the bottle and drunk the lot right there and then in the street.

The photographs that Jessica Lawrence (for Angie had now managed to remember the girl's name) had shown to her all those years ago, as jaw-dropping as they were, could not have done justice to the reality that awaited her.

She had already visited the Alcazaba, two days ago, and

had to pinch herself when she lined up the lens of her own camera to capture the view from the ancient structure.

The incline was steep towards the castle, and with the temperature lingering around the low twenties even in the early evening, she wished that she'd had the foresight to bring a large bottle of water with her in addition to the wine. Or perhaps instead of the wine, which no longer seemed like such a good idea considering how dehydrated she was likely to be when she finally made it to the top.

She kept walking, her legs aching from the effort, eager to make it to the summit in time to see the sun at its most beautiful. It was a dream she had carried with her since she was nineteen years old, and a small sob came out as she rued the fact that Graham would not be there, to share it with her like they had planned. She forced the emotion to move on quickly, and reminded herself that she had longed to come here even before she had met Graham, before she had given her white knight his face. Before they had made the promise to meet here once they'd made it to ten years.

She batted away the image of him that sprung into her mind and pushed ahead, concerned that she may not have left herself enough time, that she might miss the moment when the sun passed behind the clouds and disappeared as though it had been nothing more than a splendid figment of the imagination.

She reached the entrance and debated which way to go, which vantage point to choose. There were small groups milling around, in spite of the late hour, many of them speaking languages that she couldn't begin to identify let alone understand.

If the climb to this point had taken her breath away for physical reasons, the view she finally settled on for the big moment drew the air out of her lungs in a different way. She took the bottle of wine from her bag and placed it down beside her feet. She leaned her arms on the wall, gulping in huge breaths of warm air, desperately trying to stop herself crying. But she couldn't. It was too bloody beautiful for anyone in their right mind not to cry at what she could see.

The rest of the world was lost to her now. The other people, their languages, the faint hum of the traffic from the streets she had trod a half hour ago – none of it existed anymore. The only thing that mattered now was that she had made it, both literally and figuratively.

She let her tears flow until they reached her lips, which were upturned in a smile that she felt might never leave her face. The sun was hovering on the horizon, giving its due notice that any moment now, it would make its descent, furnishing the sky with colours that no paintbrush could ever hope to do justice to, and making way for the stars.

She felt a puff of air at her side and was broken from her reverie, furious that someone had chosen that exact moment to invade the cocoon of happiness that she had created for herself.

'Don't look at me, look at that,' the someone said, pointing to the horizon. She turned her head to where he was pointing and gasped, bringing her hands to her mouth. She had imagined it. She had dreamed it, many times. She had hoped that she would get there, one day, and that it would live up to the ridiculous expectations that she had carried with her for so long. But she hadn't *actually* expected to experience it.

It was glorious. It was more than glorious, but she didn't have the words. And the man who stood beside her, who had arrived at her side mere seconds before the most magical moment of her life, was Graham.

'What are you doing here?' she asked, when finally, she felt able to take her eyes off the sky, and to form words again.

Graham turned to look at her, his face stern. He stared at her for several moments which felt like torture, his eyes roaming over her as though he needed to see every part of her, to take it all in. Angie could feel tears stinging at her eyes again, but these were different from the ones she had just cried. These were tears of mixed emotions. Of joy that he was here, that he had remembered, that he had gone to all this effort to come to Spain and find her. But as the minutes continued to pass and Graham's face didn't change, and he didn't say anything, they were tears of anxiety, of fear that he was at this moment regretting his decision and was about to turn and walk away, leaving her alone when she felt so open, so vulnerable.

His brows were the first to relax, and as the rest of his face followed suit, Angie's fear began to melt along with his scowl. His features cracked into a smile, and he picked up the wine that lay at Angie's feet.

'I made a promise,' he told her.

Acknowledgements

I would like to thank all of my friends and family who acted as sounding boards for the book and who helped shape the story of *Embers*. I would also like to thank the team at Ringwood for their support throughout the writing and publication process.

About the Author

Born and raised on the outskirts of Glasgow, Stephanie McDonald discovered a passion for reading at a very early age, and harboured dreams of one day becoming a published author. In 2016, she wrote and self-published her first full-length novel, *Learn to Let Go*. This debut was followed by the People's Book Prize nominated *Inference* in 2019. *Embers* is her third novel, and her second to be published by Ringwood.

Other Titles from Ringwood

All titles are available from the Ringwood website in both print and ebook format, as well as from usual outlets.

www.ringwoodpublishing.com
mail@ringwoodpublishing.com

Inference
Stephanie McDonald

Natalie Byron had a happy life in Glasgow. Or at least, she thought she did. The morning after a date, Natalie wakes up inside a strange house, sleeping next to a strange man on a Scottish island.

Fearing she's been kidnapped, Natalie flees. When everyone around her insists that her life in Glasgow is nothing but a delusion, Natalie begins to doubt her own sanity.

But there is one thing Natalie is sure of. She needs to get off this island.

ISBN: 978-1-901514-68-1
£9.99

What You Call Free
Flora Johnston

Scotland, 1687. Pregnant and betrayed, eighteen-year-old Jonet escapes her public humiliations, and takes refuge among an outlawed group of religious dissidents. Here, Widow Helen offers friendship and understanding, but her beliefs have seen her imprisoned before.

This extraordinary tale of love and loss, struggle and sacrifice, autonomy and entrapment, urges us to consider what it means to be free and who can be free – if freedom exists at all.

ISBN: 978-1-901514-96-4
£9.99

Not the Life Imagined
Anne Pettigrew

A darkly humorous, thought-provoking story of Scottish medical students in the sixties, a time of changing social and sexual mores. None of the teenagers starting at Glasgow University in 1967 live the life they imagine.

In *Not the Life Imagined*, retired medic Anne Pettigrew tells a tale of ambition and prejudice that provides a humorous and compelling insight into the complex dynamics of the NHS fifty years ago.

ISBN: 978-1-901514-70-4
£9.99

ISBN: 978-1-901514-80-3
£9.99

Not the Deaths Imagined
Anne Pettigrew

In a leafy Glasgow suburb, Dr Beth Semple is busy juggling motherhood and full-time GP work in the 90s NHS. But her life becomes even more problematic when she notices some odd deaths in her neighbourhood. Though Beth believes the stories don't add up, the authorities remain stubbornly unconvinced.

Is a charming local GP actually a serial killer? Can Beth piece together the jigsaw of perplexing fatalities and perhaps save lives? And as events accelerate towards a dramatic conclusion, will the police intervene in time?

Murder at the Mela
Leela Soma

DI Alok Patel takes the helm of an investigation into the brutal murder of an Asian woman in this eagerly-awaited thriller. As Glasgow's first Asian DI, Patel faces prejudice from his colleagues and suspicion from the Asian community as he struggles with the pressure of his rank, relationships, and racism.

This murder-mystery explores not just the hate that lurks in the darkest corners of Glasgow, but the hate which exists in the very streets we walk.

ISBN: 978-1-901514-90-2
£9.99

Everyday Magic
Charlie Laidlaw

Carole Gunn leads an unfulfilled life and knows it. But in spite of her mundane life, Carole has decided to do something different. She's decided to revisit places that hold special significance for her. She wants to better understand herself, and whether the person she is now is simply an older version of the person she once was.

Instead, she's taken on an unlikely journey to confront her past, present and future.

Everyday Magic is an uplifting book that reminds us that, while our pasts make us who we are, we can always change the course of our futures.

ISBN: 978-1-901514-77-3
£9.99